The House at the Edge of the World

JULIA ROCHESTER

PENGUIN BOOKS

PENGUIN BOOKS

UK | USA | Canada | Ireland | Australia
India | New Zealand | South Africa

Penguin Books is part of the Penguin Random House group of companies
whose addresses can be found at global.penguinrandomhouse.com.

Penguin
Random House
UK

First published by Viking 2015
Published in Penguin Books 2016

001

Copyright © Julia Rochester, 2015

The moral right of the author has been asserted

Grateful acknowledgement is made for permission to reproduce lines from 'Neither Out Far Nor
In Deep' and 'Stopping by Woods on a Snowy Evening' from *The Poetry of Robert Frost* by Robert
Frost, published by Jonathan Cape, reprinted by permission of The Random House Group Limited

Typeset in Dante by Palimpsest Book Production Limited, Falkirk, Stirlingshire
Printed in Great Britain by Clays Ltd, St Ives plc

A CIP catalogue record for this book is available from the British Library

ISBN: 978-0-241-97169-7

For my parents, Ralph and Barbara

PENGUIN BOOKS

The House at the Edge of the World

'A highly engrossing literary mystery'

BOOKSELLER

—

'Gripping'

SUNDAY TIMES

—

'A slippery tale of perception and manipulation'

SCOTSMAN

—

'Poised, lightly witty novel'

OBSERVER

—

'Funny, sharp and also terribly sad'

EMERALD STREET

—

'Impressive. Carries you along – clever plotting and a startling outcome. School of Daphne du Maurier – and I mean that as a compliment!'

PENELOPE LIVELY

'I enjoyed the book so much. The writing is wonderfully crisp and funny and it's so full of vivid, surprising images that the reader almost doesn't notice the moment that deep secrets begin to be revealed'

EMMA HEALEY

The people along the sand
All turn and look one way.
They turn their back on the land.
They look at the sea all day.

As long as it takes to pass
A ship keeps raising its hull;
The wetter ground like glass
Reflects a standing gull.

The land may vary more;
But wherever the truth may be –
The water comes ashore,
And the people look at the sea.

They cannot look out far.
They cannot look in deep.
But when was that ever a bar
To any watch they keep?

Robert Frost

Prologue

When I was eighteen, my father fell off a cliff. It was a stupid way to die. There was a good moon. There was no wind. There was no excuse. He was pissing into the chine at Brock Tor on his way home from the pub and fell headlong drunk into the spring tide with his flies open.

I spent that night on the beach with Corwin, watching the moon silver the sea, and later an image lodged in my mind of our father in slow descent, turning within a glittering moonlit arc of urine. When I confided this to Corwin, he was angrier than I had ever seen him. I had fixed the image, and now he must share it with me, as if it were a memory. He hit me, which was fair, I thought – a back-handed swipe across the mouth that drew blood. I was so upset that I ran to the cabin and lay there all night half awake. At dawn, Corwin came and crawled into the bunk with me to kiss my swollen lip and say sorry. He was more generous then.

Of course, boys had been pissing into the chine for all time; atavistic squirts against the terrible indifference of the North Atlantic. But my father was not a boy, he was forty-four, and it was almost ten years before I was able to forgive him the vulgarity of his death. When, finally, I did so, I found that the imaginary falling man was more real to me than my memories of the living John Venton, and that all that remained of my sense of him was the residue of my embarrassment. I remember the exact moment of forgiveness. I was looking at a piece of sculpture in an exhibition, a model that lay on the floor. It was the perfect reproduction of a man's corpse but reduced to the size of a large doll – or a baby, perhaps. It was agonizingly tender, and when I saw the title,

Dead Dad, I felt an emotion so violent and so unexpected that it took me some moments to identify what it might be. I thought of the man who had made this, how he had sat, dispassionate, by the naked corpse that had been his father and had recorded every detail of the last of his physical presence in the world. I envied him, I realized – the emotion I was experiencing was *envy*. Oh! I thought. That's interesting!

I did not share this with Corwin. He was off and away. I did think to tell Matthew, and to ask him to explain his son, my father, to me, but by then he had become translucent with age, as if he were screen-printed on fine silk, and I did not want to risk anything that might pierce or rend. I should have asked, of course. And not only then: Matthew was always disappointed to find me so un-inquisitive.

Matthew used to say that every tribe must have a *Rememberer of History*. He often spoke in italics. It was an annoying habit, which Corwin has inherited. Matthew said that among tribal peoples myth and history are passed down as if the teller has experienced it himself, in the first person. The teller does not recount, he recalls. 'And who's to say,' asked Matthew, 'that he is not, in fact, *remembering*? What do we know of the fate of the soul?'

Here I sit with Matthew's map. The whole story is contained within it – or, should I say, trapped within it? When he was dying and we began, too late, to decode the map, I understood him better. Matthew remembered on our behalf, and he imagined on our behalf, and he perceived that remembering and imagining share agency: any story, whether or not rooted in fact, may unleash any number of real events, and vice versa. Matthew's map is a work of his imagination, his collection of myths, histories, half-truths, fabrications and omissions, but it is also a real world. When he drafted it, when he began to paint for himself his very own garden of earthly delights, he drew a circle around himself – and, it took me some time to realize, around us. Circles

2

are strong in magic and, whether he intended to or not, Matthew fixed himself upon the centre. Sometimes I indulge in upsetting myself by imagining him there, with marionette arms and legs, secured to the canvas by a butterfly collector's pin.

But before I get back to my father, I need to dwell a little longer on Matthew, to remember on *his* behalf. I'm explaining this here, now, because you might say: 'You can't possibly know that. You weren't there.' Or you might say: 'That's not how I remember it.'

It doesn't matter. This is how I remember it. This is how I have imagined it. It doesn't matter if you don't imagine it like this at all.

PART ONE

I.

The house sits at the centre of the map, framed by the Venton lands as set out in the deeds. One hundred and fifty acres fan around it: to the north, a swathe of wooded valley, tangled branches tumbling into the mill stream; to the south, gorse- and hazel-edged grazing; up and east, where the land settles into wind-washed fields, what was once Thornton Farm. But by the time Matthew painted it, most of that land had long since been lost to the Ventons. The house itself had the bones of a farm, but had been tamed to genteel Georgian proportions, and the Ventons, having forgotten that they had once been farmers, looked only west from their windows, down through the indented fields, to the Atlantic.

Long before Matthew came to contain his life within a circle, that triangle of ever-altering sea was the shape that expressed his world. Later, when he was old enough to be let loose, he added another triangle, the three points between which he ran and played: house, church, cabin. In those days, before he learned to fear the sea, this triangle seemed to point towards an exit – west across the water. Matthew sat on the cabin steps and dreamed himself agile in the rigging, toes gripping rope – a dream unimpaired by the fact that the tall ships were long obsolete.

It was Matthew's father, the wilful James, who had built the cabin. He also had dreamed of crossing the sea. He was a restless man with ideas of escape. It had been his ambition to travel to America, and he pictured himself striding through birch forests, crunching through snow with a rifle slung over the shoulder of his bearskin coat. James had saved the money for his passage and had been all packed to leave, but he had exercised his strength of will upon Matthew's mother and, instead of crossing the Atlantic, found himself standing over the Norman font in Thornton church, renouncing the Devil and all his works, with the infant Elizabeth – the first of his four children – in his arms. In the churchyard lay dead Ventons, their bones weighted down by tombstones, while in the church other names were remembered on memorial tablets, which echoed the lament 'lost at sea, lost at sea', around the cold walls. James envied them the freedom of their souls.

Matthew was the late, hope-long-given-up-for, son. His mother never quite lost her air of surprise that he should be in the world. Before him were The Sisters. He thought of The Sisters in the singular – an entity that was older and of the world in a terrifyingly practical way. The Sisters made a lot of noise – mainly a six-legged clattering of shoes on the flagstones – and moved at the centre of a storm of flying objects. Pots, pans and preserving jars circled, suspended in the air, always on the point of falling. There were flurries of wet sheets and dry underwear. Rouges, hair-pins, magazines and knitting patterns scattered in their wake like autumn leaves. Matthew often thought that if he hadn't had so many sisters, things would have been very different: he would not have spent so much time hiding in the woods on the bank of the mill leat.

He burrowed into the spaces formed by storm-tipped trees, which he transformed into earthy dens furnished with wooden crates. He hung lanterns from overhanging roots and hid there with his books and a sketchpad. He sketched the plants and fungi around him and took the pictures home to identify in the large reference books in his father's study. After a while Matthew began to sketch pictures of the creatures he saw or imagined there. Badgers and foxes became increasingly anthropomorphic; leaf-clad pixies appeared. James, who took an interest in the development of his son's mind, was horrified – it was effeminate to believe in fairies and talking animals. He called upon the Crab Man.

The Crab Man looked like Matthew's idea of Long John Silver, but without the peg-leg or the parrot. Instead, his props were the crabs that rattled around in the metal bucket at the kitchen door. Laughing saltily, he would take a couple out of the bucket, one in each hand, and, with a leathery leer, wave them in Matthew's face. Snippety-snap went the terrifying crab claws within an inch of Matthew's nose. They smelt of fish-water and engine oil.

James had conceived an adventure for Matthew, a man-making crabbing expedition. One evening, one of the Crab Man's children appeared at the kitchen door with the message 'Dad reckons tomorrow will do', and the following early morning James shook Matthew awake and they walked over to The Sands together in the dark. It was May, turning warm, the scent of ploughed soil rising from the fields and the rooks stirring in the trees. In the Crab Man's kitchen, Matthew allowed himself to be laughed at by the older children. James had told him to accept some tea and a bit of bread so as not to offend, but to decline any second offers because *life was hard* for the Crab Man, and it was Matthew's duty to note this and learn from it.

James came with them and waved from the harbour wall, quickly disappearing from view into the before-dawn. Already, Matthew knew that this was a mistake. The thick, sweet smell of engine oil had travelled through his blood to his gut and no amount of breeze would shift it. Whenever he looked back to that day, which he did often, he saw the ink-black water swelling towards him, and remembered the elastic falling away of the centre of his body as the boat dipped into the shining bowl left by the wave, and the rising and re-springing of his intestines far up into the centre of his chest as the bow lifted. As dawn greyed over, he apprehended, through the misery that burned from his throat to his navel, that the shore, obscured by mist, was not visible. He filled with terror at the vastness of the sea, and began to understand the scale of ocean and, even more terrifyingly, atmosphere and universe. It seemed impossible that this tiny molecule of a vessel could keep them safe, and he believed quite sincerely that he would die and that the sea, in her colossal, insatiable greed, would swallow him whole. The waters will close over me, he thought, and I will leave no trace. The salt water will fill my nostrils, and my lungs, and take my voice, and I will sink. And the fish will nibble at my eyes and my flesh, and my veins and arteries will float and trail like seaweed, and my bones will lift backwards and forwards at the bottom of the sea and grind to sand, and no one, no one, will know that those tiny white grains were me.

He slumped in the boat and, between bouts of hauling himself up the gunwale to empty his stomach, prayed to all the gods that were plausible to him. The Crab Man, who had expected this, did not hold it against him. He and his son dropped their crab pots into the water while Matthew vomited himself dry. Eventually, the son made Matthew a little nest of coiled rope in a locker in the bow and pushed him in with a friendly pat on the shoulder, and there Matthew lay, passing in and out of sleep.

Around mid-morning he woke to an altered pitch of the boat. It was bumping very gently on its fenders against the side of the cliff. He roused himself to see where he was and found that they were in a cove, protected from the wind. The engine was switched off and the Crab Man was holding the boat steady. His boy was standing on the gunwale and reaching into the cliff face. When he pulled out his hand there were two mottled brown eggs in it, which he handed to his father, who, seeing that Matthew was awake, held them out on the flat of his palm for him to look at.

The gulls were strangely resigned to the robbing of their nests, and Matthew, curious enough to overcome his nausea for a moment, emerged to look up the height of the sheer cliff face at the wheeling gulls and the enviably balancing boy. 'Why don't they attack?' he asked.

'I don't know,' shrugged the Crab Man. 'I've often wondered that myself.' He placed the eggs in a bucket lined with straw. And then, to make sure that Matthew understood, 'You don't take from a full nest. You take from the nests with a single egg, when they've only just started to lay – that way they'll lay again, see?'

On the way home, the Crab Man switched off the engine and put up some sail, and he and his son sang, which only increased Matthew's misery because he could not join in. In the moment that he jumped from the boat onto the harbour wall he experienced an ecstasy of love of dry land and a relief to be alive that left a deep impression on his eleven-year-old mind. The thing about land, he now perceived, was that it could be marked – you could leave upon it scratchings and scrapings, and in the future, centuries after you were dead, an imprint of you would remain and someone who knew how to read it might revive a memory of you. And the more time you spent on land engraving your story upon it, the greater the chance that there you still would be.

Matthew did not paint the Crab Man or his boat into the map, but the cipher for the day he learned to fear the sea is there, for anyone who knows how to read it.

A third of the way up Highcliffe is a ledge.

And on that ledge is a nest.

And in that nest is a single seagull's egg.

2.

On the morning of his death day my father appeared in the doorway of my bedroom holding a cup of tea. He had already been up for two hours, husbanding his vegetables, but was now changed for work, fastidiously neat in his suit and tie. He always appeared disconnected from his suit, as though he stood in sufferance behind a comedy cardboard cut-out for a seaside-pier holiday photo.

I wondered what he was doing there. He didn't usually bring me tea in the mornings. It seemed to be an impulse that he was already regretting because now he had to speak to me and, though he loved me, he preferred to engage with me – or anyone, for that matter – in companionable silence. He thrust the cup of tea at me, ready to snatch his hand away quickly if I drew my claws.

He lurked near the door and put his hands into his pockets in case he was tempted absent-mindedly to pick up anything that might, once in his hands, admit some unsettling insight into the female adolescent mind. At last he found a safe place for his fingers at my workbench and they came to rest on the handle of the book press that he had found at a junk yard, taken apart and made work – for me. That was how he expressed love: by fixing things.

'What's this?' he asked, touching the narrow spine between the plates.

'It's a leaving present for Corwin,' I said. I didn't want to tell him what it was, for no better reason than that I didn't want to tell him. In fact, it was a copy of our sixth-form Bible, *Keep the Aspidistra Flying*, which I had rescued from its scruffy cover and repaired with cloth binding and endpapers in shades of

Orwellian grey. I was unhappy about the endpapers: I had not paid enough attention to aligning the grain and now the book wouldn't close properly. On the title page I had letter-pressed the words:

> To Corwin 'Crow' Venton,
> *my brave brother.*
> *Summer 1988*

Left with nowhere to go on the subject of the book, my father fell silent. I assumed that when he had planned this conversation, he had rehearsed it with the pre-adolescent Me who lived on in his affections, not with the near-adult female who lay naked under the blankets. I took pity on him. 'Dad,' I said, 'what are you doing here?'

He summoned up about a morning's worth of speech. 'I need to have a word with you.'

'You've forgotten the sugar again!'

'Morwenna!'

'I know what this is about.'

My father looked relieved and hopeful of being spared the difficulty of elaboration. 'Do you?'

'Do I?'

'What do you think this is about?'

'I must be more considerate of my mother,' I recited.

He appeared exhausted. I could tell that his stamina for this conversation was about to expire. We all failed my mother, he more than any of us – it was somehow connected with why he looked all wrong in a suit. He hated his job. When people asked him what he did for a living, he used to say, 'I design blights on the landscape.' Which was a conversation-stopper.

'I'll try,' I said. 'I promise. It's not easy for me to be considerate of anyone.'

He sighed. He had to love me even though I was not considerate. His shoulders bent a little under the burden of it.

'Would you like a lift into town?' he asked.

'No thanks. I thought I'd walk.'

He seemed to consider placing a kiss on my forehead, but he would have had to breach the gap between himself and my bed. As he went downstairs I called out, 'Thanks for the tea.'

Over the years I reconstructed this last day. It was not a deliberate effort. But subconsciously I gave it significance. It was as though those twenty-four hours both held and withheld my father in essence – like a moth chrysalis on the point of cracking open. When I was able to articulate this thought, Corwin snapped at me. He said, 'There's nothing transcendent about death!' And, by then, he should have known. Nothing distinguished that day. Even the plea to behave better towards my mother was a regular occurrence, which inevitably followed a row.

They rarely rowed – my father made it difficult for my mother to engage him on points of difference, so their frustration with each other built up slowly until it erupted about something trivial. Corwin and I called them 'sofa rows' because the sofa always featured in them: that lumpy, scratchy, Victorian chesterfield, which had been sitting in front of the fireplace on the day that Mum moved in, and had probably been sitting in exactly the same position on the day my grandmother moved in, symbol of the Ventons' passive tyranny against her. I don't know how my father and Matthew prevented Mum from placing the slightest personal mark on Thornton – some effort of passive resistance, I supposed. They had conceded the garden room to her in order for her to pursue her crafts. Not that she had any talent for crafts, but it had been the seventies, and it was expected of her: all those poor attempts at quilting, weaving and batik – all in muddy shades of terracotta. And all those pretty, clean, new things patterned with Laura Ashley sprigs, which she sneaked into her room like contraband.

Corwin and I eavesdropped on the end of that last row.

'I really don't think,' Mum was hissing, 'that it would be extravagant to change a sofa after an entire century.'

'It would be profligate,' replied my father, 'to replace something which so adequately performs its function.'

On the stairs, Corwin and I winced. Our father was quiet in anger, so we measured the level of his rage by the number of sentences completed and how heavy the weight of syllables. Mentally, we translated. What he meant was: 'It's part of the house.' Which sounded fair enough but wasn't, because Mum wasn't part of the house. We were all organic to the house, which was organic to the landscape, and she was a foreign body. The sofa represented my mother's failure to be a good wife and adapt to Thornton, and my father's failure to be a good husband and adapt Thornton to her. It made her unhappy, we could see that. But we were ruthless. Our sympathies were with Thornton, which was immutable. We thought she should throw in the towel.

Mum retorted that it would be nice – she repeated this louder, hoping that Matthew would hear: he always made such a fuss about the 'modern insipid usage' of the word: 'It would be *nice*,' she yelled, 'to have some say in what is allegedly my own home. And it would be even *nicer* to enter the current decade before it is over!'

We squirmed with discomfort. To suggest entering the eighties was guaranteed to induce a display of wrath from our father. It was the decade of untrammelled greed, of contempt for the unfortunate, of worship of Mammon and the Devil and all his henchmen, and he would have no part in it.

'Valerie,' he said, in a tone of lacerating disappointment, 'you know how I feel about all of that.'

'It's just a bloody sofa!' screeched Mum. 'It's just somewhere to park your arse! It's hardly the privatization of British Fucking Gas!'

We heard our father move towards the door and we scuttled

up the stairs. He always gave her the last word, but by making an exit, so that she was left addressing the empty room.

When I came down to breakfast the chickens had escaped and were running all over the front lawn. Mum was sitting on a garden bench holding her face to the sun, her eyes closed. I sat next to her. She said, 'I hate those chickens.'

I said, 'I know you do.'

She smelt of henna, a dry, grassy scent. She had applied it the day before and there was a red sheen upon her dark hair, except where it was naturally grey and had turned a sad pale orange. I considered her too old for henna. She had missed a bit behind her ear when washing it out. I said, 'Hold still,' and lifted up her hair and rubbed at the grey-green crust with my thumb.

The chickens charged around on the grass, straggling behind their rust-coloured leader, like a bunch of hung-over squaddies. Mum said, 'I hate the smell – that chicken-shit smell.'

'Where's Hilda?' I asked. Hilda was my favourite.

'Behind the fuchsia,' said my mother. And then, not necessarily referring to Hilda: 'Poor thing.' She leaned her head back a little further and closed her eyes, floating on a deep pool of resignation. 'It smells of dead Tories' wardrobes,' she said. 'Mildewed tweed. That's what it smells of.'

Under the fuchsia Hilda was just visible, sitting very, very still behind a cascade of red bell flowers. I looked out beyond the combe to sea. There was no horizon: the morning mist was rising from the water.

'Actually,' said Mum, 'what you smell in those wardrobes probably is shit. All that mouse shit under the floorboards. Layers and layers of it deposited there over the centuries. The better the house, the more mouse shit there is – just think how non-U it would be to lift the boards and actually clean it out! You could probably calibrate the entire British class system on the depth of mouse shit under the floor.'

Corwin appeared in the doorway with a glass of orange juice in his hand and smiled at me. Mum sensed the smile and her eyes snapped open. 'You two and your secret smiles!' she said nastily, and stood up. 'Do something about those bloody chickens.' She pushed past Corwin and went back into the house.

Corwin sat down next to me, stretched out his long legs and laid an arm along the back of the bench behind me. I made to get up to deal with the chickens, but Corwin put out a hand and pulled me back. 'Let them enjoy the illusion of freedom a bit longer,' he said. 'They can't go anywhere.'

His leg rested against mine. We shared our skin. We were tanned and dusted with gold. This dry world was a revelation, a boon: the pale brittle grass, the hardened soil, the brown crisped leaves. For most of our lives we had been rained upon. From velvety mizzling rains to wind-propelled water darts. Even when it wasn't raining the droplets hung in the air, patient and immobile as the sheep and cattle that grazed the fields. We had rarely been away from the sound of water moving. There was always a stream or a river churning close by, winding its way, building noise, to thunder over the cliff and join the sea. But that summer, the streams had sunk into the ground. All we could hear were the bees in the lavender.

Corwin was still feeling sorry for the chickens, and was glaring at the flint garden wall. Suddenly he leaped from the bench and started chasing them around the lawn. They shot off in different directions, clucking madly and indignantly. He ran after the leader, bent over with his overlong arms outstretched. They went twice around the garden before he caught her and, grasping her firmly between his hands, returned her to the chicken run in the far corner of the garden. The others reassembled, unsure of their next move now that the pecking order had been upset. Corwin went along the chicken wire, looking for their escape route, and, finding a gap under the wire, took a stone and started hammering it back in. I went to fetch Hilda from the fuchsia. She had laid two eggs. I tucked her under my left arm and picked up the eggs. My father always said that the warmth of new eggs was the most comforting thing he could think of.

I took the eggs as an offering to Mum, who was sulking in the kitchen, martyred by her yellow rubber gloves. The role of peacemaker usually fell to Corwin, but she was angry with Corwin of late, we didn't know why, something to do with male children fleeing the nest, we assumed. We didn't assume that she would miss me when I fled the nest, or that either of us would miss her. Still, for the equilibrium of the house, it didn't do to have Mum sighing at the sink. I felt that I needed to shield Corwin and the chickens from her.

'Would you like me to boil you an egg?' I asked her.

She looked at me over her shoulder with suspicion, her hands still in the water.

'They're fresh,' I added. 'Hilda just laid them.'

Mum pulled the plug. There was a loud suck of draining water. 'You know, Morwenna,' she said, turning round, 'I really hate it when you try to be nice to me!'

I was about to say something tart when the food-timer went off, letting out an almighty wake-up trill. We both jumped. Matthew's bread had finished proving. My mother's face twisted and she ran out into the garden. I yelled, 'Matthew. Bread-timer!'

Matthew shuffled down the hall from his study. 'Oh, thank you, Morwenna,' he said. 'I thought I'd put it in my pocket.'

He took the baking tray from the boiler cupboard, tipped and removed the damp tea-cloth from the mound of dough.

'Your mother seems to be crying in the garden,' he said. 'Do you think someone should do something about it?'

'No, it's all right. Just leave her for a bit. It'll stop.'

'Oh, good,' he said. 'All right, then.'

It was hard on Matthew. Neither his mother, his three sisters, nor his wife had ever cried about anything, as far as he had been able to tell. He slashed a couple of lines on the surface of the dough before putting it into the oven. Then, setting his food-timer as he went and putting it into the pocket of his trousers, he disappeared back down the hall and behind the door of his study.

I was sliding both eggs into a pan of simmering water when Oliver appeared in the kitchen.

'Oh,' I said. 'I didn't know you were here.'

'We're going climbing,' he said, pulling his long hair into a ponytail and tying it with the hairband from around his wrist. 'Can I have an egg?'

Oliver always seemed to be there – in our kitchen – adoring Corwin from afar, which was vexing. Even so, I loved to look at him, his gentle colouring, the way that he was soft hazelnut brown all over, his hair, his eyes, his skin, his freckles. And I was fascinated by the way that he looked like a plain diffident girl from one angle, and how, in profile, his strong nose and Adam's apple transformed him into a boy. There was something otherworldly about this shape-shifting, as though he had the power to vanish, but was too modest to do so.

I cut up some buttered toast and we dipped soldiers into our egg yolks, meditatively. Corwin came in with an armful of ropes, karabiners and harnesses, and I permitted myself a moment of jealousy – it was the one thing we couldn't share. Corwin did his best to teach me to climb, but I had – have still – a terror of heights.

Before I left for work I went to make my peace with Mum. I found her in the kitchen garden, still wearing the washing-up gloves, resentfully pulling up carrots. She ignored me for a couple of minutes, so I said, 'Mum, let's be friends.'

She stood up and pulled off the gloves, then swept her right arm around to indicate the garden, palm up, in a movement I recognized from the ballet lessons I had dropped – to Mum's disappointment. She had enjoyed ballet lessons. *She* had possessed grace.

The kitchen garden was beautiful, monastically calm, divided into medieval squares. This was what my father's soul would look like in image: neatly laid out, not a weed in sight, rot and canker at bay, a billowy herbal-medicinal softness around the edges and packed with nutritious goodness. For a moment I saw my mother as she saw herself, banished to the cloister, and I felt a twinge of sympathy. She had been pretty and plucky and working as a secretary and had bought her clothes on Carnaby Street until she went on that fateful camping holiday with her best friend. She didn't even like camping. And then my father had lured her in with his strong, silent, country-squire act, and before she knew it she was pretending to enjoy long walks in the rain and to share his principles.

'Do you know why your father married me?' Mum demanded, moving her feet into third position. She liked to punish me with sudden hysterical confidences. 'It was for your grandmother. They all knew she had cancer. No one told me, of course. That's why he married me. I was a death present.'

'That's not true,' I said helplessly. My father never spoke on the subject, which, of course, made her sound shrill and irrational even to her own ears. He seemed ennobled by his silence.

'How would you know?' she snapped.

And now, I thought, you will cry. And she did. But she didn't abandon herself to her tears: instead they rolled silently down her cheeks, and her lips pressed together against the strain of her distress. I picked up the bowl of carrots from the ground by her feet and took them to the kitchen. Oliver and Corwin were still there, waiting for Mickey to pick them up in the VW van. Corwin was laughing scornfully at the newspaper, which meant that he was reading about some disaster in some abandoned part of the world in which thousands of people had died horrible, *entirely avoidable* deaths because of *Western Greed*.

'Your turn,' I said.

'For what?'

'Mum.'

He put down the newspaper. 'Where is she, then?'

'Pulling carrots.'

He topped up his mug of tea, and poured out another to take to Mum. 'Anything in particular?' he asked, as he added the milk.

'Dad never loved her.'

'Poor Mum,' said Corwin.

'Poor Dad!' I said.

3.

That morning the heat had sparked a rush on Slush Puppies at the Sea View Café and we ran out of electric blue, which upset people. 'It's all the same shit,' I told my customers. 'They're not flavours, they're just different combinations of chemicals. The virulent green tastes almost exactly the same and is just as bad for you.'

My boss took me aside and said, 'Morwenna, you are a bad-tempered, foul-mouthed little smartarse and the only reason I'm not firing you is that it's the end of the season anyway.'

'I'm terribly sorry,' I said to my customers, chastened. 'But we're out of raspberry.'

The preference for blue began to obsess me. It bore no resemblance to anything found naturally in food. I spent the day imagining us all with fluorescent blue intestines, glowing away invisibly. The beach was packed. Dozens of children ran in and out of the sea. Some of them played together, but many of them, I noticed, had marked out their own private circuit. I remembered doing that: pretending to be the only one on the beach. I served ice cream, asking, 'Large or small? Soft or scooped?' and stabbed at Mr Whippys with chocolate Flakes. One badly sun-burned man told me to 'Smile, love! It may never happen!' And I balanced his ice cream on the cone in such a way that it would fall off before he got back to the beach – a technique I had perfected over the summer.

At four thirty, Oliver came by to pick me up from work. 'Where's Corwin?' I asked.

'He's gone back with Mickey. He'll catch up with us later.'

I was resentful to be an errand of Oliver's, but we grabbed a couple of pasties and went to sit on the sea wall. I told him about the Slush Puppies.

'Everyone knows it's not natural,' he said, 'so they go for the most appealing colour.'

'What's your favourite Slush Puppy flavour-colour?' I asked him.

'Blue. What's yours?'

'Blue.'

The tide was very flat, just lapping gently onto the sand, no foam on the edge of the water.

'But why do they call it raspberry?' I asked. 'Why not something bluish, like blueberry or plum or something?'

Oliver ignored me and wrapped his half-eaten vegetarian pasty in the greasy white paper bag and lobbed it into a litter bin, alarming a couple of young seagulls which had perched there. They had not yet mastered the use of their wings and flapped clumsily to the pavement, bouncing once or twice upon impact. Oliver sighed and leaned forward to prop his head in his hand. I assumed that it was Love of one sort or another.

'Are you OK?' I asked dutifully.

'Don't you feel sad?'

'About what?'

'About leaving.'

Stripy windbreaks and ice-cream wrappers littered the sand. I looked out over the rainbow of plastic buckets and spades, the inflatable dolphins, the massed beer guts and blistered breasts, and wondered if I should be feeling sad.

'No,' I said. 'Why? Do you?'

'I'm not sure I want to go to university. I'm thinking of deferring while I make up my mind.'

I was horrified. For the last two years I had been dreaming of nothing but the filthy city where I would know no one and no one would know me. I was going to wear anonymity like a well-cut trench-coat and conduct life in angular urban grey tones.

23

'You can't be serious!'

'Why not?' His heels kicked gently against the wall. 'I'm just not clear why we're all in such a huge hurry to leave.'

We both stared hard at the sea. A woman in a white bikini fell from a windsurfer with a loud scream and a smack of pea-green sail on the water. The windsurfing instructors kept a count of breasts exposed in the undignified struggle to get back on the board, and later bragged their tally in the pub. The woman shrieked with embarrassment as she hooked a leg over the board and tried to pull herself back on. The instructor gave her a shove, one hand on her left buttock. He would get extra points for that – they counted hands on buttocks too. She sprawled face down on the board. I was furious with her for making a fool of the entire sex. She should have been made to wear a wetsuit. This was the kind of thing I thought about. Oliver, on the other hand, was busy honing his nostalgia, looking further out to sea, where the light popped on the horizon, and thinking how beautiful it was.

'So, what will you do?'

He blushed. 'I'm not sure I want to go to university at all. It's just more endless chatter. Crow is the only one with the courage of his convictions. He's going to India to actually do something. The rest of us – we're not doing anything. I want to do something practical – farming maybe, but sustainable farming.'

'You are joking!'

'You're such a snob, Morwenna!'

'It has nothing to do with snobbery,' I said. He moved his head and shifted from female to male. His androgyny seemed to preclude a practical career. 'I just think of you as . . .'

'As what?'

'I don't know. I just can't see it.'

The beach was emptying of families and beginning to fill with damp dogs chasing slimy tennis balls on the wet, rippled sand. The sea was edging out of the rock pools. Old Arthur came down the hill in his blue flannel dressing-gown for his five o'clock swim. We watched him walk out into the shallow red tide, stringy muscles under slack, mottled skin, the white down of his hair lifting in the breeze. He waded right out until he reached a depth at which he could begin his slow, lopsided crawl along the length of the bay. Eventually, Oliver said, 'Well, I don't think I can just stand by while we rape the planet. But it's obviously not something I can talk to you about. And, anyway, we should get going.'

'I'm sorry,' I said. And I was. I contemplated life without Oliver in it, and came to the conclusion that I was sad about it. 'I will miss *you* when I go,' I said.

Oliver smiled sadly, put his arms around me and hugged me. 'And I'll miss you too,' he said.

We both knew that he didn't really mean me, but Corwin. I didn't mind. It was almost the same thing.

Oliver and I made our way up into town and let ourselves in at Willow's house. A number of small children, some of whom might or might not have been Willow's half-siblings, scattered up the stairs. The sound of Joni Mitchell drew us into the garden, where Willow's mother reclined on a picnic blanket, surrounded by a number of her sometime lovers, the last of her beauty evaporating mistily from her. None of them reacted to our arrival. The household was so fluid that we might well be living there, for all they knew.

'Is Willow around?' I asked.

'Oh, hello, Morwenna,' said her mother. 'I think so. I think she's in the greenhouse.'

One of the lovers waved a joint in our direction, which we declined. I wished I were the kind of person who knew how to accept casually offered drugs. I wished, in fact, to be Willow, who was blissfully unencumbered by a conventional family structure, and whose father might or might not have been a Beatle, her mother having been a Maharishi Mahesh Yogi groupie at about the right time. Willow occupied a wonderland of uncertainty in which everything was possible.

We went up to the end of the narrow scruffy garden and found Willow in the greenhouse, spraying the cannabis crop. 'At last!' she said, when she saw us. We were not late, but she had little sense of time. 'Get me out of here!'

Saturdays were always like this. We gathered ourselves up, pub by pub, half cider by half cider. We drank the cider because it was cheap. We found Mickey playing pool in the First and Last, but Corwin had said he was going to the Beacon. Corwin was not at the Beacon but there we found a crowd of school-mates so we stopped there for a while. In the meantime we had lost Oliver at the Ship, but found him again later at the Mason's Arms where Corwin was reported to have been seen drinking outside the George. By around nine thirty we were all united down at the harbour at the Lighter and that was where I last saw my father.

I had forgotten that he would be playing there, partly because Mum, who ordinarily enjoyed a night out, was smarting in front of the television at home. If I had remembered, I would probably have avoided the Lighter. He was sitting in a corner of the lounge with four or five of his friends, playing his fiddle. Bob Marsden was sitting next to him, holding his ear, and singing in a quavering voice, some ancient song that is certain, either directly or indirectly, to have been about the Green Wood.

Bob Marsden, in the role of 'Dad's best friend', required explanation, but Corwin and I had never been able to find one for him. Since my father's fortieth birthday party when Bob 'forgot himself' (my father's words at the time) and placed his hands on my budding breasts, Corwin and I referred to him as 'Fuck Off Bob' (my words at the time), which enraged Mum and saddened my father. There was a permanent whiff of the locker room about Bob Marsden, a sticky stench of lewd boasts exchanged and female parts appraised and compared. We assumed that he enjoyed spending time with my father because it allowed him to talk about himself uninterrupted, but whenever we challenged my father as to what he gained from the friendship he would just say, 'We've known each other a very long time.'

My father saw me at the bar and smiled. He had three pints lined up in front of him, paid for by appreciative members of his audience, and I could tell that he was still upset, from the speed at which he was drinking them. My father was a good musician, but his elegies didn't chime with our idea of Britain, which, from our remote white corner, appeared to be populated with Real People, who fought to keep the mines open and suffered class prejudice and racism and sang angrily in industrial accents of life in the suburbs of the big cities. Some of us had even been to a big city and met Real People, some of whom had even been black.

If Fuck Off Bob hadn't been there, I might have gone over and asked my father to stand me a pint. But instead I just waved and, suddenly irritated by his sprigs of thyme and fair maidens at gates, I thought: Mum's right. You live in the past. (Afterwards, that thought took on the force of something spoken aloud, and I lived with the sensation of having wounded my father with my last words to him, when, in fact, I had simply thanked him for tea.) And then there was a plan and we turned to leave, Corwin hooking his arm around my neck. We waved at our father, and he, mid-fiddle, nodded, with a sad smile, which might simply have been in response to the passage of music he was playing. My father was a still man. He moved in the same way that he talked: only the necessary minimum. But when he played music he danced, which always made him appear as though under enchantment, and that was my last sight of him as we left the pub: my father seated and swaying, rapt in movement.

Corwin took the lead. We made our way back into town, stopping at the off-licence for a couple of bottles of Strongbow, and at Mickey's bedsit for a bag of Willow's home-grown, and we ambled the length of the seafront and up onto the cliff path. The dark was beginning to settle in the hollows of the sand-dunes and on the surface of the sea but the sky was still blue. Three angry weals of red had been scratched into it by the sun. By the time we had climbed to the cliff-top they had faded away. We walked in single file along the cliff, and each of us must have glanced down into the blackening bowl beneath Brock Tor as we began to descend to Thornton Mouth, where night had already wrapped itself around the cabin and was creeping out from the cliffs to meet the water.

That night we built a fire within a ring of white- and grey-scribbled boulders, just above the high-tide mark. Once I had imagined that an ancient language was expressed on the stones that one day I would learn to decipher. We dragged long pieces of sea-bleached driftwood across the shingle and set them on end, carefully weaving them into a cone two metres tall. We stood back and found our work beautiful, seeing there a group of dancers, arms aloft, curves white in the moon, momentarily entwined, on the point of springing apart.

Then Mickey set it alight. The fire amazed us with the speed at which it caught, twisting itself around the wooden limbs, shooting flames twice their height into the sky. I look at eighteen-year-olds now, their unformed faces, their smooth pebbles of certainty clutched tight in their fists, and I remember our faces in the fire-light, how, for once, the Atlantic was outdone and the fire entered our senses with the force of an autumn storm and held us in an ecstasy of awe at its destructive power as, one by one, the branches of driftwood submitted, staggered inwards, collapsed glowing into the centre.

When the fire was subdued we swam on the high water. For the last seven years our little group had clung together on our raft of cleverness, navigating a school in which book-reading was considered posh, and to be posh was a congenital and incurable affliction. We were, I think, the whole world to each other. And yet, that night, as we floated in the moonlight, shivering on the eerily tame tide as we counted satellites, the ties between us were lifting. Strand by silken strand, they rose softly from the water.

We warmed ourselves by the fire. Mickey rolled a joint. I remember the tip of his tongue as he patchworked the Rizlas together, the way that he passed the joint to Willow. Oliver was pressing his hair dry with a towel. He let the joint pass him by. He disliked drugs and alcohol: they unleashed words that could not be retracted, and he was usually the first to leave. But tonight was special: it was almost all over and he was making allowances.

I lay with my head in Corwin's lap. He was preaching. It would be our burden and our duty, he said, our generation, spawn of Thatcher. We must look to the south and see the damage we wrought there. We must undo, reduce, redistribute. We must battle with our inflated egos, make ourselves small. For soon, he said, the south would rise up against us, and its vengeance would be just and terrible. We were making a hell of the earth, the sun would burn through our atmosphere, and lo! The waters would rise and engulf us.

'Christ, Corwin!' said Willow, suddenly. 'Shut the fuck up, will you?'

'You could start by becoming a vegetarian!' said Oliver, quietly but severely.

'Oh, God!' I groaned. 'Here it comes. "How meat is destroying the planet".'

Oliver ignored me. 'Meat production is a really inefficient and wasteful use of land,' he lectured Corwin. 'So even if you enjoy chewing on dead, tortured animals, you should think about the amount of land in Third World countries that is being given over to your disgusting hamburgers. Do you know how many square miles of Amazon are chopped down every year for cattle farming? Do you?'

There was a huge hole in the ozone layer and the rainforest was in flames.

A gloom was settling on the group. Willow turned to Corwin. 'You see what you've started? Now he's at it!'

'You forgot the farting cattle,' said Mickey. 'All that flatulence introduces warming gases into the atmosphere.' After a joint and more than his fair share of cider, he found himself hilarious and started to giggle.

Oliver said, 'It's not the farting, actually. It's the belching.'

His earnestness was too comical – we were all laughing now.

'I don't know why you think it's so funny. That's just how they want you, you know. Stoned and amused and disengaged.'

The accusation of 'disengagement' hung dangerously in the air. I deflected it with a catty swipe of indiscretion. 'Oliver wants to be a farmer!' I announced.

Oliver flinched as everyone fell silent and looked at him. I thought he might at last do his vanishing trick but instead Corwin pushed me from his lap, leaped up and started waving his long arms around like a fairy godfather, shouting, 'And so you should, Oliver. So you should! That's exactly where to start. Small-scale farming. Reduce our impact on the environment.'

Oliver said quietly, 'Exactly. It's like I said to Morwenna. It's a question of conviction.'

'Morwenna doesn't have any convictions,' said Corwin, sadly. I thought about raising a protest, but I was tired, and I knew even then that he was right – all I had was dislike. Then he squatted behind Oliver and put his arms around him and kissed his cheek. 'Oliver,' he said, 'you've convinced me. I'm going to be a vegetarian from now on.'

Oliver shot me a look in which agony and resentment that I had witnessed it were mixed. I felt irritated with Corwin. Really, he was quite ruthless with his demonstrations of affection. People wanted to mistake them for love.

Willow and Mickey were arguing about whether or not it was time to go home. A mile to the north-east our father fell to his death. You would have thought that we might have felt some jarring of the soul, but we didn't.

Willow stood up. 'We're off.'

The light was so strong that we were able to watch Mickey and Willow cross the beach and disappear into a moonshadow at the foot of the cliff. Oliver, Corwin and I were left watching the embers. After a while, Oliver fell asleep under his jacket, his head on his arm, his face covered with his long hair. 'Should we wake him?' I asked.

'No, leave him,' said Corwin. 'He'll wake up when he gets cold.'

We guarded the privacy of the cabin with superstition, and never invited our friends to sleep there, so we left Oliver by the fire, crossed the cove to the cabin and took the key from its hiding place under the eaves, let ourselves in and curled up together under the great-aunts' crocheted bedspread and fell asleep to the shingle sighing.

4.

No one noticed that my father was missing. He had not come home the night before, but it was traditional, after the annual row, for him to spend the night on Bob Marsden's really quite comfortable modern black-leather sofa, before recovering enough speech to apologize – he was always the one to apologize, with flowers from the garden. And Mum always accepted. And then there was a truce during which my father tried to be more present and my mother went up to Barnstaple and bought new shoes.

It was another beautiful day when Corwin and I woke up. We made tea and walked out to meet the tide, then swam until we were overcome with hunger and ran back to the house and to Matthew's bread.

Mum lay on the front lawn, sunbathing. When the phone rang, at about midday, Corwin and I lay at either end of the hammock, reading. Neither of us made a move to answer it. At last Mum, as ever incapable of leaving a phone unanswered, leaped up angrily, tying her sarong around her waist as she went. We recognized, from her acknowledgement of the caller, a note of sarcasm, which indicated that she must be speaking to Bob. And then something – not a sound, but a quality of attention – that caused us to look up and at each other. We rolled out of the hammock (I remember Corwin holding it steady so that I wouldn't fall) and crossed the lawn. There was no hurry. It was as it is in dreams: we were not the agents of our own movement. In the hall, Mum stood, the old-fashioned Bakelite receiver to her ear, not speaking. It was dark; the flagstones were cool under my bare feet. Mum seemed to be glowing red: the henna in her hair, the tan shiny with coconut oil, the sarong over her hips. We moved closer to her. I could smell the coconut oil on her skin. I heard her say, her voice hissing like water falling onto hot coals, 'Yes. I'm sure! You'd better get over here.' I knew that I needed to sit down for this. Mum was glowing redder and hotter, and the smell of coconut was making me feel ill. I sat on the stairs. Corwin had his hand on Mum's shoulder. She replaced the receiver and turned towards me. A flame-ball of fury rolled from her and engulfed me whole.

There is a gap in time. Corwin tells me that he wanted to run to Brock Point, but that Mum, already dialling the police, said, 'No. I need you here.' And that I sat on the stairs and didn't move. But all that is gone from my memory. The next thing I remember is Fuck Off Bob sitting in our armchair, crying and emitting hangover fumes. Even I am prepared to admit that on a normal day he was a good-looking man, big and dark, with those shoulder-length brown locks, which he claimed to be an inheritance from a washed-up survivor of the Spanish Armada. But hung over and crying, his carefully cultivated piratical appearance took on the quality of a dishevelled morning-after fancy-dress costume. Corwin and I sat at either side of Mum on the chesterfield, facing him, and watched him snivel. 'I'm so sorry!' Snivel, snivel. 'I'm so sorry.' The tears ran into the handsome crags of his cheeks and dripped off his chin. All I could think of was how much I hated him; that, if my father was dead, I wanted Bob to be dead as well, or maybe even instead, but just very painfully, brokenly, dead.

Bob had woken up on the shag-pile rug (bought so that he could say *shag*-pile) with the feeling that something had happened – something awful and irrevocable. He said – more than once, 'It was such a good night!' He was trying to give it some context: all that jolly good fun, we were to understand, was an essential element in the story. My father had been *happy* as he

33

fell off the cliff, or he had fallen off the cliff *because* he was happy. It was hard to distinguish the subtleties. Bob sounded like a Devon rustic – all those years of taking the piss out of Devon rustics saying what a 'good noiyt' it had been, and the accent had stuck.

The part of the story with which we were grappling was that Bob had watched my father fall off a cliff, then gone home. We expressed this conceptual difficulty. Why had it not occurred to him to call the police? 'You don't understand,' he sobbed. 'I was out of it! I didn't know what was going on . . .' His manly frame convulsed in the armchair, a bagpipe wheeze of despair filled the room, and he started apologizing again.

The shock had brought out our default characters. Mum was too angry to speak. Corwin was trying to be civilized. In the end it fell to me to say, 'Look, Bob, we don't give a flying fuck about how sorry you are. Just begin at the beginning and take it from there.'

So, this is the story of my father's death:

It had been a good night. There had been much merry, merry monthing of May and still more pinting of Old Peculier and even my father had cheered up by the time they rang the bell. He and Bob were laughing all the way home. ('Not quite,' I interrupted. 'What?' said Bob. 'Not quite all the way home,' I said.)

It was such a beautiful night, so beautiful, that when they got to Brock Tor they were overcome with nostalgia and a need to urinate into the chine, for old times' sake. So they wandered off the main path and down to the cliff edge below the tor and they both took a piss. And my father was laughing, and Bob himself was laughing so hard he almost passed out – in fact (this bit took some intellectual effort), he must have passed out. And when he came round Bob just got to his feet and stumbled home. And it wasn't until he woke up that it seemed to him strange that one moment my father had been there, and the next he hadn't. And then it seemed that it was all a bad dream, but when he called Mum it became less and less like a dream and more like something that had really happened – my father was laughing at the edge of the cliff and then he fell forward and was gone.

At this moment two versions of the story were equally true in my mind. My father was dead, but also, this was a colossal fuck-up of Bob's that we were going to have to sort out and my father lay on a ledge somewhere with a broken leg and a fearsome hang-over and the coastguard would find him. Already, there was a helicopter buzzing about over Brock Tor.

Then Matthew came in. He had been off on his morning walk. It was so natural for him to be gone at that time of day that we had forgotten about him. He already knew that the house was all wrong, that none of us was where we ought to have been. He came in and said, 'Something has happened to John, hasn't it?'

Mum spoke for the first time since Bob had started crying. She said, 'I need a drink.' She stood up, walked past Matthew and left the room.

Matthew said, 'Corwin?'

Corwin was strangely alert, his normal lassitude gone, his limbs neatly arranged. He said, very precisely: 'Dad fell off the cliff last night.'

The familiar face of my grandfather dropped away, the face I always saw because it was the beloved face that was always there, and I saw him as he looked to the world: old and thin-haired, his brown-splashed hands shaking slightly. He remained standing and looked down at those hands, lifting them and holding them apart.

'Where?' he asked.

'Brock Tor.'

Bob was crying again. Matthew looked around for a chair, and Corwin jumped up to find him one, taking it from the writing desk in the corner and supporting Matthew's arm as he sat. His hand remained on Matthew's shoulder. Matthew looked from

Corwin to me to Bob. I heard the clink of ice falling into a glass in the kitchen.

At last, Matthew said, 'Morwenna, dear. Bob seems to be in some distress. Why don't you make him a cup of tea while Corwin tells me what has happened?'

In the kitchen, Mum was drinking gin. I put on the kettle and fished around in the cupboard for tea. 'Who's that for?' she asked.

'Bob,' I said.

'Oh, for Christ's sake,' said Mum. 'Give the poor man a proper drink!' And she grabbed a glass and opened the freezer door and pulled out the ice tray and pressed ice cubes out with her thumbs as if she were strangling the chickens. Then she filled the glass with gin and shoved it into my hands.

The cold of the glass on my palms woke me up. 'I don't want to go back in there,' I said.

She opened her mouth to say something, but instead glared at me and tutted as she snatched the glass from my hand and strode off through the hall. I sat at the kitchen table. The sky was thrush-egg blue, the triangle of sea beyond the church spire a deeper velvety damson. Somewhere over the coast path the helicopter buzzed, but I could not see it.

The doorbell rang. Corwin went to answer it. I heard him greet the policemen and lead them into the living room. Then he came to the kitchen, took my hand and led me upstairs, where we lay on his bed. I rested my head on his shoulder and he stroked my hair for a very long time. On Corwin's bedroom wall Che Guevara gazed off into the distance in a revolutionary reverie. And suddenly I began to laugh. Corwin said, 'Morwenna! Stop it. What the hell are you laughing at?'

But I couldn't stop it. Through my laughter I managed to say, 'Che Guevara!' And then he saw it too. And he started to laugh and we rolled over onto our stomachs and buried our faces in the pillow so that no one could hear us and we shook as we laughed into the pillow because it was the end, you see, of all

our surrogate sympathies. We were going to have to experience
pain for ourselves.

On the edge of our world people searched for my father. The
coastguard were sending abseilers, we had been told, down the
chine 'to have a look', which I took to mean, 'for bits of your
father's brain'. But that brilliant day turned out to have been the
last day of summer. In the afternoon the rains came over. If there
was anything to find, it had been washed away.

After two days of rain came the sea mist. Trapped in our attic,
Corwin and I watched it roll up the combe towards us and wrap
itself around the house. It sat there like the suspension of time.
Three days after my father's fall, Matthew called us all together.
The police wanted to speak to us. They were not hopeful of find-
ing him alive, they said, as though this was not obvious to us.
Matthew said, in pain, 'Ah, well. We have lived so long with the
sea. The tribute is long overdue.'

Mum let out an incredulous choking 'Christ!' And Corwin,
not meaning to, laughed – but not unkindly, and not at anyone in
particular.

Matthew placed his hand over Mum's and said, 'Valerie dear,
it's time to call off the search.'

Her hands flew to her head, but he insisted. 'The sea has had
him now,' he said. 'Believe me, dear. We don't want what's left
over when she's done with him.'

I thought of my father in the sea's embrace. He once told me
that mermaids mate with drowning men and that he remembered seeing a mermaid from the cabin steps. He knew that they
didn't exist, he said, and that she could not have been real. But
still, he said, the memory was clear. She was very dark, and not at
all pretty: 'Sly, she was,' he said. She scowled at him and slid into
the water. There she is, on Matthew's map, sitting on a rock, her
tail in the water. She is the colour of granite, of mackerel.

*

37

When Matthew said that we owed the sea tribute, in the moment between Mum's choke of despair and Corwin's laugh, I thought: She was jealous. The sea was jealous of our moment of inattention, our one act of fire worship, and she took my father in retribution.

But, of course, I had to remind myself, it would probably not have been the water that killed my father. It would have been the rock.

5.

The house was besieged by well-wishers. There are few cruelties to compare with the solicitude of concerned neighbours. We hid in the house, not daring to go out. Offerings began to appear on our doorstep: chicken pies and apple crumbles and Lancashire hot pots, labelled with freezing instructions, as unwanted as the little corpses left there over the years by our semi-feral cats – mice, voles, the odd disgusting rat, birds (always to my father's distress) and, once (to mine), a rabbit kit.

Some of the bolder and more curious simply opened the front door and strode into our house to tend us. May Rowsell, whose purple rinse cunningly disguised her steely meddlesomeness, took to dropping by, coming in without knocking and chirruping, 'Just checking to see how you are, dears!' When she talked to Mum her voice took on the same Edwardian music-hall contortions that she applied to her appearances in those village entertainments, which were never over before she had minced across the stage in a hat and embroidered shawl, swinging a birdcage and squeaking out 'My Old Man'. Corwin and I thought about rescuing Mum from her, but didn't feel up to it.

We didn't dare lock the front door, as though conscious that this would cause offence. Our bereavement placed upon us the duty to receive sympathy. Matthew hid in his study, Corwin and I in our rooms. On the rare occasions when I ventured downstairs I encountered yet another familiar face doing 'something useful', like dusting, or mowing the lawn, or carrying a tea tray in the direction of my not-quite-widowed mother.

Finally, as if summoned by incantation, Mum's sister, Jane, materialized out of the mist. She appeared in the hallway one day, just as May Rowsell was busying around collecting up untouched mugs of cold tea. May and Jane appraised each other and immediately Jane had May's measure and May disappeared on the spot, leaving behind only the faintest puff of Devon violets-scented talcum powder and a tray of mugs abandoned on the table next to the telephone.

Jane was even angrier than Mum, if that was possible. This was what came of descending to the country. She stood in the hallway and projected her voice: 'Hell-O in there! It's safe to come out now!' Corwin and I jerked to attention, as though someone had pulled on our strings. We went downstairs, where Jane glinted, petite and neat, in a shiny mackintosh and patent leather kitten heels.

'Where's your mother?' she asked.

Corwin jumped the last two stairs and attempted to wrest the advantage from Jane by pretending that we had asked her to come. 'Thank you so much for coming,' he said, kissing her cheek. 'Mum is going to be so relieved to see you!' He put his hands on her shoulders. 'Let me take your coat.'

Mum had not wept a single tear since the day of my father's fall. But the heat had gone out of her, and she was now sheathed in a cool, crisp shell, which restricted her movements. Jane assessed her, and said, 'You look terrible! I'm running you a bath.' Mum didn't argue. Soon the scents of lavender and rose wafted down the stairs from the bathroom – aromatherapeutic weapons in Jane's constant battle against the twin evils of ageing and dowdiness.

Corwin and I were left alone in the living room for the first time since Before. The room felt all wrong – counterfeit. It was missing an essential but intangible element that made it our family room; my father's part of its spirit, I presumed. I felt quite detached thinking this thought. The spirit of a house is organic – it seems a little lopsided after pruning, but it soon grows in.

'She'll be able to replace the sofa now.'

'Lay off, Morwenna!' said Corwin.

I sat on the sofa. It truly was lumpy and scratchy and uncomfortable. I was determined to love it.

When Mum and Jane re-emerged, Mum had a damp, propped-up look about her – like a rag doll that has been dropped in a puddle, put through the washing-machine and leaned against the radiator. Jane had blow-dried Mum's hair and made her put on the shift dress that she had bought for my father's Christmas work do.

Jane ordered a light supper from me and aperitifs from Corwin. I put on some boots and went to garner salad. The mist still hung over the garden, which drooped and dripped. It was in mourning. There were weeds among the root vegetables, the courgettes had swelled to marrows, and a number of overripe tomatoes had fallen from the vines and lay rotting on the soil. I pulled at the weeds in a half-hearted attempt at rescue, but it was no good. The garden was doomed. As I snipped at the salad leaves I thought: She will dig up the vegetables. She will get rid of the chickens. She will replace the sofa. And then I realized. Mum could do none of those things because she could never, now, win the argument. The deep unfairness of this struck home. No wonder she was so angry.

There was no bread. Matthew had not been seen for the last two days, although I had heard him moving around the house in the early hours of the morning. I could hear him thinking in the pauses in his shuffle. I went and pressed my ear to the door of his study. I feared hearing the sounds of grief, but there were none, so I knocked tentatively at the door.

'Come in!'

I opened the door to the mingled smells of oil paint, white spirit, linseed oil and pipe tobacco. He stood on a set of library steps in front of the map, his paintbrush poised beneath the magnifying-glass.

'Ah! Morwenna!' he said. 'Have you been sent to extricate me?'

'Jane's here.'

'Yes. I can sense her presence!'

He carried on painting.

'I've just come across something very interesting,' he said. 'A blasphemous pamphleteer! He seems also to have had a line in daubing slogans on walls. I found him in that funny little tract there – no, not that one. The one on the left.'

I picked up a dog-eared tract published by the Village Sermon Society for the Publication of Village Sermons.

'He's referred to as "the infamous blasphemer of Barnstaple". So then I went looking for him elsewhere, and it occurred to me that I might find him in the memoirs of that old magistrate, Ezra Hargreaves – you remember, he had one of those beards that you hate so much, where the upper lip and chin are shaved. Unfortunately,' said Matthew, 'we don't have the wording of the blasphemies – they were too toxic to record.'

Matthew's sketchbook lay open on the table, the one I had made him for Christmas: hand-stitched, bound in a soft brown leather so that it could easily slide into his jacket pocket, numbered on the spine. It lay open at the page where three cartoons of the unfortunate blasphemer were sketched: a forlorn Hogarthian figure with the mad gleam of the proselyte in his eye – a working man, rumpled and resentful.

I had stopped seeing the map. When we were younger Matthew used to hand us the magnifying-glass and say, 'Look, children. Tell me what you can find.' That was the game: discover something new on the map and be rewarded with a story.

Now Matthew said, 'What do you think was the very first thing I painted on the map?'

'The house?' I ventured. I had always assumed that he had started with Thornton, but Matthew said, 'No. Of course, everyone tends to make that assumption. But I started here,

Morwenna. With the Devil. It is Thornton's founding myth, as you know.'

On the map, the Devil peered back over his shoulder, pointing the apple-red cheeks of his naked backside at the church and farting. Above the steeple the gilt-haloed head of St Michael floated on a pair of wings, wearing an expression of great decorum.

I knew Matthew's devils. They danced all around the map. The Devil had left stories all over the county. He liked to leave his hoof-prints on our roofs: trip trap, trip trap, over the slates, softly, softly, over the thatches.

I said, 'Matthew, you have to come out for supper.'

Matthew sighed. 'That Jane,' he said. He put down his palette. 'She always wears such noisy shoes!'

'Are you OK?' I asked.

'Morwenna!' he said. 'Must you be so lazy with language? And what a silly question!'

He climbed down from his ladder. 'You know, Morwenna,' he said, 'I have always been terrified of drowning.'

'I know,' I said. 'The Crab Man.'

'Yes,' said Matthew.

'But I doubt that Dad actually drowned.'

He looked at me sharply. 'I'm not sure, my dear, that that thought helps.'

'No,' I said. 'I suppose not.'

'That Jane,' said Matthew. 'She has always been so *purposeful*.'

Jane had insisted that we lay the table in the dining room. We never ate in the dining room, but this was not really a meal: it was a parley. Matthew sat at the head of the table, Jane and Mum on one side, Corwin and I on the other. The polished mahogany of the furniture and the red velvet curtains and brown Edwardian wallpaper all made me think of a coffin – a red-velvet-lined mahogany coffin, with brass handles. A wave of claustrophobia swept over me. My father would not like it in there. Then I remembered that there would be no coffin.

Matthew smiled at us all. 'Please,' he said, to Jane, 'tuck in.' He held the bread basket towards her. 'I'm sorry that there's no bread,' he said. 'I've been neglecting my duties.' She took from it a piece of damp Ryvita. Corwin cut himself a huge chunk of the cheese that we had found lurking at the back of the fridge and from which we had removed the mould. I understood that we were hungry, and that this salad in front of us, bursting with tomatoes and radishes and spring onions and boiled eggs, was somehow miraculous – blessed even. Suddenly I had an appetite for the commiseration food in the freezer. I was going to eat it all. Matthew said, 'I'm sure we must have a bottle of wine somewhere. Corwin, would you find some wine to offer our guest?'

Corwin, whose charm had been slipping a little, revived and jumped up from the table. He was reminded that there was no weapon in Jane's arsenal as powerful as Matthew's amiability, and this cheered him enormously. Matthew turned to me. 'Morwenna, dear. Glasses.' I took from the sideboard the crystal glasses that had last been used for Christmas dinner. Jane pushed the salad around on her plate. She had nibbled a tiny cardboard corner of Ryvita and abandoned it. Mum ate nothing. She sat and glared with a furious despair at Matthew, who was eating heartily, as though she were about to hurl herself upon his sword.

Corwin came back with wine and poured a glass for everyone, even Jane, who attempted to demur. She was about to say something, but Matthew lifted a glass and said, 'I think, don't you, that now that we are gathered, we should say a few words about John?'

Corwin and I stopped eating. Jane sat back in her chair and murmured embarrassed assent. Mum's expression, fixed on Matthew, remained combative. Under the table, Corwin took my hand. Matthew said, 'We can't pretend to share our grief. Each of us is alone with our own sense of loss and we may not intrude upon each other's emotions. However, we may make a simple toast: to our beloved John. May his soul find peace.'

Corwin and I muttered, 'Dad!' Jane pushed her nose towards the glass with a cat-like sniff, and Mum laughed and said, 'Christ, Matthew. You always were a pompous old arse! But here's to John – or what's left of him.' Theatrically, she lifted her glass and took a good challenging swig. 'You and John!' she said. 'All that tramping over the cliffs communing with the elements!' She stopped herself. 'OK,' she said. 'That's enough of that! What happens next?'

'Well,' said Matthew, pushing off gently on Mum's wave of hostility. 'In the absence of a body, we have to petition the court to issue a death certificate.'

'I know all of that,' said Mum. 'I'm not an idiot. I was there when that infant policeman was explaining it all to us. I meant, what happens with me? Your pleasant arrangement with John was based on the assumption that you would cop it first, which you haven't.'

Corwin opened his mouth to frame a question, but Mum said, 'Shut up, Corwin. You keep out of this.'

'Keep out of what?' I asked. I was beginning to realize that I was the only person in the room who didn't know what was under discussion.

'Your dear father and grandfather held the view that it was too vulgar to discuss money and property,' hissed Mum. 'They just did this tasteful, gentlemanly "One day, son, all this shall be yours" thing. Only it shan't.'

Jane allowed herself a smug little sip of wine, as though modesty prevented her taking any credit for the quality of Mum's performance.

'Mum, don't you think you're being just a little bit melodramatic?' asked Corwin, in his best conciliatory voice.

'Oh, hark at you, Little Lord of the Manor-in-waiting!' retorted Mum.

The room darkened a shade or two. Outside, the mist was thickening, and, while our attention had been diverted, the days had shortened. The coffin lid was closing on us. I shouted, 'What's wrong with you? Why are you taking it out on Corwin?'

'Ah! And the chatelaine springs to the defence of her beloved brother!' Mum's voice was beginning to sound metallic. Jane put a hand on her arm. Mum reached for the wine and poured herself another glass.

Matthew said, 'Valerie, dear! Please! This is your home. There is no question of you being asked to leave it.'

'But it isn't, is it?'

'Mum!' Corwin said. He looked older. I looked older. I could feel it on my face: all the skin was pulling down around my eyes. 'Please stop this.' He reached across the table and took her hands. 'Please, just calm down. We don't understand why you're bringing this up now.'

Mum returned his grip and looked at him sadly. 'You – plural – don't understand? Are you speaking for Morwenna too?' She laughed. 'Look at the two of them! My beautiful cuckoo children!' And she pulled her hands away and stood up.

'This is what will happen,' she explained. 'Your grandfather will make arrangements for the house to pass directly to you two when he dies. In the meantime, until such time as I can claim your father's life insurance – which will not be straightforward without a body – I am dependent upon your grandfather's charity. Not that he could ever be uncharitable.'

I looked at Matthew. It was true, of course. He said, 'Valerie, what else can I do?'

Something stirred in the mud of my belly – a loathsome creature squirmed there: the house would be ours, mine and Corwin's. No one else could mess with it.

Mum shrugged her shoulders. 'Nothing, Matthew. There's

nothing else you can do.' She moved towards the door. 'I'm going to pack. I'm going to spend a couple of days with Jane.'

Matthew stood up. 'We need to talk about a memorial service for John. It has been almost a week. People will wish to condole with us.'

'You sort it out,' said Mum. 'I'll be there.'

Left alone with us, Jane allowed a flash of panic to cross her face. Corwin said, 'Nice one, Aunt Jane!' It was a measure of his anger that he called her 'Aunt' – it made her feel old.

'It has nothing to do with me!' she protested.

Corwin laughed his scornful laugh. Matthew was packing his after-dinner pipe as he always did, but I knew that he was upset. I said, 'I'm going to talk to her.'

She was in her bedroom, packing, surrounded by things of my father's: his book and reading glasses on the bedside table, a jumper thrown over a chair. I said, 'How can you go away at a time like this?'

'I can't breathe here with all of this . . .' She gestured around the room. 'It's too sad. Look at the window – there's no air here. I need air.'

The darkening sea fog hung against the glass. Nothing was visible beyond it. I said, 'You're always so weird when Jane's around. It's as if you revert or something.'

Mum straightened up, dangerously. '*Revert?* Revert to what, exactly?'

'To Jane!' I was shouting. I had not felt outraged until I started shouting, but once I did, it seemed to me that she was unnatural, distorted – abandoning her own children to their bereavement. 'She's so fucking . . .' I reached for the worst insult I had in my vocabulary '. . . bourgeoise!'

'*Bourgeoise!* Christ! You even put an *e* on the end? You two are so monstrous! Well, here's the thing, darling. Now that you and Corwin are eighteen I think you're old enough for me to reveal that you are both, whether you like it or not, fully paid-up

47

members of the *bour-geoi-sie!*' She began counting out knickers. 'You don't mean *bourgeoise*, darling. You mean something else.' She always took one pair of knickers for each day she planned to be away and an extra pair. I noticed that she was packing seven. '*Suburban*, perhaps. Your father was fond of that one. Or what do you and your friends call people you think are beneath you? *Aspidistra*? Isn't that it?'

I flinched. That was *our* word. She had no licence to use it. 'It's all right,' said Mum, comfortably. 'One day, when you grow up, you'll look back and realize what a disgusting little snob you were.'

She closed the lid of her suitcase. 'Now, here's some advice for you, mother to daughter – and you can take that indignant expression off your face. You and Corwin are fine with each other. You always have been. This is the best advice I am ever going to give you. Get yourself a career. Don't give it up for your husband. Don't give it up for your children. Never, ever allow yourself to be financially dependent on someone else. Do you understand?'

I nodded. It was something I had believed that I believed, but now I saw that there were practicalities involved. I said, 'Don't go, Mum. Please.'

'I need a break, darling. You can see that, surely? I need to get away from your grandfather and his fucking map. All shut away in that room of his. What kind of a person works on the same painting for fifty years? It gives me the creeps.'

She gave me a hug and a kiss on the cheek. There were no tears. In fact, I never saw her cry again.

After she had gone I sat on her bed. I wondered if she would ever sleep there again. I thought about stripping the linen so that she could come home to clean sheets. In the corner of the room a patch of damp was causing the wallpaper to peel off the previous wallpaper, which was peeling off the one before, and so on. That's interesting! I thought. All those forgotten wallpapers. Matthew would like that. I must remember to show him.

Corwin was standing in the door. 'What are you doing?'

'Nothing. Has Mum gone?'

'Yes.'

'Do you miss Dad yet?' I asked.

'Not yet. Do you?'

'Not yet,' I said. 'But I suppose we will.'

'Yes,' said Corwin. 'I suppose we will.'

6.

Our friends had all written to say that they didn't know what to say. I missed them. I missed them more than I missed my father, which began to alarm me. In my room I worked on my parting gift for them, an edition of five little accordion books, which unfolded to reveal the wavering length of coast from the head-land to Thornton Mouth blind-stamped into the thick soft white paper. Above the coastline, printed in blue and staggered in a way to suggest waves, I had set the lines of a poem by Robert Frost about looking out to sea. I had surprised myself by creating something pretty. It was called 'Neither Out Far Nor In Deep':

> *The people along the sand*
> *All turn and look one way.*
> *They turn their back on the land.*
> *They look at the sea all day.*

I had planned to make an extra copy for Matthew, but he had reminded me of how much he feared the sea and I didn't want to appear tactless.

On Corwin's desk a pile of envelopes in pretty pastel colours accumulated, which sighed at the gorgeous tragedy of it all. By the time we took our A levels Corwin had trysted with most of the girls in the fifth and sixth forms. They all fell for his big warm black eyes and thick dark lashes and he was so chivalrous – our father had taught him always to hold the door open and to offer to help with heavy bags. Sex was an extension of courtesy for Corwin – it seemed impolite to brush off a girl who was going to such great lengths to be liked, and he submitted to their need for affirmation in various wind-sheltered dips in the beaches, or corners of houses vacated for the weekend by parents. No one seemed to resent him for it.

He began to experience cabin fever. We were still imprisoned by the weather and our fear of meeting people who would ask us how we were. At last he broke down and demanded that we leave the house. 'We'll take the bikes,' he announced. 'That way we won't have to talk to anyone we don't like.'

The mist had thinned to a half-hearted rain, and we were soaked even before we got to the top of the hill. Corwin took off ahead of me, his black drain-piped legs pedalling maniacally. Then he swooped down the hill between the curving hedgerows, his arms outspread, his outsize black jumper flapping like wings – Crow, liberated. I followed more slowly. I didn't like to take my hands off the handlebars. Corwin disappeared around a bend and by the time I had him back in my sight we were out from under the rain, and the town lay below us around the curve of The Sands, backing up into the hills, brightened from a gap in the clouds by a wash of cool blue. Corwin stopped to wait for me.

'Only three more weeks!' he said.

'Why do we hate it so much?'

Corwin shrugged his shoulders. 'It's a seaside town,' he said. 'They're essentially unlovable. They never deliver what they promise.'

'Oliver doesn't hate it.'

'Oliver is inclined to love.'

'What does that say about us?' I asked, suddenly panicked.

'I love you,' said Corwin. 'That's enough.'

'Yes,' I conceded. 'I suppose so. And Matthew,' I added.

For the first time, I felt apprehensive about being separated from Corwin. 'I wish you weren't going so far away,' I said.

'I'll be back.'

We laid down our bikes and sat on the wet grass at the edge of the road. The sea was iron – hard and unforgiving.

'Matthew hasn't said anything more about a memorial service,' I said.

'He thinks Mum should be involved.'

'There's something wrong with us.'

'They just need time.'

Suddenly I could not bear the idea of town. 'Let's go to the cabin,' I said.

Corwin winced. 'We can't go down to the cabin.'

'Why not?'

'Haven't you noticed that Matthew hasn't been down since?'

I had not noticed. How had I not noticed? Matthew normally went down every night after dinner. The bile burned at my throat. I suddenly understood why he had stopped going. He was worried about what the currents might deliver. Corwin slotted his fingers between mine and for a while we said nothing.

'What will we do when Matthew dies and we inherit the house?' I asked.

'I guess we'll end up living in it, eventually, when we're older. When we've done something with our lives. We'll feel differently about it. It will be ours.'

'What? With our spouses and our hordes of children in some kind of hippie commune?'

'I'll never get married,' said Corwin. 'Or have children. The world is overcrowded enough already. No – I mean when we're old and run out of steam, when we've seen the world and are ready to watch the sea and grow vegetables. I've always just assumed that you and I will end up back here somehow. I picture you with your hair in a grey bun and wearing a long apron, with me standing next to you holding a pitchfork!'

'Oh, please! And what if I want to have children?'

'You should have children if you want.'

I was not sure that I did want. But a future without husband or children and with only Corwin in it – and a few chickens? Maybe a goat? My father had always wanted a goat. I could not see it. On the

52

point of escape Corwin was talking about return. I could only imagine walking on and out, out of Matthew's circle and away.

'Let's make a vow,' Corwin said, suddenly and enthusiastically. He liked big binding promises. 'Let's swear never to marry or have children and to be old together at Thornton.'

'How are we going to afford Thornton? We're going to have to sell it eventually. And, anyway, no! I can't swear to that.'

'We have to keep Thornton going. We have no choice.'

'Yes, we do. We have a choice!'

Corwin's calm assumption that he and I would decay and die at Thornton whispered dread into my ear. A world twenty-four miles in diameter might be sufficient for Matthew, but not for me. Until that moment, Matthew's map had always been an endearing eccentricity: one man's one painting, never to be completed. 'A whole world is contained here,' he preached. 'Sufficient for a lifetime of discovery.' And then he would wave his walking stick at some shy patch of colour in the hedgerow, and shout, 'What's that, then?' And, when we didn't know, we were like the unbelievers in *Peter Pan*: somewhere, the flower of a rare fleabane or speedwell wilted on its stalk; Matthew heard its dying scream. 'You are appalling children,' he would say good-naturedly. 'Ignorant as stone! Which might be excusable, if you possessed any curiosity whatsoever!' Now, for the first time, I saw the map as perhaps Mum saw it: slightly sinister – as if he wrought some subtle magic in the unending painting of it that bound us to Thornton.

'This is an absurd conversation,' I snapped. 'Stop it!'

'OK!' said Corwin, and stood up, pulling me to my feet after him. We picked up our bikes. 'Still want to go back?' he asked.

'No,' I said. 'Let's carry on. It's time to face humanity.'

Mum returned from Jane's composed and generous, just after our A level results came out. 'Darlings,' she said. 'I'm so proud of you!' Her hair was a silky chestnut bob and she had acquired a jacket with shoulder pads. 'I really had been letting myself go,' she confided to me. 'You know, your father never exactly embraced change. And now you're leaving!' she added, startlingly. 'It's a good thing, darling. Really. I should have persuaded your father to move. I wasn't doing any of us any favours by being so biddable.'

Corwin and I suspected Jane of arranging for some doctor to prescribe anti-depressants for Mum, and we went through her things one afternoon when she had gone into town, and through her handbag when she returned, but we found no evidence to support our theory.

Matthew had resumed his evening walks to the sea. Time was pooling into the space left by my father. Soon that space would fill and I would not have mourned him. The thought filled me with panic. Mum and Matthew were still standing off over the memorial service. Corwin began to pack for India.

'There's something wrong with us,' I said. In the kitchen Mum hummed along to a couple of bars of the *Archers* theme tune. 'It's because he's not at rest,' I said. 'There's a reason people have funerals. You have to send their souls across.'

'Across what?' asked Corwin.

'Across whatever is between us and the other side, wherever that is.' I imagined a flaming boat on a still tide.

'We need a ceremony,' I said. 'I can't bear to think of his soul being stuck.' At the bottom of the sea, I thought, entangled in seaweed.

Corwin rolled up a pair of patched jeans and stuffed them into the battered old Karrimor rucksack that had been the crowning gift of Christmas 1983. 'I don't believe in it,' he said.

'In what?'

'In any of it – the after-life, the soul. And neither, incidentally, did Dad.'

'Yes, he did! He believed in the soul, at least. He thought everything had a soul.'

'No, he didn't,' said Corwin. 'He believed in some overarching principle of nature, but not in individual souls.'

'That's it, then? We just leave? I can't bear it,' I shouted. 'I can't bear the nothingness of it. There's something wrong with us!'

'Why do you keep saying that? You're getting hysterical. There's nothing wrong with us!'

But there was. 'I think it's a good thing we're going our separate ways,' I yelled, and ran downstairs to comfort myself with Matthew, but he was not in his study. I was just about to leave the room, when it occurred to me to consult the map. I wondered, fearfully, what it would have to say about all this. I forced my gaze to Brock Tor and braced myself to see a falling figure, but there was none. Matthew could hardly be expected to paint his own son's death, but the omission upset me. I wondered if he had put my father in the water, and reached for the magnifying-glass on the desk. But I lost courage, and didn't seek him there. I replaced the magnifying-glass and left the room.

Instead I searched the house for a box with a key, and emptied it of its contents and took it to Corwin and Matthew and Mum and asked each to put in something associated with my father. 'So, you have John's sentimental streak, after all!' said Mum, but sadly enough for me to forgive her the aspersion. None of us was to look in the box – simply slip in the object, so that we would not know what had gone into it. It had to be a secret between each of us and my father's memory. It still is a secret. Then I took the box to the kitchen garden and blindly inserted a trowelful of soil before locking it.

On a rising tide I walked to Brock Tor and pushed through the gorse patch to stand above the chine. Fed by all that rainfall, the stream now shot out of the cliff. To the north-east there was a black sheet of rain, but where I stood the sun shone and there was a light onshore wind. I forced myself close enough to the edge to be able to hurl the box over the waterfall and into the cove below. It floated there for a while, slowly nudged by the tide

55

towards a fissure between two up-facing blades of granite at the base of the cliff. What if it didn't sink? Or break up? What if it washed up on the beach? That was not what I wanted at all. A wave came over and ground it into the rock. It bobbed back up, a dark smudge on dark water, as though in defiance – of me, so it seemed. But then another wave hit hard and, withdrawing, dragged the box along a jagged ridge, where it twisted and bounced violently in the white water. The next wave slammed it under the cliff, out of view. The rain had reached me now, but I stood and waited for a long while to see if the box would reappear. It didn't.

At home Corwin asked, 'Well, did it work?'

'No,' I said. 'Not really.'

'Well, there you go,' he said. 'Don't say I didn't tell you.'

But perhaps, after all, the box performed some act of release, because that evening Matthew called a family summit and we set a date for a memorial service. The conventions soothed us, and we were kinder to each other. We agreed to ask Mark Luscombe to deliver the eulogy, mainly because, as local GP and chairman of the Thornton Players, he could be trusted to be heard in the back seats. We booked caterers, and informed people of the date, and chatted with the vicar, and chose passages from the Bible that sounded secular enough for our tastes, and generally behaved as if there were a body to bury or burn and take our leave of.

We dressed in black. I put on each item carefully – black tights, black blouse, black velvet skirt, black shoes. It was fitting and calming, and when I looked at myself in the mirror I saw someone in mourning and felt relief. At the church porch we greeted people in the honeyed autumn sun. The air smelt sweet, of leaves on the ground.

Inside the church, we sat in the front pew. 'Lost at sea,' whispered the church walls. 'Lost at sea.' The church was full. I had never noticed that any of these people knew my father. They cried at the moving bits. Mark talked about my father's love of music and nature, his gentle smile. Then he said, 'John always made me think of Sir Galahad. He was uncorrupted by the vices of our age. He was chivalrous. He was pure of heart. And he was on a quest – for his personal Holy Grail, his perfect fifteen acres.'

This raised an affectionate melancholy laugh, but it was unfortunate. The closest my father and Matthew had ever come to a row was two years earlier, when Matthew insisted on selling off the remaining acres of what had once been Thornton Farm to the farmer who leased them from him, and who promptly acquired planning permission to build a caravan site. My father had always harboured ideas that he would farm them himself one day. It was not a realistic dream. Mum never believed that he could make it work. In the dry-eyed front pew, I took Matthew's hand and squeezed it. But at the same time I caught a glimpse of something dark and formless, the beginning of a thought that I could not yet complete.

A procession of people passed into our house and before my eyes in a jumbling of fragments of my childhood that made me feel, for a moment, as if I were the one moving into the next world with my life unfolding before me. I was hugged in turn by Willow, Mickey and Oliver, who would, or could, not stop crying, perhaps, I thought, because he felt it his duty to cry on my behalf. He sobbed on my shoulder: 'I really loved your father!' I had had no idea. I could not imagine when he had had the opportunity to love my father. Corwin chatted with Sandra Stowe, which was a gross betrayal. Sandra and I were old, old enemies. She probably couldn't remember why any more than I could. As soon as I had the opportunity I hissed at Corwin, 'What's *she* doing here?'

'She was fond of Dad.'

'What do you mean she was fond of Dad? She didn't even know Dad!'

Clearly, Corwin had slept with her when I was not paying

attention. 'Of course she did,' said Corwin. 'She used to come over with her dad when we were small. Try and be nice!'

'She was a little thug!'

'No. You were a little thug – you used to beat everyone up with words.'

'She started the whole "Morwenna the witch" thing.'

'I doubt that,' said Corwin. 'And if she did, you probably provoked her. Anyway, you were both about seven!'

'Well, I'll give her one thing. She's not pig-faced and pregnant yet. Although it can only be a matter of time.'

When most of the guests had left we sneaked up to our rooms with our friends. Mickey sat drunkenly on the floor next to Corwin's record player, putting on songs and taking them off again before they were finished. He was trying to find the definitive song, the one that would suspend the moment in amber, but he failed.

Oliver, I thought, had left early, but the next morning when, after a restless sleep, I went down at six, I found him in the kitchen making tea.

'I thought you'd gone.'

'I crashed on your sofa,' he said. 'I didn't think you'd mind.'

'No,' I said. 'Of course I don't.'

Oliver's face was full of concern for me. 'How are you doing?' he asked.

'Fine. I think,' I said. 'Yesterday was nice . . .' I corrected myself, 'I mean, it was what it ought to have been, don't you think?'

He nodded, but in a slightly masculine, disapproving way. My answer had been inadequate.

'When are you off?' I asked.

'Thursday.'

'Wait there,' I said. 'I've got something for you.'

Oliver had not been in the room when I had handed out my

leaving presents. I went upstairs, retrieved the last accordion book and put it into his hands. He gently pulled on the slender ribbon that held the pages in place, and unfolded it on the kitchen table. His eyes scanned the verses. When he looked up they were tearful.

'Don't be sad for us, Oliver,' I said, because he couldn't speak. 'We'll be all right.'

'It's lovely,' he said finally. He smiled. 'It's our childhood.'

I was pleased. You could always trust Oliver to understand the important point. He folded it back together and carefully tied it up. 'Thanks,' he said. 'I'd better be going.'

'I'll go with you as far as the footbridge,' I said.

We walked down the hill in silence; the morning was chilly, blue edged with gold. As we passed the lichgate Oliver asked, 'Do you think this has changed you?'

'Probably,' I said.

I remember, now, his look of slight disappointment. I ought to have been transfigured by something so momentous. At the footbridge we hugged goodbye, and he walked on towards the coast path, his long hair shining in the low sun.

I stopped at the church on the way back up, sat and read the memorial tablets for a while, then ambled home. And a week or two later we all scattered off to our adulthoods and began to forget each other.

7.

Corwin left for India. I gave him the copy of *Keep the Aspidistra Flying*. I re-read it recently and, of course, it is a completely different story from the one I remembered. In the sixth form we read it as a noble battle against the Money God. Gordon Comstock was our hero. I had forgotten that he fails to escape the conventional course of job, wife, child, and aspidistra on the occasional table.

I went to London. Nowadays, it is all shiny, with pale pressure-washed pavements and *al fresco* foamy coffee. We have stopped worrying about Mutually Assured Destruction and the demise of the trade unions and we worship the Money God without shame. But the London that I found when I first arrived was depression grey with tired, smoke-filled buses. Coffee was instant, the pavements lined with *al fresco* sleepers, young, male, northern or Scottish. There were no Poles, Bulgarians, Estonians or Russians. They were all corralled behind the Iron Curtain, which at the time seemed unfair on them, but also to keep them safe, at least, from Margaret Thatcher and The-Americans. There were three student tribes: the Political (donkey jackets, Dr Martens boots), the Apolitical (vintage pillbox hats, mohair batwing jumpers) and the Tories (stripes and pearls, rugby shirts). Safely beyond the range of Corwin's social conscience, my sense of outrage at injustice, both national and global, dissipated. It was sad, it really was, for all those lost young men along the Strand and under Waterloo Bridge, but it had ever been thus (I took comfort from the phrase – it lent a certain historical distance to the problem). I took to rooting around Oxfam shops and wearing diamanté brooches and clicked on uncomfortable sixties stiletto heels past the buckets rattled at the university gate on behalf of The-Palestinians and The-Sandinistas.

Already by the Christmas break of my first year, Thornton seemed improbable. I was far more comfortable alone among the shoals of solitudes slipping through London than I had been intimately sharing the cavernous loneliness of the coast. I began to think of Thornton as a caricature of itself, one populated by the creatures that inhabited Matthew's map.

Mum suggested that we spend the Christmas holidays in London. 'It will just be too grim in Thornton, darling! I'm going slightly mad – I actually miss your father pottering about in his vegetable patch! And Matthew and I have nothing to say to each other so we have to be meticulously polite all the time, which is utterly exhausting! Let's go out. I'll take you shopping.'

I was glad. I had been dreading Christmas. Matthew wouldn't come up, of course, so Mum stayed in a hotel and we met up on the steps of the National Gallery. 'Darling, you lucky thing!' she said, over tea. 'I used to love coming here. My parents used to bring me – as you know, they didn't have an imaginative bone in their bodies, but they had the idea that young ladies should look at art.'

My maternal grandparents had been old parents, and my memory of them was fragmented. I remembered houses side by side, sloped driveways, hydrangeas, acres of carpet, a lot of rules. Children were not allowed in the drawing room.

'Actually,' Mum said defiantly, 'I'm thinking of signing up for an art-history degree.'

'Oh, God, no! Really?'

'Why,' asked Mum, icily, 'would you say that?'

'Well, it's such a cliché, isn't it? Bored, middle-class, middle-aged housewives and all that.'

'Thank you, darling. You're always so tactful!'

But when we walked around the gallery, I could see that she

responded to the paintings – drew energy from them. She sighed as we left. 'Of course,' she said, 'I could never persuade your father to come to London. He didn't see the point.'

'I don't see why that stopped you coming.'

Mum smiled. 'Well, Morwenna. You're eighteen. You wouldn't.'

As I settled into my London life, I thought often of Corwin and Matthew, rarely of my mother and almost never of my father and began to resign myself to my limited capacity for love. It was sufficient, I told myself, to love only two people and not to whore around with my affections. The enthusiastic and indiscriminate flirtations of my fellow students appalled me – their profligate copulations, all that mascara-streaked post-coital regret. I made . . . not what I could call 'friends' yet, but close enough. We met between lectures in the Nelson Mandela Bar and drank half-pints of Guinness, and at the weekends we took never-ending bus journeys to go to parties in Victorian terraces in parts of town too obscure even to be labelled unfashionable. We danced earnestly in flock-wallpapered rooms; the cheap lino on the kitchen floors swam with beer. We slept on sofas. It took all of Sunday to find the way home.

To Corwin I wrote of other, more important, things. How, on these homing Sundays, I gathered gifts to myself: the circles of gas holders against thunder clouds; the profane poetry of a drunk's rantings; the blue of painted angels' wings. His replies came on flimsy airmail paper. After a while I noticed that his letters were full of people and mine were not.

That first summer, when Corwin came back from India, I found him a little less like himself. Or, perhaps, he made me feel less like myself: pallid, too sharp in my movements. Or, perhaps, we were each more like our own selves. There was an Indian languor still in his limbs, and his skin was very dark. With his black hair and eyes he looked as though he had been claimed for the south. He shivered in the July sunshine. (It passed. His skin paled and he soon speeded up again. But later, when his periods away became much longer than those at home, he would find it harder to reset himself.)

The house was a little shabbier – this was how we felt our father's absence, in the stiff door handles, the swelling of the wooden draining-board around the sink, the drip of the bathroom tap. A fox had taken advantage of the neglected chicken run, and had made off with the chickens. My father had been so quiet that we only noticed now how his constant activity had resounded like a bass note through our lives. Thornton was strangely silent without him. 'I must get a man in,' said Matthew, sadly.

On the anniversary of our father's death, Mum held a family dinner in the garden. She laid out a white tablecloth and the ancestral dinner service, all set off with a vase of flowers freshly picked from the garden. We ate summer food – gazpacho and fresh bread, lightly steamed courgettes tossed in olive oil and lemon juice with char-grilled chicken, late strawberries. When we had finished eating, Matthew brought out the coffee and the porcelain tea cups. He had saved the cream from the top of the milk for the occasion.

Corwin talked. He had discovered his vocation. He would move water! All that water, all his childhood, how could he ever have imagined, clinging to his hot-water bottle at night, under the damp, scratchy blankets, the desert and the drought? How the soil turns to dust? 'They use sprinklers to keep the country clubs green!' he said. There was a new note to his scorn, I noticed, a quiet, tensioned zeal. 'The water mains are only switched on for twenty minutes a day, and the rich have lawns! It's some *insane colonial hangover!*'

Matthew was stuffing his pipe with tobacco. He didn't know what to say. He had spent decades training himself to avoid the unpleasant. In the vase were bright orange crocosmia, red and pink roses, purple salvia. I thought of all the colours of India, the dusty bangled ankles. I would never go there. I thought of the constant unconscious adjustment of the saris of the women picking over the vegetable stalls of Brick Lane, and of those saris hidden under winter coats, of all the greys of London.

'And swimming-pools!' added Corwin.

'Well, I think it's admirable!' said Matthew, standing up. 'Most admirable. Water engineering! John would have liked the sound of that.' He excused himself and went to pay his evening homage to the sea. There was less of him. My father's death had diminished him, worn him away at the edges.

Mum leaned back into her chair and smiled and sighed, 'My beautiful children!' And meant it, for once. This was a gift from her to her twins – food, wine, maternal pride – a reprieve. Because coiled up in her breast was the news, which she delivered to us over the thick dregs of the coffee, that she was moving in with Fuck Off Bob.

'Well, darlings,' she said, 'I wasn't exactly expecting you to be over the moon about it. But I am entitled to love after widowhood. You can't expect me to squat here with Matthew for the rest of my life.'

Corwin gave my ankle a lazy kick before I could refer to Bob's repugnant groping hands. He didn't pretend to be discreet about it. It was simply that we all knew what I was thinking and that there was no point in revisiting the subject.

'Of course not, Mum,' he said. 'We're glad you've found someone. We'll get used to the idea. And you're looking great, by the way.'

She *was* looking great. Some of it, presumably, was merry widowhood, but some of it was new, expensive, clothing. Bought, I realized, now that I was paying attention, with Bob's money, which he had made from his lucrative antiques and architectural salvage business, built up by prising family heirlooms from senile widows entering nursing homes. So much for impassioned speeches about financial independence, I thought to say, but I restrained myself.

'I won't,' I said, recalcitrant. 'I won't ever get used to it.'

'Well, darling,' said Mum, magnanimously, 'graciousness has never been your strong point.'

Corwin laughed, took Mum's hand and kissed it. 'Ah, it's good to be home!' He sighed and, keeping hold of Mum's hand, reached to take mine. I acquiesced. I found that he was not so altered, after all. His virtue was still intact. It was still the most irritating thing about him.

'Does Matthew know?' I asked.

'Of course.'

'And?'

'And what? What does he think about it? Is that what you're asking? Well, darling, he's far too polite to tell me what he thinks, but certainly he understands about widowhood, and about loneliness. And he'll be glad to see the back of me.'

A vast bank of ludicrously puffy clouds had formed above the trees and had taken on a shade of gold so fierce that it appeared as though a heavenly host was about to erupt from them to deliver blessing upon Mum and Bob's treacherous couplings. Mum smiled at the skies and basked in the warmth of her own indifference.

I let go of Corwin's hand. 'I'm going down to the cabin,' I said.

At Thornton Mouth, Matthew sat on the cabin steps watching a couple of surfers. I sat down next to him. It was so restful, the way that he rarely commented on arrivals or departures. The surfers were seal-shadows on the darkening swell; they were losing their light, but still they waited for the just-one-more. 'How patient they are!' said Matthew.

'They should come in.'

'Ah!' said Matthew. 'You are too timorous! It has always been the Venton curse.'

65

'I thought seasickness had always been the Venton curse.'

'Well, in the Ventons it amounts to the same thing. We dream of crossing the sea, but we are constitutionally incapable.'

'Corwin's not timorous.' I picked up a black pebble with a thick white stripe running through it and balanced it on the flat of my palm.

'Well, he gets that from your mother.'

'She just told us about Bob.'

'Yes, I can see that.'

Suddenly, one of the surfers found a wave and was up on the board, zigzagging his way along the edge of the sunset.

'I actually feel sick!'

'How you exaggerate, Morwenna,' said Matthew, mildly.

I put the pebble in my pocket. 'I do! I feel sick!'

'It's all mind over matter,' said Matthew.

'Doesn't it bother you?'

'Why should it?'

The surfers were paddling in. Matthew's pipe glowed in the twilight as he sucked on it. I found myself resentful of the pipe: it seemed unnecessarily anachronistic.

'Bob was Dad's best friend!'

'Well, then. That gives them a lot in common.'

'And it's so soon!'

'Morwenna, dear, I do wonder sometimes at your simplicity. Your mother is only forty-two. She is too young to sit in mourning. That would be the last thing John would have wanted. He always regretted that it was not in his nature to be more . . . *demonstrative*. Valerie suffered a little under his self-sufficiency, you know.' He knocked out his pipe, then patted my knee. 'Let's go back up.'

'No.' I sulked. 'I'm going to sleep here.'

I watched him disappear into the dark below the cliff, and listened to his footsteps on the shingle until the sound went under that of the waves. The surfers, too, were making their way up the beach towards the steps. I went inside and lay down, below the photo of Great-grandfather James, who never made it to America, alone with my ill-feeling. I was the one who suffered under Corwin and Matthew's sanctimony. I felt homesick for London, where their judgement of me evaporated into the polluted air. It took me a long time to fall asleep, and when I woke it was to the sound of seagulls squabbling beneath the window. They were fighting over something rotten, retched up by the tide.

It was daybreak and I was cold. I made my way home through the gorse and the sleepy sheep. My feet were soaked with dew. At home I sat on Corwin's bed, willing him to wake, staring at him so hard that eventually he opened his eyes and asked, 'What time is it?'

'Five-ish.'

'I'm not prepared to talk about it,' he said, turning over. 'It has nothing to do with us. Go to bed.'

'Can I crawl in with you?'

'As long as you don't move or speak before nine.'

I climbed in beside him, fully dressed, and lay very still on my back. It began to rain. The water was sliding down the slates, along the gutters, down the pipes and into the drains. So much water.

8.

Two days later Mum moved out, taking nothing more with her than would fit into the back of Bob's car. Bob's locks had been shorn – a directive of Mum's, I had no doubt. Corwin helped to load her bags into the boot, and Bob was so grateful to him for releasing his mother without a fuss that he accidentally called him 'mate', then blenched with embarrassment. I scowled at them all from the doorstep. Bob pulled out of the driveway with Mum's hand waving from the open passenger window.

In the parental bedroom, the duvet was folded back to air. I opened the wardrobe doors. On my father's side was a neat stack of cardboard boxes, on Mum's a single box. Corwin lifted it out and put it on the bed. At the top of the box lay a cardboard folder labelled 'C & M documents'. It contained our birth certificates and old school reports and exercise books. Beneath this folder were layers of the framed family photos that had sat on Mum's dressing-table and on the window-sill in her craft room. At the bottom of the box was her wedding album.

'Bitch!' I said.

Corwin picked up the album and opened it. 'Have some under-standing, Morwenna,' he admonished. He leafed through the pages. 'Poor them,' he said. 'Look at them. They were barely older than we are – practically children!'

'Oh, fuck off!'

Corwin grabbed my arm, pulled me down to sit next to him and gripped me around the shoulders so that I could not move. 'Look at them,' he commanded. He lifted his hand to my head and twisted it so that I was forced to look at a picture of our parents flanked by our grandparents. They all appeared very solemn – not unhappy; rather, grave with import.

'It's just a picture,' I said.

'Exactly,' said Corwin, triumphant. He ruffled my hair aggressively, released me and lay back on the bed.

'I suppose the house is ours now,' he said. 'What shall we do with it?'

'I think, technically, that it's still Matthew's,' I said, unforgiving.

'No,' said Corwin. 'It will be ours now. You'll see. He'll want to secure our loyalty to the place.'

'I never realized that you put so much thought into these things.' I looked out of the window at the decayed kitchen garden, remembering how Mum had told me that when they married it had been a rose garden, and that my father had dug it up. I imagined her staring out of that window and seeing there the ghosts of roses. Then I turned and started putting the photos back into the box. I struggled a little, trying to fold the four leaves of the lid into each other. Corwin didn't offer to help me.

'Look at that!' he said, pointing to the corner of the room. 'Look at all those old wallpapers. I wonder if Matthew knows about that.'

Corwin was right. The following day, Matthew invited us to join him for coffee. He asked us to grind the beans, just as we had when we were children, taking it in turns with the handle of the grinder. Matthew put the coffee on a tray with milk and sugar, and squares of the darkest chocolate on a saucer. We followed him into his study. The coffee was thick and grainy; the milk sank into it as through sand.

'So . . .' he said, handing me a cup and offering the chocolate. I took two squares and balanced them on my saucer. 'Here we are.'

Matthew's desk was uncharacteristically tidy, his sketchbooks ordered on his shelves – more than half a century's worth of them. He didn't sit down. This was a solemn occasion and what he wanted to say must be delivered standing. 'Your mother was right to blame me,' he said. 'I made no contingency for your father dying before me. I don't quite understand why – it was foolish of me. There is no recent family precedent for sons pre-deceasing their fathers but, of course, that is highly unusual. What can I say? There was no obvious threat to John. When I was your age – you can't imagine. We were so fearful. But since then the world has come to feel so fixed. Safe, almost.'

Corwin's foot twitched. 'Here, maybe.'

'Yes,' said Matthew. 'Here – but here is where we live. Or where I live, perhaps I should say. But let's not become distracted. Today we must talk about the house.'

Matthew stood, the map an iridescent halo encircling him. His head obscured the picture of our house, but the original farmland radiated around him. Matthew was never meant to be a farmer. My father had been, though. Again, I glimpsed the shadowy thought that had visited me at my father's memorial service and I wondered for the first time if my father had hated Matthew for destroying his plans for a smallholding when he sold those last pretty fifteen acres. There had been a copse. My father had taken us there to watch fox cubs. I couldn't imagine that my father had had any hatred in him, but it was the closest I had seen him come to tears. He said, 'It was always a pipe dream, if I'm honest with myself.' And then he started to laugh. 'It's all right, Morwenna! Don't panic!' I had been pan-icking: betrayal, grief. I was not equipped for big, quiet tides of emotion.

Matthew had the deeds to Thornton on his desk. 'I'm making them over to you,' he said. 'There will be issues around inherit-ance tax, of course. But we will take legal advice on that.'

Corwin was smiling. This made him happy. I was simultan-eously thinking: Mine, ours! And: It's not so simple, maintaining this house, which has been paid for by a century of attrition of land. There was no land left with which to top up the mainten-ance fund. But I didn't want to spoil the moment, and I supposed, vaguely, that by the time we would have to worry about such things Corwin and I would be earning salaries. Matthew said, 'You may do as you wish with the house, but the kitchen and my study are sacrosanct. Oh, and you will ask before removing any books, won't you?'

He beamed down upon us from the map. Suddenly, his trouser pocket started ringing shrilly. 'Ah,' he said, contentedly, pulling the timer out of his pocket. 'The bread!'

It was too much to take in, sitting there in the house, which was now so overwhelmingly ours. We walked down to the beach without speaking, apart from when Corwin enthusiastically greeted oncoming walkers with comments about the weather. I suspected that he was doing it simply to annoy me.

We threw stones into the sea. Corwin's forearms were covered with goose-bumps; the bleached hair stood on end in a fine golden fur.

'Well?' he said.

'Oh, I don't know.'

'We could sell cream teas,' he teased.

'Jesus, Corwin!'

We threw more stones. A rising wind pushed the cloud-shadow across the surface of the sea.

'We could get a dog.'

'I hate dogs.'

'Well, a goat, then. Dad always wanted a goat.'

'I thought you wanted to save the world.'

'What I want to do is to earn my comfort and my peace, not simply have it handed to me.'

'This time last year we were saying how much we hated it here.'

'That was The Sands we were talking about – that's not the same thing.'

'I can't keep up with your fine distinctions,' I said. I had had enough of the conversation. 'Have you heard from Oliver at all?'

'No, I haven't. Have you?'

'No. Strange! He loved you so much. He was always at your heels. He must have found someone else to adore.'

'Why are you always so catty about Oliver?'

'Oh, I don't know. He has so much integrity; he wants to save the world too, only he's so much more severe about it than you. He's a permanent reproach. It's exhausting.'

The sky had opened into sunshine. I lay back on the shingle. 'I have no interest in saving the world,' I said. 'But it doesn't seem to bother you.'

Corwin laughed. 'Oh, it does,' he said. 'But I can't change that about you. You've always been the detached one.'

'I'm not the one who goes running off around the world. I'm still here.'

'No, you're not. You're in London. London is nowhere.'

'London is everywhere!'

'It amounts to the same thing.'

'Well,' I said, 'I like Everywhere-Nowhere.'

We bumped into our old friends in the pubs, but they seemed to fade with each meeting. Soon they would disappear altogether. Over a pint at the First and Last, I said, 'Well, I guess what held us together was our wanting to leave.' This insulted Willow, who believed in Friendship and had written amusing letters to me in generous spiky handwriting about student life in Manchester. She had a new boyfriend, who had been arrested 'for possession', which made her ever more glamorous. Mickey took refuge at the pool table, heartbroken. No one had seen Oliver. Back in the autumn he had sent postcards from Wales, where he was volunteering at the Centre for Alternative Technology, but there had been no news of him since.

Corwin and I went looking for Oliver at his parents' house in one of the new cul-de-sacs that were refuted by Matthew's map. His father opened the door to us, and, when he saw us there, yelled down the corridor, 'Sarah! Friends of Oliver's!' and shut the door again. We were used to this and waited for Oliver's mother to answer. We had always terrified her, and she fluttered on the doorstep twisting the discreet silver cross that normally hid beneath the housecoat she wore to do the hoovering. Oliver was very protective of his mother; Jesus was her friend, which exposed her to ridicule. He expected his own friends to be gentle with her. Corwin put on his most spiritual smile. 'Hello, Mrs Finch, how are you?'

'Corwin!' She flinched. 'Gosh, aren't you brown!'

'We were wondering when Oliver's going to be around.'

She looked a little confused. Perhaps she had thought that we knew more of her changeling child and his movements than she did. 'Oh,' she said. 'He's still in Wales. I don't know when he's planning on coming home.'

She attempted a smile at me. 'Hello,' she said, and added hopefully, 'He seems to like it there.' Oliver had once overheard her telling his father that 'there must be a place for him in the world'. Perhaps she prayed that it might be Wales.

Oliver had been the first to cut loose. We were a bit hurt, but there had always been something ephemeral about him. We continued to forget him and the others. It didn't happen quickly. It was like outgrowing skin: as though we left on the coast path tissue-thin casts of ourselves that desiccated and broke up in the wind.

PART TWO

9.

We left Matthew on his own in Thornton for the first time in his life. He had tried to leave, once, at the age we were when we left, when we stepped so blithely onto the trains that took us on, on to whatever came next. Matthew had thought vaguely that he might go to university. It seemed like a natural extension of school, which he had not much minded – had enjoyed even, at times. But then came the war, which set off a ripple in the universe. It passed over the planet and even Thornton, nudged deeper into the ground by its force, could not withstand it. Whenever Matthew climbed out of the combe he sensed imbalance.

He was nineteen and, without vanity, his body pleased him. He was confident of its design: the muscle under the skin, the bones under the muscle, the heart and lungs and intestines within their perfect casing. But did he have courage? He worried at this question, because now that The Sisters had left to marry he was in a time of joyous, almost spiritual, solitude, and it was tempting not to be concerned with courage. He had experienced fear, but was that the same as lack of courage? He suspected that he might have a certain kind of courage, the kind that only the self-sufficient possess. There was less to break in him than in a sociable man, he thought. He would be prepared to risk more.

His father had been too old for the front in the last war. It was another experience missed; James's soul was riddled with the lacunae of missed experience. Matthew's soul, by contrast, was so full that he did not have room for it in his body. It spilled out into his sketchbooks, onto page after page of annotated drawings. He wished to propitiate his father's disappointments, and started a portrait of him, seated before a wall of books in his study. Matthew thought that if James could see himself, he might feel more substantial.

One April night in 1941 a storm hammered at the door – a great thuggish giant of a storm, flailing in an ecstasy of violence. From his window, Matthew watched it bend the trees. There was a challenge in its diatribe, and he wondered if this was his test, because he was sure he must be tested sooner or later, so he went out to meet it.

It mocked him all the way down to Thornton Mouth, shrieking in his ears, and cuffing him now and again into the furze. At the top of the cliff steps it kicked Matthew's legs from beneath him, and he slid down in a scrambling reversed crawl. Once on the beach, Matthew began to fight the wind in the direction of the cabin, but it was too strong, and pressed him up against the cliff face. Matthew's head was full of the storm. The waves assumed faces – demons charged him from the sea. They scooped up handfuls of pebbles and flung them up the beach, where they ricocheted around him, off the cliff face and off the steps, with the crackle of artillery fire. Matthew closed his eyes and listened to the pebbles smashing against each other, against the cliff, imagining the vortex of battle, imagining himself in the middle of this storm in the middle of the Atlantic and he realized that the thought of battle terrified him less than did the sea. This was the test. For the integrity of his soul, he must enlist with the navy.

The military doctor was barely older than Matthew, and fresh out of medical school. He made Matthew walk up and down in his underwear. Then he made him walk up and down again. He stood behind Matthew. 'You have the slightest scoliosis!' he announced, delighted with himself for spotting it. 'You have an almost imperceptible limp.' And, tracing Matthew's spine with his forefinger, like a reverse faith healer, he placed a crook in Matthew's back. 'Too bad!' said the doctor, cheerfully. 'Otherwise, you're in perfect health.'

Matthew did not go straight home. Instead he went to sit on the bench in the churchyard, beside the lichgate. The rain had let up. Within his view was expressed an entire myth of England, one he cherished and had been prepared to defend. The hawthorn was in blossom, there were crocuses and daffodils. Water dripped onto a gravestone from the snout of a gargoyle. Sheep grazed on either side of the V of fields that framed the sea. He did not blame the doctor, who had worked hard for his knowledge and could not be expected to keep it to himself, as an older, more experienced man might have done. No. The slight, Matthew knew, was returned to him by the sea, which lay before him, smooth, slate-grey, mockingly calm. Eventually he made his way back down to the beach and the cabin and lit the stove and set a kettle on top of it, and sat on the cabin steps waiting for the water to boil. The clouded sun laid shadows on the sea. The tide was withdrawing in long hisses of tumbling shingle; the shifting stones eroded infinitesimally. The sound of the waves swirled around in the deformity in the small of his back with narcotic effect and he began to see all things in their true scale, just as he had in the delirium of seasickness. It had not been a test, after all. It had been an admonition.

The day after he acquired his limp, Matthew set out at dawn. On the way out of the house he paused where he had never paused before, at the stick stand, which contained the collected walking sticks of generations of Venton men. He tried out a few, swinging them exaggeratedly around the porch, and selected a thorn-stick – it was apt, he thought, and he liked the feel of the round nub of wood in his palm.

He had hoped for a dramatic soul-cleansing sunrise – he had read that in some languages the sun does not rise, it is born daily. However, he had to make do with a sluggish tonal adjustment from dark to pale grey. In his rucksack were bread, cheese and apples, and he carried a compass. He paused for a moment outside the heavy oak door and considered whether to walk along the coast or to head inland. Then he turned his back to the sea and began to walk directly away from it. The path took him uphill and along the brook, past the old manor house, and into the soon-to-be bluebell woods. A couple of deer, startled, jumped the stream and disappeared into the trees.

Very quickly, surprisingly so, he came to land that he did not recognize. As far as possible, he followed a straight course, but the hedgerow forced him left and right, sucking him along the high-banked lanes. Without his compass he would soon have lost his bearings. After a while he dipped into a wood, then out again. He was passing houses and farmyards he had never seen before, yet nothing was quite unfamiliar, so that he began to feel this was like dreaming, when the known shifts into the unknown and back again. Every so often he stopped to check a landmark against the map – a task made harder by the wartime removal of all the road signs. But he was a good map-reader and was able to plot his wavering course in a series of pencil marks against bridges and crossroads and farmyards.

Mid-morning his reverie was broken by the foul blood-and-urine stench of a tanner's yard, and then he was walking through a small market town that he recognized from some childhood visit. And because all the signs had been removed it was as if he secretly knew its name but could not speak it, and he walked through the town from one end to the other, where everyone was going about their business, buying bread and buttons and newspapers, as though he were invisible. Only then did it occur to him that what he was doing was a very suspicious activity in wartime, and the marked map in his rucksack suddenly acquired a great weight. He walked on past the school, where the shouting children were on their morning break, through the churchyard and on out of the town into more fields and hedgerowed lanes until eventually it was midday exactly and he stopped.

He was in the middle of a field of cows. An enormous chestnut tree stood in the centre. He walked over to it and touched it with the flat of his hand. He could make out the roofs of some farm buildings and was able to work out his position on the map, which he now marked with a large cross. Then he sat down under the tree to eat his lunch and retraced his steps all the way home.

A crack of light had opened on the horizon when he got home – a white line upon the sea. It was about six thirty. He took off his boots and went to his room and rolled out the map on the floor. He took a pair of compasses, stuck the point into the cross of Thornton church and opened them out to meet the mark in the chestnut-tree field. As the crow flew it was only about twelve miles. The lead turned around the compass point, and the circle was drawn that would contain him for the rest of his life.

Matthew gridded up the circle and transferred the lines of the map onto a six-by-six-foot canvas. It hung, untouched, on his wall for several weeks before he decided how to start. In the meantime, he finished the portrait of James. It turned out truer than he had intended – he had brought his own disappointment to the painting. That was Matthew's last portrait. He used to say, 'Worlds in grains of sand, Morwenna. Worlds in grains of sand.'

But the war came to him anyway. Matthew performed his secret service, for ever unacknowledged. The Atlantic war dead washed ashore, in pieces, and he gathered them up, brought them up the cliff face to the churchyard for their anonymous interment. He never dropped his ritual of stopping when he passed a war memorial to say each name out loud. 'Because you never know,' he said to me, 'how and where they might have ended up. Their names may be all that was left of them.'

No one ever suggested that we put up a stone to my father. I imagined Matthew on his evening walks to the cabin, standing at the edge of the tide and saying his son's name out loud, into the wind: 'John Venton!'

For seventeen years after my father died nothing much happened, and then a pigeon flew through my window. It still feels to me now as though it was the pigeon that precipitated events, as though it had been winging its way towards me for years. It was like the butterfly in the Amazon that launches the avalanche, or tidal wave, or whatever it's supposed to launch. Of course, it was Corwin, not the pigeon, but the pigeon's entrance was more dramatic. Perhaps it was part of Corwin's subconscious, unleashed. Or perhaps even of mine.

After Mum moved out, Corwin and I claimed Thornton for ourselves. Corwin declared that he was taking over our father's desk, which had always fascinated him with its secret drawer in which our father had allowed him to conceal a hundreder conker and a Swiss army knife. Corwin swept the contents of the desk into a box and placed it on top of the box on Mum's side of the bedroom wardrobe. Then I took down the Laura Ashley curtains from the garden room and moved my workbench down there. That was how it started.

During term breaks, we dared to do what had never been permitted our mother. We filled boxes with the domestic clutter of centuries: dusty single balls of saved wool, battered fans, bunches of dried lavender. We threw nothing out. Some superstition prevented us actually removing anything from the house and upsetting the delicate chemistry of its atmosphere. We stored everything in what had been our parents' bedroom. At first we stored the dusty, broken, useless things. Then we began to curate. We asked Matthew, 'Do you mind if we move this or that?' And he never did seem to mind, so we stopped asking. Over the next three years boxes piled up under the bed, on the floor, on the bed.

And we cleaned. We applied buckets of lemon-scented Jif to every surface. We lifted furniture and hoovered up the mouse droppings. We pulled woollen blankets out of the corners of cupboards and released clouds of moths. We hung the rugs over the washing line and beat the dust out of them. When the house was clean, we painted. We started in the attic – we painted everything in my room white: the floors, the walls, the mantelpiece, the furniture. I took down the curtains and left the windows undressed so that when I woke in the mornings I could tell from the light in the room what colour were the sky and sea even before I opened my eyes. We boxed up everything from Corwin's room: Che Guevara and *The Communist Manifesto* and *The Dark Side of the Moon*. We took his bed apart and rolled up the carpet and shoved it in with everything else. All that remained in Corwin's room was a mattress on the bare floorboards and a wardrobe. Then we shut the door on our parents' room and locked it. We hung the heavy key in the key cupboard in the kitchen.

After storm-tides we collected debris from the beach: wraiths of driftwood, which we balanced on string and hung over the landings; runic stones and spheres of rusted iron, which we placed on the ledges. We strung garlands of sea-perforated pebbles on frayed fragments of rope and arrayed bleached bird and sheep skulls on the mantelpieces.

Matthew never objected to this desecration of the ancestral seat – occasionally he would ask after a painting or an ornament that had been part of his home-scape for seventy years. When we said, 'We packed it up,' he would say, 'Oh, did you?' It was as though the house slumbered in hibernation behind the door of my parents' bedroom. Matthew didn't change a detail of our arrangements, although I noticed, with each visit, that something we had packed away had found its way into his study, things that must have had sentimental value – a decanter that had once sat on a shelf in the living room, a picture that had once hung in the hall, a porcelain figurine of a shepherdess, which must have belonged to our grandmother.

We began importing new acquaintances for weekends in the country and made them drink strong cider and laughed at their inappropriate footwear as we dragged them up and down the coast in all weathers. In the mornings we took coffee and chocolate with Matthew. Sometimes we visited Mum, Corwin more often than I. She was always smiling and made us take off our shoes in the hall.

But this little game of domesticity didn't last because Corwin had the addict's craving for pure experience. Immediately after he grad-uated, and without ceremony, so that at first I didn't grasp the magnitude of his defection, he banished himself to the rainless, warring places where he moved through seas of confused, displaced human beings, digging and piping and irrigating. And the number of such places was infinite. He spun off so far into the unknown that I assumed he would eventually rewind in my direction. But then he had been gone for a year or two, and soon five, and, before long, ten. Of course, every so often he returned laden with gifts and he spoke as Corwin always had done and cracked the same jokes at which Matthew and I laughed overmuch and gratefully.

My bedroom at Thornton filled with objects that spoke nothing to me of my brother, the family peacemaker. Red and gold Afghan rugs patterned with tanks and Kalashnikovs; unlovely fertility figures with swollen bellies and knife-hacked genitals; strings of enormous crude beads of crackled blue and coral red and embossed silver. They intruded so violently upon the white of my room that I began to believe they were given not in love but in anger.

I turned out to be a villager after all – I made of London my village and lived there quietly. That gift of my father's, that first book press, turned out to be the gift that shaped my life. One morning in the autumn after I graduated, I walked into the bindery outside which I had been hovering for the preceding three years, like a street-child outside a bakery. It was one of those places that occupied its own temporal dimension: you could find it only if you knew exactly what you wanted from it. When I entered I sensed immediately that it was a place of great discretion, somewhere safe from intrusive questions and uninvited confidences. It was no bigger in floor-plan than the living room at Thornton, but with twice the ceiling height, and every square inch of wall and floor was taken up with chests of drawers and shelves of papers and cloths and leathers. At the back, squeezed between presses and piles of books and slip-boxes, was a large table at which three or four people worked in silence. The owner of the bindery perched behind a high counter, which was shoved into a corner by the display window. She was small, very thin. Her hair was pulled back into a plait, and the scattering of grey in it made it impossible to determine her age. She might have been anywhere between forty-five and sixty. She wore dark makeup around large eyes and a bright red lipstick, which, strangely, had the effect of austerity. Her name was Ana. She looked at the books that I had bound and brought to show her, said nothing about the many imperfections that I now know them to have contained, and took me on as an apprentice. And there I stayed put and there nothing ever changed. All around us London primped and preened while we sheltered in our time-loop. I began to understand Matthew better.

Still, shiny London was more enjoyable than grim London had been. Grey buildings returned to pale limestone, light bounced off multiplying panes of glass. I permitted myself some vicarious sparkling. In the semi-legal jerry-rigged industrial spaces that were my homes, I strung up fairy lights and held parties to which my few slow-won friends came, bringing with them smiling strangers.

Corwin came home to see in the new millennium with us. That Christmas, I unwrapped from a paper printed with robins and snowmen a malignant fist-clenched figure. It was about two feet high and was pierced all about with spikes of different shapes and metals. I placed it on the coffee table, where it bristled aggressively.

'Goodness!' said Matthew.

'Powerful, isn't he?' said Corwin, smiling affectionately. 'These,' he said, gently fingering the end of a metal shard, 'are petitions. They're driven into the statue to bring down curses. It's a bit like the principle of a wax doll, except that he doesn't represent the victim. He's the spirit who has the power to exercise the curse.'

I put the curse spirit on my bedroom table and contemplated him. I thought of Corwin's weightlessness: how little he carried with him; how I was his proxy consumer of interesting ethnic artefacts, so that he might drift through the world alleging passion but committing to nothing. I thought about Thornton and how firmly it sat in the combe, how weighted it was with a heavy ballast of furniture and books, and I set to devising a counter-punishment. I knew how to slow Corwin down. I would send him books. And he would not be able to give them away because I would bind them myself and make them personal to him, and over time his bags would fill with books and they would all be about Here, and he would have to take Here with him, wherever he went.

I raided Matthew's collection of forgotten local histories, excavated from the dustiest corners of failing second-hand bookshops, and started with *Cove and Combe: Secrets of the Devon Coast*, a gentleman's vanity publication, as so many of them were. It had been nicely produced, with engravings of looming cliffs and fishing vessels tossed on unlikely waves, but the cover was coming apart, which was the only reason that Matthew allowed me to wrest it from his collection. I gave it an inappropriate periwinkle-blue cover and overdid the endpapers with extravagant marbling – the books must be conspicuous and the materials too expensive to discard. I wanted the periwinkle blue to mass, book by book, so that Corwin might take measure of the extent of his abandonment of me. At the base of the spine I tooled a device: it was Matthew's farting Devil.

Later, as Matthew receded, I stopped asking permission to remove books from the shelf. I sent Corwin *West Country Myth and Mystery* and *Tales of the Moors* and *Fairies, Pixies and Knockers*. I plumped up earnest limp-bound parish histories. They were as you would expect: a lot of health-giving striding of the coast punctuated with amusing bursts of buzzing Devon dialect.

Every time I went down to Thornton and lifted another book to weigh down Corwin, my curse spirit seemed to grin at me a little more obscenely, as though I had tasked him with another metal spike to his head. I would grin back, and think, as I drifted to sleep: I curse you, Corwin Venton. I curse you to Here.

II

I didn't see Corwin again for five years. Perhaps (although I was still sending him books) I had almost learned to do without him. The weather had already turned cold, and I sensed another eviction coming, if you could call it an eviction when you didn't have a tenancy agreement. I was beginning to wonder if, at thirty-three, I wasn't getting too old for this. My homes had become precarious – every last garage in the East End was being bought up by developers and turned into a construction of sheets of glass set in a material that looked like the grey plastic from which Corwin used to build model aircraft. My landlord, Linton, had begun to look shifty. He ran a factory that made things out of fake fur from the three floors of warehouse beneath my flat. Rolls of artificial leopard and bear leaned stacked against the walls on all the landings and moulted onto the worn stair carpets. There was a layer of synthetic lint on every surface of the building. Maybe 'shifty' was unfair. Linton had always been considerate of me. When we met on the stairs we danced awkwardly around rolls of pretend zebra, which lodged between us and caught in the wobbly banisters. I had seen men with expensive mobile phones and stripy suits looking up at my window, but didn't want to upset Linton by asking about them. 'Regretful' was a better description of his expression – he didn't want to displace me.

I began to spy on my own front door. I had to stand on my workbench to get an oblique enough view into the narrow cut of street below. One Sunday morning there was a man pointing his camera up at me, taking photographs. I pulled on a jumper and sheepskin boots over my pyjamas and sprinted down the four flights of shaky stairs to confront him. He was taken aback by the sudden opening of the door of a building that had been shuttered up for the weekend. I said, 'What are you doing?'

He was strangely rectangular, I noticed. It was the coat he was wearing, some kind of military surplus parka. He said, 'I don't think that's any of your business.'

I said, 'You're photographing my home. I think that's my business.'

'Well,' he said, 'that's my point . . . sort of.'

He pointed up to a glass-studded ledge level with the second-floor window – an area of flat roof between my building and the next. 'That's what I'm actually taking a picture of. There's a CCTV camera up there.'

'Oh,' I said. 'I hadn't noticed.'

'You should pay more attention,' he said sternly.

'I prefer not to,' I said. 'Paying attention just makes me anxious. Why are you taking a picture of the camera?'

'It's an act of resistance.'

'To what?'

'Did you know,' he said, 'that the average Londoner is captured on CCTV three hundred times a day?'

'Yes,' I said, although it wasn't true. 'And?'

'I'm capturing them back.'

'What? All of them? Is it conceptual art, or something?'

'Not at all! It's about basic principles of civil liberty.'

'You sound like my brother. What are you, then? Some kind of urban *guerrillero*?'

'Not really,' he said. 'It's private. A sort of secret subversion – like spitting in soup.'

'Do you spit in people's soup too?'

'No!' He sounded offended. He looked far too noble to stoop so low. 'I was speaking metaphorically.'

'What do you do with the pictures?' I asked.

*

That was how I acquired Ed: by accident, in November, over a bacon butty under the railway arch. His hands were strangely delicate, protruding incongruously from the block of khaki that he was wearing. He said that what he did with the pictures was print them off, passport-photo size, label them with date and time, and stick them to the wall. He had been doing it since January. It had been his New Year resolution to photograph every CCTV camera that he walked beneath.

'I'm surprised you haven't been arrested,' I said.

'Oh, I have,' he said proudly.

'Well, there you go!' I said, not asking for details. 'Can I see them?'

A new landscape opened up to me as I looked for CCTV cameras. At ground level, London was a flickering sequence of shop windows, or the same front door flashing up in different colours, but now I looked up and it became more geometric, stepped and zigzagged, embellished by rolls of barbed wire and boastfully inaccessible graffiti. There were unexpected ornamentations and vanities: a mosaic panel of birds; the face of a woman in relief above the arch of a doorway. I felt pleasantly dizzy. We stopped to document six cameras.

Ed's flat was in the basement of a terraced house; a weak winter light came in through the bay window. Two entire walls of his living room were covered with a wallpaper of tiny squares, pictures of cameras against brick wall or concrete or glass. The effect was surprisingly soft; it looked like cloth.

'Don't you find it oppressive?' I asked.

'I found it more oppressive not knowing where they were.'

'What happens on New Year's Eve?'

'I haven't decided yet.'

'My grandfather has a map on his wall,' I said, running my fingers over a row of the photos. 'This reminds me of it. He walked as far as he could go and still get back in one day and then he used a pair of compasses and marked a circle around himself.

He says that there's nothing outside his circle that can't be found within it. He paints at it all the time – every time he finds something worth recording it goes into the map.'

'Sounds cool,' said Ed. 'But it's not the same thing.'

I scanned the wall of cameras, all pointing at him. I liked the futility of his project – he tilted at windmills. 'You're both in the middle,' I said, without rancour, shrugging my shoulders. Clearly he was one of those annoying people who correct you all the time, but I was raised on pedantry. I elaborated, 'You are each the point to which you return.' I myself didn't seem to have a middle, I reflected, suddenly seeing myself with a doughnut-hole where my abdomen ought to be.

He said, 'Would you like a coffee?'

'Yes, please.'

Without his coat he seemed less obsessive. He hadn't commented on the fact that I was still in my pyjamas; perhaps he hadn't noticed. When it grew dark Ed made a law-abiding fire of smokeless-fuel briquettes in the grate and lit some candles. The walls of photos transformed into velvet drapes. It was the start of something: brushing fingers, sighs in and sighs out, all of that. I found that I didn't object.

On New Year's Eve, Ed and I drank cava with an Indian take-out and liberated ourselves from the cameras by removing the photos and burning them in a midnight ceremony. Afterwards the room was bigger, blanker. Tiny bits of BluTack were left studding the wall. It felt a little lonely.

'What's next?' I asked.

'I'm going to give up alcohol for twelve months.'

'No! Really?'

'It's something I've always wanted to do.'

'It is?' I couldn't help feeling that the timing was poor. He was the first person in my life to eclipse Corwin – a moon passing in front of the sun. I wasn't sure that sobriety created the right conditions for an experiment in attachment.

I now think of that time as my aspidistra year, when I was determined to give myself up to a future of traditional domesticity. We would go to Ed's parents for Sunday lunches along with his brother, sister, in-laws and their offspring. They were gracious and drew me into their conversations while I helped to peel potatoes. Over lunch the parents told amusing stories about when Ed and his siblings were young, and Ed and his siblings told amusing stories about their parents' eccentricities.

One Sunday, to enter into the spirit, I told the story of my parents' engagement. 'Your grandmother,' Mum would say, 'couldn't wait to marry your father off.' And my father would smile at her while she talked. 'And she knew that he'd rather die than go into a shop and buy an engagement ring.' We understood her perfectly – it was inconceivable that our father should discuss anything as personal as a marriage proposal with a stranger, a shop assistant. 'So as soon as she caught whiff of a girlfriend she foisted this hideous ring on him!' Our great-grandmother's emerald ring would glitter on Mum's waving hand.

They had taken tea in what was then the rose garden. And Mum had sipped from a porcelain cup in a haze of rose scent and thought: Yes. This would be a nice way to live. And after tea my father took her to the cabin to watch the sun go down. He knew, he said, that the sunset would be more articulate than he, and he offered it to her as a betrothal gift. Being June, it was a gentle, peachy, undemanding sunset, very flattering to my mother's complexion.

And Mum had cried a lot and her mascara had run. That was our favourite part of the story: our weeping mother. Her generous sobbing seemed exotic to us, free-spirited. But the story wore out. We learned to feel embarrassed about our mother's incontinent tears. And my father came to realize, after he had dug them up, that it had been the roses that had moved her, not the inexorability of the sinking sun.

As we drove back to London, Ed was quiet. Eventually he said, 'I don't know how you managed to turn that story about your parents into a bad story.'

I said, 'I don't know either.'

'You're pretty hard on your mother!'

'Well, you've never met her.'

'Well, I'd like to.'

This was a sore point. I wanted to keep Ed separate.

'You never talk about your father. What was he like?'

'I don't know.'

'What do you mean, you don't know?' Ed was upset – I had drawn a shadow down on the afternoon.

'I was eighteen when he died,' I said. 'Did you know what your father was like when you were eighteen?'

'Yes,' he insisted. 'I think I did. Go on. Give it a go.'

I wanted to say that I didn't really know how to describe my father without Corwin there to help me, but I had noticed that Ed didn't like Corwin. He was the only person I knew who didn't like Corwin, and I assumed that that was simply because he had never met him.

'Well,' I said, 'he was quiet, but not antisocial – he liked gatherings. He loved the pub. He loved the wall of smoke as he walked in and he loved the nicotine-stained ceilings and the smell of beer-soaked nylon carpet. And he loved being able to sit for hours on his own in a corner if he wanted to and be left alone with his one slow pint. Or he could sit in a group and say nothing and just smile and stand his round, or play his fiddle.'

I stopped, suddenly realizing that I was describing my last sight of him. 'He was very thrifty,' I said, trying to redirect my memory. 'Everything was done sparingly: speech, movement, everything. He liked to fix things. He made things grow. You didn't really notice him until he spoke – when he spoke it meant that he expected something of you, and you'd be anxious that you wouldn't be able to meet his expectation. I don't know how to describe it. And then he wanted to share his enthusiasms, and Corwin and I didn't really care to know the things that he knew. He was always trying to drag us off to observe a badger's set or to take an interest in growing aubergines or something.

'He was out of his time, I think,' I said. 'He studied architecture, but everyone was building high-rises. He wanted to design houses with turf roofs that disappeared into the landscape. He always talked about "simplifying". Nowadays, he'd be right with the zeitgeist. As it was, he was stuck in an architect's office making technical drawings for shopping centres. He found it soul-destroying.'

I ground to a halt. 'It's pointless trying to describe him,' I said irritably. 'It won't make sense if you haven't met Matthew.'

Ed allowed my irritation to subside, and said, 'He sounds like someone I would have liked.'

I thought about that. 'Yes,' I said, surprised. 'I think you and he would have got on well.' I looked at his profile. He was a safe driver: eyes on the road, hands at ten to two on the steering wheel, and now he had my father's phantom approval. 'Yes,' I said again, in connection with nothing in particular. Something about the conversation called for the affirmative. Yes, I thought. I can learn this. I can grow into this. I can put out little shoots and they will thrive on his generosity, on his competence, and that will be enough. That will be plenty.

12.

But it was London winter, and, try as I might, I could make nothing grow.

I was still in my flat – Linton must not have been offered the right price for his building, after all. All colour was leached from the city apart from in the street below, where the Bangladeshi wedding-shop windows shone bright light onto sequined red saris and gold-embroidered turbans. I bought myself armfuls of flower garlands and hung them about my bed, swathes of vermilion and gold and cinnamon to brighten my mornings.

It was a Sunday and I was sitting at my window reading. I intuited the pigeon before it hit the window. Some presentiment caused me to look up as it resolved itself out of the February grey and smashed through the glass sideways, wings askew. It must have tried to turn at the last moment. The window shattered at the centre sending cracks out to the corners of the frame and the pigeon hurtled over my shoulder in a shower of glass fragments. My hand flew up protectively and a shard sliced across the skin. I grasped it in pain and already the blood welled up between the fingers of my right hand. The pigeon, panicked, flung itself from wall to wall shedding feathers and shooting out great streams of green-grey shit all over the room, then landed in a heap in the middle of the carpet, shook itself out and hopped about a bit. It didn't seem to have come to any harm.

I recognized it immediately as a bird of ill omen. My coffee had spilled all over the table. I looked at the pigeon, harbinger of what, I didn't yet know. The feathers around its neck rippled iridescent pinks and purples and blues. I have always liked the idea of birds: the beauty of flight, the great mystery of their navigation systems. But pigeons can't escape their verminous associations. It fixed me with a rodent eye.

Shaking, I poured myself a glass of wine and sat dazed at the kitchen table watching the blood seep through the twenty layers of kitchen paper that I had wrapped around my hand, until I heard Ed's key turn in the door.

I had given Ed a set of keys as a New Year gift – an act that now seemed to me inexplicably sentimental and which I was regretting. He had taken it all very literally, and now used the keys without warning. It would not occur to him to ring the doorbell before invading my privacy. He had also suggested that we share his New Year resolution for 2005 and both learn Mandarin, with a view to taking a three-month sabbatical in China, an idea I didn't like at all. I heard him go into the living room and mutter, 'Jesus!' Then there was some scuffling and he appeared in the kitchen doorway clutching the pigeon in both hands. He looked at the mess of bloodied tissue on my hand, and muttered, 'Jesus!' again. Then he said, 'How about opening the window?' I fumbled with the window lock, clumsily slid up the sash with my left hand, and Ed released the pigeon into the iron sky with a dramatic flourish, as if it were the dove of peace. Then he carefully scrubbed his hands with soap and hot water before addressing himself to my wound.

'What the hell happened?'

There was no point in stating the obvious. I was the only person of Ed's acquaintance who would lure a pigeon through a pane of plate glass. I was talking – it was happening quite without volition: 'You know, I read something recently about flight. They found some fossil in China or somewhere that was the missing link between dinosaurs and birds. There have been decades of disagreement, you see, between scientists who think that flight developed by creatures leaping from tree to tree and those who think that it developed from running around and jumping up to catch insects or something.'

Ed found a bandage in a kitchen drawer and began to clean the cut. 'Anyway,' I continued, 'it turns out that the running and jumping faction were right – there they are, these dinosaurs, running around through the bubbling Jurassic forest, jumping away, and, hey presto, they take off! Imagine the surprise.'

'Wen,' said Ed, 'please shut up.'

I hated to be called Wen. It made me sound like an abbreviated Wendy. I said, 'Poor tree-top leapers. All those decades of research. All for nothing.' Ed looked up sharply. He suspected that this was a snipe against his career as an academic.

I looked at my neatly bandaged hand and wanted to do something for him. Something tangible – a kiss, perhaps. Some unbuttoning. But then the phone rang.

It was Mum.

'Mum!' I said. 'To what do I owe this rare and unexpected pleasure?'

Mum sighed. 'You really can't help yourself, can you?'

My hand had begun to throb. 'No,' I said, contrite. 'I'm sorry. It just slips out.'

'Have you spoken to your grandfather recently?'

'Yes. A couple of days ago. Why?'

'Has he said anything?'

'Christ, Mum. Stop being so cryptic. About what?'

'Well, we dropped in at Thornton over the weekend.'

'Ah! The cosiness of that word "we".'

'Oh, just drop it for five minutes. Matthew's clearly not well. He's lost a lot of weight. So I went and had a chat with Mark Luscombe and he told me that obviously he couldn't tell me anything but he did say that we ought to start preparing ourselves.'

'But . . .' I said. I knew the futility of this 'but' and stopped speaking. Then I said, 'Mark's discussing Matthew's health with you?'

'No. He's not. But he's very fond of your grandfather and he knows that Matthew won't ask for help.'

'He has no right to discuss it with you. If Matthew doesn't want us to know, then he should respect that.'

'Whatever, darling!' said Mum. We both knew that Matthew was my problem, not hers. 'Anyway, how are you?'

'I *was* fine,' I said. 'A pigeon just flew through my window pane.'

'The strangest things do seem to happen to you,' said Mum, clearly, like Ed, thinking that it was somehow my fault. 'How's Ed?'

'He's fine.'

She sighed. 'Poor Ed.' Corwin had told me that Mum called Ed 'Morwenna's Last Chance'. There was a pause in which she contemplated my lack of accountability. 'Well. Let me know how Matthew is. Have you heard from Corwin recently?'

'Not for a while. Have you?'

'Oh, you know what a dutiful son he is. He emails every week and tells me absolutely sweet FA!'

'Oh, well!'

'Indeed. Well, bye, darling. Come and see us – me – soon.'

Ed had found a piece of hardboard that I didn't even know I had – perhaps he had brought it to my flat without me noticing because he thought it might come in useful one day. He was screwing it to the window frame using the cordless screwdriver that he had given me for Christmas. Buzz. Buzz. Buzz. I wished he would go. I dialled Thornton. Matthew took a long time to pick up.

He said, 'Ah! Morwenna.'

I said, 'I'm thinking of coming down soon.'

'Oh, good! Remind me when you get here that I have something to show you.'

'What is it?'

'You'll see.'

I said, 'How are you? Is everything all right down there?'

'Everything's fine.'

'OK, Matthew. Bye. See you soon.'

I wiped coffee and bird shit off the cover of my laptop and logged on to my email. In the subject line I wrote: 'Matthew dying. Time

99

to come home.' I was just about to press 'Send' when the phone rang again. I let it ring. Ed said, 'Aren't you going to get that?'

'No,' I said. The feeling of portent had suddenly returned. 'Don't answer it,' I said, too vehemently. 'It's Corwin.' But this was an error. A frown formed on Ed's forehead – now he had to check. It bothered him that I always knew when it was Corwin. He put down the drill and answered. 'Corwin! Yes. She is.' Ed handed me the phone. Corwin's voice oscillated on the crackly satellite waves. I always felt, during these calls, as though I were at a Victorian séance, communicating through layers of ectoplasm. Corwin said, 'Can you go down to Thornton and meet me there?'

'Did Mum tell you about Matthew?'

'No. What?'

'He's not well.'

'What's wrong with him?'

'I don't know. He won't talk about it.'

'Oh. Well, I'm on my way home anyway. I need to see you. You go on down.'

'OK,' I said. 'Travel safely.'

When I put the phone down, Ed was looking at me. He distrusted the brevity of my conversations with Corwin.

I said, 'Can I borrow your car?'

'Why?'

'Corwin's coming home. I need to go to Thornton.'

'When?'

'Now.'

'What? Just like that?

'Something's up with Corwin.'

'What?'

'I don't know. I just know.'

'You two freak me out!' he said. 'How long will you be gone for?'

'I don't know. '

'I think I'm going to need it this week.'

That simply wasn't true. He never needed it during the week. He walked or cycled everywhere. In fact, he pretty much only drove his car when he needed to take it to the garage to repair a wing mirror that had been smashed while it was parked on the road. But I couldn't be bothered to argue.

When he finished with the window he produced a bowl of hot, soapy water. He told me to leave the carpet – he said that with carpets you have to let things dry otherwise you end up scrubbing the dirt further into the pile. While he was wiping down the bookshelves I packed some clothes. Ed had left his jacket over the back of a chair in the kitchen. His car key was in one of the pockets. I took him a cup of tea, gave him an I-don't-deserve-you kiss, and sneaked out.

After Bristol the Sunday traffic began to thin out. A mean, mizzling rain had kept everyone at home, nursing their seasonal affective disorder. I stopped once for coffee and petrol and left a message on the bindery voicemail to say that I wouldn't be at work for a couple of days. It was a family emergency, I said. I bought an enormous packet of crisps and ate from my lap as I drove.

Corwin was about to make something go wrong. I could sense it. One phone call from him from some godforsaken part of the planet and I had lied to Ana, who was a fair boss and might not be able to tell. And I had stolen Ed's car. And it was raining.

The rain squatted above me all the way from Taunton, a cold sleety rain. But around the headland the sky cleared. A single bolt of pink unfurled across the blue. Sudden stunted bare trees reached over the lanes like supplicant souls. By the time I arrived in Thornton the dark was rising up the sides of the combe. There was light in the hall and in the kitchen – Matthew still had the habit of putting the hall light on at twilight; some ritual of regard for the stray wanderer, perhaps.

Matthew inhabited only a part of the house now: the kitchen, his study, his bedroom. When we came down he would venture with us into the living room, which smelt damp until we cranked up the heating. Mum never visited us there.

He was at the kitchen table, reading and nibbling on a plate of bread, cheese and tomato chutney. He looked up and I searched his face for sign of illness. He was a little more drawn, perhaps. 'Ah! Morwenna!' He wasn't expecting me so soon, but he couldn't be sure that I hadn't told him I was coming straight down and, anyway, he had long since given up being surprised by anything. I kissed his forehead.

'Are you hungry?' he asked.

'Starving!'

He fetched a plate and put the cheese and the butter dish in front of me and sliced a piece of bread. It was fresh, elastic under the butter.

'How's Corwin?' asked Matthew.

'He's on his way home.'

'Oh, is he?' Matthew looked up. 'From where?'

Once Matthew had kept track of Corwin in an old atlas, which acknowledged neither the independence of African states nor the break-up of the Soviet Union. But Corwin had been gone so long that he had given up trying to distinguish between the different kinds of elsewhere that held him. There was only Thornton now. Unchanging, set in granite against the Atlantic. He no longer even quite believed in London, although he was occasionally persuaded of it by me.

'Sudan,' I said.

'Goodness! How fascinating that must be. What has he been doing there?'

'Oh. The same thing he does anywhere – everywhere else but here.'

We washed up. 'Let's have a nightcap in the study,' Matthew suggested. 'Have you anything to read?'

'No,' I said. 'Why don't you find me something, and I'll get the fire going?'

I switched off the light in the kitchen. For a moment I stood in the dark and listened. There was nothing but ancient sound – the rushing of the brook, the hoot of an owl – then Matthew's step in the hall. He had found something for me.

I lit a fire in his study, and brought some logs in from the wood shed. Matthew poured two glasses of malt whisky. He laid a book on the coffee table – a tatty limp-bound book called *The Ghosts of Dartmoor*. 'I thought you might make something of that,' he said. 'It has some lovely woodcuts. You could turn it into a nice little book.'

'Thank you,' I said. 'Oh, and I've brought you a present – chilli chocolate,' I added, handing the bar to him. 'I thought we could try it tomorrow with coffee.'

'Goodness!' said Matthew. 'Do you really think so?'

I stood up and took my glass over to the map. 'Is there anything new?' I asked.

I expected him to say, 'You'll have to use your eyes.' That was the old game – catch him at it or find it yourself. But instead he said. 'Ah, yes! I knew I had something to show you. Stand back. No. Not there. Further back. So that you can see it all.'

Taking my arm he steered me around his desk and man-oeuvred me until my back was against the bookshelves on the opposite wall. 'Now,' he said. 'Look at it. Really *see* it – as a whole.'

I tried to see it. All of it. All at once. Somewhere beneath, all that glowing colour was anchored on the contours of the Ordnance Survey map. I tried to intuit them, to disregard the painting's wandering saints and wronged women and poet priests; its contradictory seasons, snowdrops and roses, fruit and blossom, spring cubs and autumn hunters. I thought, belatedly, that it was interesting that Matthew had allowed the half of his circle that was sea to be blue, when it was almost never that. More often, almost always in fact, it was the colour of cloud and rain, of bruised skin. Bisecting his circle of land and sea were the cliffs, rising out of the water and receding into the top right quarter of the circle, as they would appear to a walker approaching from the south-west. Off the coast was the jagged line of a reef. Except that I knew that this reef was a ships' graveyard, and that Matthew had recorded every ship wrecked off our coast by painting their watery ghosts, in full rig, and, though this was only visible under the magnifying-glass, I knew that he had written each of their names in his minuscule hand along with the dates of their deaths. And I knew all their names: they repeated themselves. *Perseverance*, 22 April 1842, and *Perseverance*, 30 June 1866, and *Perseverance*, 24 October 1897. There was *Hope*, and again *Hope*, and yet still more *Hope*. There were *Hannah*s and *Elizabeth*s and *Mary Ann*s. The world had sent its ships to die there: the *Pacquebot de Brest*, and the *Maria Kyriakidis*, and Matthew's favourite, the *Dulce Nombre de Jesus*. And, of course, the *Constantia*, out of whose entrails Great-grandfather James had constructed the cabin.

'Now,' said Matthew. 'Let me show you.'

He rummaged around in his plan chest and pulled out a large roll of tracing paper. Then he pulled up his library steps and began to tape the top edge of the roll to the top of the canvas with masking tape. Carefully, he unrolled the paper and secured it to the edges of the stretcher so that it overlay the whole painting, but tightly, so that the painting was visible beneath a pattern of pencil lines. As he smoothed it over the map and fiddled with the tape and the edges until it fitted tightly, he said, 'I can't believe I'd never seen it before. Do you see it yet?'

I didn't. He came over to stand beside me. 'This is quite extraordinary. If you join up these points, church, Devil's Stone and cabin, you mark a triangle from which you can build a pentagram that fits exactly within the circle. There it is, Morwenna. Divine Proportion!' You're mad, I thought. Quite mad. You have placed yourself at the centre, and now you detect divinity in your design. And at the same time I thought: I want to grow to be old and mad and afire with conviction.

We contemplated Matthew's golden secret for a couple of minutes, until Matthew asked, 'When are we expecting Corwin?'

'Oh, I don't know. He just told me to meet him here.'

'What brings him home?'

'Perhaps he's homesick,' I said. 'Do you think he gets homesick?'

'How could he not?'

Carefully, I removed the tracing paper. The firelight flickered over the figure of a sleeping giant, almost invisibly folded, like a foetus, into the belly of Squab Rock. When I turned back to Matthew, he was in his armchair and his eyes were closed. His pipe, unlit, lay loosely in his hand. I sat by the fire, sipping whisky and waiting, as ever, for Corwin.

13.

The curse figure was grinning at me when I woke up in my room. It was another leaden day. I could hear a Hoover banging around in the hall below and wondered when Matthew had taken on a cleaner. Corwin and I had been nagging him to do so for years, but until now he had insisted on looking after himself. By the time I got downstairs the mystery vacuumer was no longer there. Matthew, also, was gone, off on his meanderings. I made myself tea and toast and walked out into the garden to look for signs of spring. The trees were poised and secretive. I went from bed to bed, bending every so often to push away the covering of decayed leaves from emergent bulbs.

My circuit brought me to the entrance to the kitchen garden and, wrapping both hands around my mug of tea for warmth, I wandered through the brick arch and into a perfectly cultivated plot, all dug over, ready for planting. At the far end a skinny woman in blue dungarees was pushing a wheelbarrow. For a moment I didn't recognize her. I had last seen her from a distance in some pub or other, plump with puppy fat in skinny white denims and silver heels – or, at least, that was how I chose to picture her.

'Sandra?' I said, too late to suppress the outrage in my voice.

She glanced over her shoulder without stopping and continued to push the wheelbarrow in the direction of the compost heap. Then she turned and came towards me.

'What brings you home, then?'

She was able to sink the 'you' to an enviable depth of disdain, by losing the *h* in 'home'.

'I wanted to see my grandfather.'

'Well. Fancy that!' she said, in reproach.

'Sandra – what are you doing here?'

'Your granddad needs keeping an eye on – that's what I'm doing here. And the arrangement is he pays me a little and I get use of this garden.'

'Oh. He never mentioned it to me!'

'Well, he probably thinks he did. His memory's not so good these days.'

'I know that!'

I wanted to say that it was *my* house, *my* garden, and that Matthew ought not make arrangements without consulting me and Corwin, but while I was not saying that, Sandra had already become bored with me and asked, 'Where's Crow to these days?'

'Sudan,' I said.

'He doesn't stay put for long, does he?'

'No,' I said. 'He doesn't stay put for long. But he's on his way home.'

'About time,' she said.

'I didn't know that you were a gardener,' I said.

'Well, you wouldn't, would you?'

She was snipping cuttings into small pieces with secateurs; they piled up in the wheelbarrow. 'Did you want something?'

'No,' I said, retreating. 'I was just out for some air. I didn't know you were here.'

'See you, then,' she said.

I had forgotten about the existence of Sandra Stowe. One summer at primary school – I think it was the year of the Silver Jubilee – she fixed me with a pointing finger in the playground, framed by the Gothic window of the infants' classroom, and declared me 'Wi-itch! Wi-itch!' in front of the whole school. 'Witchy face!' she shouted. 'Witchy name!'

The day before, each of us had been asked to draw up a family tree as a homework assignment. Our teacher, Miss Arden, a pretty young curly blonde incomer who basked in our adoration, had enthusiastically pieced together the jigsaw of cousins, aunts and uncles and established that two-thirds of the class could trace a line back to only four sets of great-grandparents. A neat diagram connecting them all together was displayed on the classroom and the class was invited to marvel at its inbreeding. The Venton name was not on it – we didn't marry into the village. We were posh, and my poshness, I vaguely sensed, even at the age of seven, lay at the root of the attack on my given name. The objection was not simply that I was posh, it was that I was posh and not at posh school, where I belonged, and where I was not, despite my mother's protests, because my father had hated posh school.

All the other kids joined in: 'Morwenna Venton is a witch! Morwenna Venton is a witch!' I don't remember minding. Matthew had us living in our imaginations in a magical netherworld and it was appealing to be ascribed supernatural powers. The sun was warming my back and I felt my spine curve up and my neck contract into my shoulders and I raised my arms, spreading out all my fingers – my ten pointing digits for Sandra's one – and produced from deep in my chest a rasping, cursing kind of voice and said quietly: 'I know *your* name, Sandra Stowe. I know your name and the names of your father and your mother and your grandfathers and your grandmothers. I know all your names.'

Suddenly Miss Arden stood in front of me. I knew immediately that I was in trouble – it was clear that I had been ill-wishing my classmates. She couldn't exactly punish me for invoking curses, so I was sent to sit in the book corner for 'being mean', which was not much of a punishment as I preferred to be in the book corner.

Remembering this now, having forgotten it for almost thirty years, I wondered if Sandra also remembered it in this way. Probably not. I thought that it would be interesting to ask her, one day.

A couple of nights later a north-easterly wind blew in, a lullaby gale that sang me in and out of my sleep. At around three o'clock

I woke fully for a minute or two and lay there. I thought of Mum and how she used to lie fretting awake on storm nights, resenting the rest of us who had been born to these storms and who wrapped ourselves up in them, deeper and warmer in our dreams. I realized that my heart had been missing this sound and that I had not known it. Then I turned over and slept through the rest of the night.

In the morning the wind was gone and the grey air was languid with exhaustion. The faint arrhythmic squeak of Matthew turning the handle on the coffee grinder came from the kitchen. I had given him an electric grinder as a Christmas present one year, but he never used it. I got up and looked out of the window. A hire car was parked on the driveway below. Corwin – blown in on the storm.

I crept into his room. The bed was in disarray and a duffel bag was thrown in the corner, but he wasn't there. He wasn't in the kitchen, either.

'Where's Corwin?'

'Oh,' said Matthew. 'Is he back?'

'He's back, but he's not in his room.'

'Goodness,' he said, pouring out a cup of strong black coffee and applying a significant amount of sugar. 'How you two come and go!' Then, 'He'll be in the cabin, I expect.'

I filled a Thermos flask with coffee and ran down to the beach. At the bottom of the combe an oak lay, up-tipped across the mill leat, its violated roots obscenely exposed. On the beach the storm had done its usual work of dragging up a tideline of battered Atlantic plastic, entangled blues and reds and greens – snapped fishing line, lost net buoys, discarded bottles and abandoned buckets and spades.

A weak column of smoke dribbled out of the chimney. Corwin lay asleep, his face hidden under the multi-coloured bedspread. Only a hand and forearm and some strands of dark hair were visible on the pillow. I put some pieces of driftwood in the stove and blew the fire back to life, then poured myself a cup of coffee and sat and waited for him to wake up. What had changed in him in the last five years? What had changed in me? Less in me, I thought. There had been less to change me. There was Ed, of course. But he was not so much a change as a logical progression.

A drum tap of light rain fell on the metal chimney cap and echoed down the stovepipe. The soles of Corwin's boots were caked with mud, but the creases around the ankles were packed with a fine dun-coloured sand – African dust. I hated to think of Africa. It made such enormous demands on the conscience.

The cabin was heating up. Corwin turned, pushed off the blankets and opened his eyes. 'Hello,' he said.

'I've brought you some coffee.'

He sat up. He was thinner, but more muscular. There was a military tautness to his face, dark rings under the eyes, and he had grown a beard, which was still dark. 'I couldn't sleep in the house,' he said. 'The bed felt too big.' This only added to the impression he gave of being a recently released hostage.

I handed him his coffee. 'How's Matthew?' he asked.

'Mum says Mark implied that he was dying, but he seems just the same. He doesn't change. As eccentric as ever.'

Corwin laughed, but a little cynically, I thought.

'You look different,' he said. 'Smoother and shinier. I hope you're not going to go all soignée on me, like Mum did.'

'How can you possibly tell? I've just got out of bed! I'm still in my pyjamas! I hope you're not going to go all sanctimonious on me just because you're a fucking war junkie.'

'Ah!' He smiled. 'My lovely foul-mouthed Morwenna. I really have missed you. Come and cuddle up.'

He shifted over on the narrow bed, and I slipped off my boots, climbed in next to him and laid my head on his bony shoulder. I could smell coffee and sleep on him. 'How long are you back for?' I asked.

'Sh!' he said, 'Listen!'

I listened: rain, wind, waves, shingle, seagulls.

Matthew was cooking breakfast when we got back to the house. Yesterday's left-over potatoes were frying with onion. He had obviously been watching out for us, because he came to meet us on the steps at the kitchen door, holding out his hands to Corwin, solemn and joyful like a priest on Easter Sunday. They clasped their hands together, Corwin stooping slightly, both beaming – with relief, I realized: they had not been sure that they would see each other again.

Matthew broke some eggs into the potatoes. 'I will have to ask you all about it, but we won't know where to begin,' he said, 'so we'll just let it all come out in its own good time. Morwenna, dear, would you grind some more coffee?'

'There's a tree gone over, down by the footbridge,' said Corwin.

'One of the old oaks? What a shame!'

Corwin tucked into an enormous pile of potatoes. I had never seen him eat so fast. I turned the handle on the coffee grinder. Matthew put some ketchup on the table and wandered off to the pantry to search for brown sauce.

'How long are you staying?' I asked.

'I don't know,' said Corwin. 'It depends on a lot of things. I'm in no hurry to leave. What about you? Can you stay for a while?'

'I can sort something out, I guess.'

'How's Ed?'

'I don't know,' I said. 'I stole his car.'

'You should marry him and have children,' he said, with his mouth full. 'Lots and lots of children. And live here. With chickens and geese and that goat Dad always wanted.'

He was concentrating very hard on pouring ketchup.

'Are you trying to tell me you've got married, or something?' I felt quite sick at the thought. 'Is that what this is all about?'

Corwin laughed. 'No, Morwenna. It's not what this is all about. But I release you from our vow.'

'But I never made that vow.'

'So much easier,' he said. 'I only have to release myself. Can I, please? I want to fall in love with someone – anyone. It doesn't look that difficult.'

'It's much more difficult when you love all of humanity,' I said spitefully. 'You spread yourself too thin.'

'But that's the point,' he said. 'I've lost my love of humanity. There's too much of it, you can't possibly keep it up. Unless you have God, of course. God helps. But, anyway, it's gone. All my *grand pity*, dissipated.' He stabbed a potato, and shoved it into his mouth.

'Why, then, you are bereaved!' I said.

'Actually,' he said, 'that's exactly how it feels. It's a terrible thing to lose.'

'Are you sure anyone wanted your pity in the first place?'

'Morwenna, my love, sometimes you are such a superficial little bitch. I don't mean, "I feel really sorry for her because she's so fat." I mean that quality of human understanding that raises us *above the beasts*.'

'Perhaps it will come back.'

'Perhaps. But, anyway, I needed a break. I got homesick.'

Matthew returned with the brown sauce. There was a faecal-like coagulation around the lid, which he wiped off with a damp cloth before handing it to Corwin. Corwin slathered the sauce over his potatoes. Matthew did likewise.

'Talking of the human condition,' said Matthew, 'here is one of life's great mysteries. Brown sauce. What do you think it is?'

'Best not to enquire,' said Corwin.

'I quite agree,' said Matthew.

I felt depressed, all of a sudden. Somehow we were talking as though we were at a 1930s house party. I almost expected to be jollied off to play tennis. Matthew broke the yolk of one of his eggs and brown sauce pooled into it.

'I thought I'd take a walk after breakfast,' said Corwin, mopping his plate with a piece of Matthew's bread. 'Anyone want to come?'

Matthew and I looked over to the window. It was raining heavily.

'No?' Corwin jumped up from his seat. His jeans hung from his belt. He really had lost a lot of weight. 'I'll be back for lunch.'

When he'd gone, Matthew took my hand. 'I think he wanted to be alone,' he said consolingly. 'It's hardly surprising. Still, I don't remember him being quite so . . .' he paused to find the word '. . . so . . . *brisk*. Do you?'

When Corwin came back he went straight upstairs to take a bath. He passed me on the stairs, and stopped to give me a rain-drenched hug. Then he lay in the bath for a long, long time. Every so often the plumbing whistled into action as he added hot water. When he reappeared, with his beard trimmed close and smelling faintly of grapefruit, he was calmer again, gentler. We alternated tea and wine all afternoon by the fire, talking of everything and nothing, while Matthew sat with his crossword, tuning in and out. That was Corwin's homecoming present to me: one last unspoiled lazy afternoon.

14

The book that Matthew had pulled out for me lay on the coffee table and Corwin picked it up. '*The Ghosts of Dartmoor.*'

'Matthew wants me to rebind it.'

'Were you going to send it to me?'

'I hadn't thought that far ahead. Anyway, you're here now. Do you want it?'

'Do you remember when we went looking for the Devil?'

'Of course.'

This was one of our favourite stories. Only Matthew knew it – or if our parents had ever known, they pretended not to.

'You were so scared,' said Corwin.

'No, I wasn't!'

Corwin had packed a Thermos flask of hot chocolate and for each of us an apple and a KitKat. He had bought the KitKats with his own pocket money in order not to *arouse suspicion*. In his rucksack were also a torch, spare batteries, two umbrellas, a Swiss army knife, a reflective blanket, in case of hypothermia, and 50p in 10p pieces for the telephone, in case of emergencies. Our parents were watching *Brideshead Revisited* – I remember the programme because my father usually refused to watch television, but everyone was talking about *Brideshead Revisited* and he had been seduced into watching it. Corwin wanted to be at the Devil's Stone well before midnight because, he argued, if midnight was the witching hour then you had to get there before the witches, who would need to get there early themselves in order *to prepare*. I had no wish to meet the Devil, and was alarmed by the hiatus following the words 'to prepare'. 'For what?' I wanted to ask, as I pulled my boots over my pyjamas and zipped up my quilted jacket. It seemed to me that at the end of that sentence was a bubbling cauldron big enough to fit two eleven-year-olds, but I was tractable and, as ever, I followed where Corwin led.

'You had some questions for him,' I remembered, laughing.

'I was going to ask him how old he is, and what's the worst thing you can do without having to go to Hell, and what his real actual name is.'

'And then,' I recited, 'you were going to punch him in the nose.'

We hid behind the trunk of the big oak tree that stood in the middle of the field, and we ate our KitKats listening to the rain falling on the leaves, wrapped up against hypothermia and watching the stone. It disappeared and reappeared as the clouds moved across the moon, and I experienced for the first time the immeasurable loneliness of transgression. And that's the end of that cute story because Matthew was out on his wanderings and came limping over the field towards us, attracted by the shining silver blanket, swinging his walking stick. We looked up at him and he looked down at us and whispered, 'Boo!' Then he dragged us back down the hill before we had even been missed. The following day Matthew added to the map a tiny picture of Corwin, wearing his tan and orange T-shirt and raising his fists at the Devil.

'Do you remember how much you cried over that because he didn't paint you too?' said Corwin.

'At least two hours. And then Matthew came upstairs and said, "Pull yourself together, child!"'

'He said, "You were just tagging along. It was Corwin who went looking for him." And you said . . .'

'And I said, "But he could never have gone looking for him without me."'

'Which was true,' said Corwin, quietly.

'Which was true,' I echoed.

*

I might have simply stayed in Thornton with Matthew and Corwin. Matthew, I had been told, was dying. And Corwin was unsettled. I felt responsible towards them both. Perhaps it was time to move back. In winter Thornton felt completely cut off; it was possible to imagine an existence protected from the rest of the world.

Corwin could not relax. He would disappear before I woke and return at nightfall. Once or twice I went down to the cabin expecting to find him there, but the cabin was empty. He would not talk about Africa, except to say that he had no intention of going back for the time being. He said he had come back slowly, covering as much of the journey as possible overland. He had not wanted simply to fall asleep in an aeroplane and wake up at Heathrow. He had needed to put enough hours and miles into the journey to place distance between There and Here.

Then one night, about a week after he had returned, and after Matthew had gone to bed, he asked, 'Did you ever read that last book you sent me?'

'No,' I said. 'It's just something I found on the shelf. I liked the engravings.'

'You should read it.'

'I never read them,' I said.

He seemed to change the subject. 'Did you ever see that movie, *The Gods Must Be Crazy*?'

'No. I don't think so.'

'The one where an empty Coca-Cola bottle falls out of the sky and it lands on a Bushman's head?'

'No.'

'So, someone throws an empty Coke bottle out of a plane and the tribe thinks it's a gift from the gods because it's such a useful tool. It's great for mashing yam and breaking nuts and stretching hide but there's only one, so pretty soon they're fighting over it and on the verge of killing each other with the thing. So they hold a council and send one of the Bushmen on a journey to the end of the world to return the bottle to the gods, because it has brought *strife* where before there was *harmony*. I laughed like a drain the first time I saw it. But then I watched it again, a few years later, and that time it just didn't seem that funny any more because it was such a neat metaphor for the central contradiction of my career, which is that something that appears helpful often just makes things worse.'

I contemplated my brother, his restlessness, his irritability. I didn't believe in talking about things. I believed that talking about things only inflated problems, but just in case it was something I ought to do, I ventured, 'Did something happen, Corwin?'

He ignored the question. 'It's like time travel – you might go back in time and interfere in order to avert a tragedy, but how can you possibly know what your interference might unleash? Dozens of bad films have been based on that premise. Anyway, the answer is, you can't. You can't know.'

I said, 'I wish you'd shave off that beard. I don't recognize you with it.'

'Are you listening?'

'You're speaking in parables. You know how much that pisses me off.'

He pretended that I had said something else. 'Let me tell you about my first Coca-Cola-bottle experience.'

At the heart of the house the central heating clanked off with a shudder; it was as if I could see the heat beginning to seep out through the cracks around the window frames and to see the sucking cold pull in under the door of the living room from the stone hall floor.

'It was in Mozambique,' he continued. 'I was living in this village in the hills. These hills were like nothing you see here – imagine vast termite mounds, and as red as termite mounds, and orange dust everywhere, and the sun going down as orange as the dust.'

I said, 'I've never seen a termite mound.'

'Of course,' he said, his voice getting harder, 'I was deeply in love with the country and had made valiant efforts to absorb the lore and dialect of the district. I had learned how to wash my underpants, clean my body and brush my teeth using only a single cup of water and I had been made aware of the explosive radii of various types of landmine.'

I said, 'You've told me that before, at least five times, your single-cup-of-water story. I bet it's one of your pick-up lines.'

'I shared a house with this German girl called Inge, who had the most beautiful feet. We slept together whenever we'd had too much to drink. There was no electricity and we were a long way from town and there was very little to do in the evenings. Inge, like me, was enchanted to be in a place where, only about a year before, the population had been at each other's throats, murdering, raping, and dragging each other's children off to be soldiers. All that sublimated violence in the air made for great sex. Some nights, when the rains came, we would sit on the veranda and listen to the thunder and watch the lightning play around the hills. We'd be totally transported, as if we were watching a firework display.

'Anyway,' he said – fixing the word, like a threat, 'I was there to dig a well – or, rather, to supervise the men of the village in building the well, and to teach them how to maintain it. The women of the village were having to walk about eight miles to the nearest source of water, carrying babies and pots. There was this one woman who limped along on a badly fitting prosthetic leg, and there was another who was so ancient and so thin and so folded over that her shoulder-blades rose out of her back like wings. They liked me, because it had been explained to them that I was about to improve their lives for them, and because I was something exotic. People used to reach out to touch me to see what my white skin felt like. Sometimes, in the morning, when they walked past my veranda they sang and clapped out a rhythm and my heart swelled, because I wanted them to love me, each and every one of them, especially the girl who had lost her leg.

'So we built them their well. And do you know what happened? No? Haven't I told you *this* story before? Well, what happened was, they stopped singing as they passed my veranda. Instead, whenever I came near they made that sound, which is the most efficient and devastating expression of contempt on the whole planet: the sound of sucked teeth. Inge and I used to try to imitate it, but we could never get it right. It's a kind of inverse snake hiss, and only the centre of the lips may move. And then you have to get the head movement, a sharp but subtle bird-like jerk away from the object of your disdain.

'You see, it turned out, after I'd been to a couple more outlying villages and dug a couple more wells, that, while it had seemed a good idea at the time not to have to spend five or six hours a day fetching water, the women had discovered that they had liked being away from the men. I had lost them their hours of freedom and they blamed me for interfering.'

'Are you going to tell me what all this is about?' I asked. 'Why are you back?'

'She went south – Inge,' he said. 'Married a Dutch peacekeeper.'

He stopped abruptly, and composed himself. 'All of which,' he said, looking at me kindly, 'is a rather long-winded way of saying that it is extremely difficult to know if and when to intervene in the course of things and it is not something that I take lightly. I am a cautious time traveller.'

'You've lost me,' I said. 'I don't understand a word you're saying.'

'Two things happened,' he said. 'And I don't know which happened first or if, perhaps, they're interdependent. But the first is what I've told you already, although you thought I was being flippant. I lost my compassion. It is the greatest loss I've ever experienced – my whole life, you see, I've had a tenderness for my fellow human. It was what I had instead of faith – my belief in human dignity, in the value of doing what you can to shore up the dignity of others. And then that sense just disappeared. The noise, the fucking noise, you can't imagine, those refugee camps – radios and dogs and chickens and screaming children and constant arguing and bickering. I began to feel this deep, corrosive contempt. It was like a virus. It completely took me over. For years you think of the children as beautiful and exuberant and vulnerable, and then suddenly you see them as voracious parasites who would kill you for a packet of paracetamol.'

Corwin stopped again. 'It's getting cold,' he said, and stood up to get some more logs. While he was out of the room I moved closer to the hearth and fiddled with the dying embers. I desperately wanted to go to bed but that would have been unforgivable. He came back and stoked up the fire into a flaming roar.

'You're very quiet.'

'You're very talkative. You sound like you could do with a proper break.'

'Well, like I said, I got homesick.'

'What was the second thing?'

'Ah, yes, the second thing. That concerns us both. You see, this idea lodged in my head, and I couldn't shake it free. I need to test it on you.'

'On me?'

'Yes. I want you to think about what it would mean if Dad's fall wasn't an accident.'

This came at a complete tangent. 'What do you mean?'

'We never questioned what happened,' said Corwin. 'And then one day I did – the question was there. What if it wasn't an accident? What if there was *deliberation*?'

'Why are you saying this? What are you saying, exactly?'

'I just need you to give it some thought – I don't want to influence you. But I need to know from you, if it wasn't an accident, what was it?'

'You're not making sense,' I said. 'Nothing you're saying makes sense to me. Dad was pissed.'

Corwin said, 'Please, Morwenna. Just think about it. Did we miss something?'

I stood up. 'I'm going back to London. It's time I got back to work. I'm going to lose my job and my boyfriend if I carry on like this.'

'He knew every square millimetre of that coast path!' Corwin said quietly. 'He could have danced home backwards with a bottle of vodka inside him and not fallen off!'

'This is your mid-life crisis. I'm not sharing it with you.'

Corwin said nothing more. He was *allowing his words to settle*. I left him sitting on the floor beside the fire. I packed my bag, then made myself a coffee, wrote my excuses in a note for Matthew, which I placed on the kitchen table, and left the house.

Outside I caught my breath. I had forgotten the moon. The combe was glowing, as though revealing its soul – the daguerreo-type plate of itself. The sharp shadows cut into the fields, like deep, dark secrets. It was as though the moon were not casting the light but drawing it from the sea. And it was then that I asked myself for the first time: Did, on such a night, my father deliberately step off the cliff at Brock Tor? The doubt was seeded. I climbed into Ed's car and lanced the moon's enchantment with the slam of the door and the yellow of the high beams and drove back to London. I could not have slept now even if I had wanted to.

In London the moon was lost in the streetlight glow. I parked Ed's car on his street and posted the key through his letterbox. At home all trace of pigeon was gone, and when I went into the living room, I saw that Ed had had my window re-glazed.

15

At the bindery no one, not even Ana, commented on my two weeks' absence. I experienced a delirium of love towards everyone there, even though there was an atmosphere of disapproval and no one was commenting on my absence because no one was really speaking to me. This was the only safe place left. I worked through my lunch break and long after everyone else had gone. I thought quite seriously of simply lying down on the floor and sleeping there, but was able to laugh off the thought and cycled home late, stopping off at the corner shop for soup and sliced bread. And that was how I spent my week. I unplugged the landline, kept my mobile switched off and ignored my computer. But on the Friday, as we all drifted off for our weekends, a fear set in. This was a feeling I had never experienced before – anxiety, yes, and jolts of adrenalin, but not this. This sat like extreme cold in my pelvis, which ached with it. I couldn't shake the idea that somehow Corwin had become dangerous to me.

With the fear came an animal furtiveness and alertness. I noticed smells I had not noticed before – the Friday-night stench of end-of-week cigarettes, exhaled Pinot Grigio, and happy-hour perfumes sprayed on in workplace washrooms. The girls looked unsafe on their enormous heels. I felt acutely concerned for them. How would they run if they needed to?

As I manoeuvred my bike into the hall, I noticed that there was light on the stairs. It would be Ed. Fair enough, I thought – and so tactful of him to wait until the weekend. I hoped he would forgive me, and I noticed that I hoped and, at the same time, assumed that he would.

He was sitting at the kitchen table, as though it would be inappropriately informal to wait for me on the sofa. I poured us each a glass of wine and sat opposite him.

'So,' he said. 'Are you going to tell me what's going on?'

'I don't think I can,' I said. 'I don't really know what's going on.'

He drank his wine and waited for me to come up with something better than that.

'I'm very cold,' I said. 'I'm going to have a bath. You can come and talk to me if you like.'

I ran the water and lit candles and lay there drinking my wine. Eventually Ed came in and sat on the edge of the tub.

'You seem upset,' he conceded.

'Yes.'

'Corwin?'

'Yes.'

'What's wrong with him?'

'He's brooding over my father. But I don't want to talk about it.'

'You and he have a very strange relationship.'

'Possibly,' I said. 'But I have no point of comparison. We just *are*. There has never seemed to be an alternative.'

The blind at the bathroom window glowed a weary orange from the streetlamp below. I wondered what Ed required of me for normality to resume. To offer an explanation of Corwin? To denounce him? Strange, how that word popped into my head: 'denounce'. What for? Ed was strangely colourless – like a moth. I wondered if it was deliberate camouflage, so that the CCTV cameras would not pick him up.

'What about me?' asked Ed. 'Aren't I an alternative?'

That was far too difficult a question. 'Did I ever tell you,' I asked, 'about how Matthew came to draw the map?'

Ed sighed a patient sigh. He was counting to ten. I thought about all the hundreds and thousands of tens he had counted to since we met. They stretched out into a long, long line, disappearing off into outer space. But then they re-formed to make clumps of pinpricks in time – tiny voids, which merged together to form an awful soul-sucking black hole.

. . . nine . . . ten. Deep, self-controlling breath. 'Yes,' he said.

I ignored him. He was missing the point. Some stories are meant to be told more than once – they have multiple applications. This was one of them.

'First of all,' I said, 'you need to understand that Matthew is absolutely terrified of the sea. He loves it – or "her", as he would say. But she terrifies him. Why that is, is another long story, which belongs elsewhere.'

I let in a little more hot water. Ed was sitting on the edge of the bath. His fingers were pushed into his hair and he leaned his forehead against the palms of his hands. His eyes were closed.

'So, this is the story of Matthew's Disappointment,' I continued – not at all discouraged by Ed's despair. 'Matthew was nineteen, and he liked being in Thornton, although he thought perhaps he should go to university, or something character-developing like that. But there was a war on, and even in Thornton it *could not be ignored.*'

'And the doctor told him he had a limp, and the very next day,' said Ed, 'he set out at dawn and walked as far as he could by midday and marked it on the map and came home and made a circle around himself and that's how he came to paint the map.'

'Matthew tells it better.'

'I don't want to talk about Matthew.'

'My mother thinks,' I said, 'that it's "egotistical, bordering on hubristic" to place himself at the centre of the world like that.'

'I think I'm probably on her side.'

I was sorry that Ed looked so forlorn. I said so. I said, 'I am sorry. Will that do?'

'It looks like it's going to have to, doesn't it?'

'Do you want to get into the bath?'

'No, thanks.'

'Let's do something different tomorrow,' I said, deciding that that was enough for the time being.

'Like what?'

'Let's go to the Saatchi Gallery. I haven't been there in years.'

'You hate all that stuff.'

'Yes, I do,' I admitted. 'But I'm bored with myself. I think I should challenge my own prejudices.'

'Why are you bored with yourself?'

'Corwin once described me as a "collection of detachments",' I said. 'Do you think that's fair?'

Ed stood up. 'I think "a collection of self-indulgences" would be more accurate!'

'Ed!' I called out. 'You're cross!'

But he was already gone.

Poor Ed.

Morwenna's Last Chance.

It was a couple of weeks before I visited the gallery. I had made up with Ed, but our truce still felt a little fragile and I thought it better to go on my own. The figure was smaller than I remembered it. It appeared waxen, pliant, as if the cold, blue-veined flesh of it would dimple under the warmth of my finger, but the label said 'silicone and mixed media'. A hard material, then – unyielding. I sat down on the floor next to it and crossed my legs. In the few years since I had seen it I had given it my father's face; or the approximation of my father's face that had settled upon my memory. It came as a surprise to see another man's face there, an older man's. One who had taken death slowly, given himself to it piece by piece, rather than launching into it whole and healthy.

As I thought that word, 'healthy', its antithesis launched itself into my mind: 'diseased'. Matthew was diseased, probably – cancerous, probably – although he had told us nothing and we could only speculate.

The gallery was filling with disappointed damp people, who had been looking forward to a turn on the London Eye but had found the queues too long for a rainy April day. Dead Dad and me on the floor, the smell of wet trainers, a small child's arm being pulled back by her father – her instinct was to touch the figure.

Could my father have had cancer? I wondered, fully giving myself up to the thought that he might have committed suicide. What if death had been inside him already? What if he had been growing it somewhere in the strange universe of his body, massing an invisible malignancy, and he had wished to spare us all?

The thought would not quite complete. Spare us all what? Leave-taking? Certainty? I could not make it make sense – my father was not a messy person: he liked order. His death was not orderly.

I left the gallery and went out into the rain and leaned on the embankment wall. Even after all these years of living in London I was surprised by the river, its rise and fall, its secret tributaries, flowing beneath the tangled traffic, cascading from the embankment walls. And the boats – somehow I always forgot that there were boats, and that there had been boats long before there had been a city, and that the river connected with the sea, and that its connectedness with the sea was the whole history of the city. Matthew never lost sight of these things. He would chide me if he knew.

My father had never seen this river – nor ever wanted to. Mum came regularly now, as she had done before she met my father, to visit the galleries, to shop. We lunched together in West End restaurants. ('Making up for lost time, darling,' she said. 'Thanks a lot, Mum!' I said. 'I didn't mean you, darling. It's not always about you.') I forced my thoughts back to my father. If suicide, then why? Was that Corwin's question? I could not imagine that our father would wish us to poke around asking why – he was too private. And then that struck me as the answer – he had wanted a private death!

I rang Mum, and when she answered, I said, 'Mum. My battery's about to go. Can you get me Mark Luscombe's number quickly?'

Mum didn't ask why. She assumed that I wanted to talk to him about Matthew. She gave me the number, said, 'Call me soon!' and I hung up.

'Mark! Hi. It's Morwenna Venton.'

'Morwenna! What a nice surprise.'

'I need to ask you something.'

'Is this about Matthew?' His voice was cautious.

'No. It's about Dad.'

A hesitation. 'About John?'

'Yes. I've been thinking . . . about Dad. Was he ill when he died?'

Another hesitation. He was working out where this was leading – had worked it out. There was sadness in his voice when he replied: 'No, Morwenna. There was nothing physically wrong with him.'

There was a spasm in my chest. My heart was hurting. Hearts could actually hurt!

'"Physically"? What does "physically" imply?'

'Morwenna? Are you still there?'

'I said, "What does "physically" imply?"'

I was shouting, but he couldn't hear me. 'Morwenna? Morwenna?'

There was rain inside my phone. A boat full of tourists went by on the churning brown river. I remembered someone telling me that there is a reward for fishing bodies out of the Thames – she was a rower, and more than once, she told me, a dawn training session had been interrupted to tow a suicide to the bank. I remembered this, now that the word 'suicide' had introduced itself into my thinking. No one, in the last seventeen years, had so much as whispered the word in relation to my father – at least, not in my presence. And yet now there it sat, right in the middle of my forehead, pulsing gently.

Back at home I called Corwin. It was the first time we had spoken since I had left him by the fire.

'OK,' I said. 'Let's say I allow the possibility that it wasn't an accident. Then what?'

'What do you think?'

'Well, you've planted the idea now. I'm stuck with it.'

'What idea?'

I forced myself to say it: 'Suicide.'

'Is that what you think?'

'Fuck's sake, Corwin. Just stop it!'

The rain was on my window and sneaking into my flat through the warped frame. 'Is it raining at your end?'

'Pissing down!'

'Good! But why would Dad kill himself?' I asked. 'It doesn't make sense. Why would he?'

'Perhaps he did, perhaps he didn't,' said Corwin, infuriatingly. 'I don't know. But we ought to know. Clearly, we missed something.'

'Do we need to know?'

'I need to know.'

'Why? What does it change?'

'That's what I need to know.'

'Christ, you're being annoying. How's Matthew?'

'Old. Increasingly absent.'

'I suppose I could come down for the weekend.'

'Yes. That would be good.'

Perhaps, I thought, my father had not been to see Mark but had been to see some other doctor in order to preserve his secret. Or – another thought – unhappy people commit suicide. Had my father been unhappy? Was that what Corwin was brooding about? We – all of us, Mum included – had cast Mum as the

Unhappy One. It had been selfish of him to be unhappy, to feed and indulge his unhappiness, when he was the one who had got his own way. Privacy. Unhappiness. Either way he had been secretive and selfish, and Mum knew it. That was why she had been so furious. I had been too hard on her, and it was my father's fault. Now I was furious too. I resolved to go and see her, make friends. It was time that we made friends, anyway. It was the grown-up thing to do.

16.

I didn't dare either to ask for more time off or to borrow Ed's car, so I rented a car for the weekend and set off before sunrise on the Saturday. I baulked at my first approach to Mum's, veered off-course and ended up stomping through bluebell woods with mud up to my ankles, preparing myself to behave well. When the woods opened out, I could see Mum and Fuck Off Bob's newly built oak-framed house tucked into the hill, and acknowledged, painfully, that what Mum had chosen for herself was a version of the life she had already had: a large country house, but dry and warm and unburdened by any history – including that of Corwin and me.

At last I got back into the car and made my way up the gravel drive and parked below a row of fashionably pleached horn-beams, which I intended to remember to admire. Mum came to meet me at the front door, saying, 'Look at the state of you. Take your jeans off – they're soaked and you've got mud all over them.'

The house was supernaturally clean, even the crystals on the chandelier, which Bob had no doubt wrested from some ancient widow, sparkled dust-free. Mum had an arsenal of sprays under the kitchen sink lined up ready to zap any incipient stain. I imagined a pixie living in the cupboard, held captive housekeeper by an imprudently granted wish, waiting to be released from his magical bond. I imagined his sleeping malevolence, tucked beneath the weary face of servitude.

'Oh, I'm sure Bob would love that! Me in my knickers,' I said, before I could remember to be nice, but Mum wasn't rising today.

'Bob's out. And in any case you can borrow something of mine.'

I took off my jeans in the hall and Mum came down with some trousers for me to put on. They were a little too small.

'I was expecting you earlier!'

'I was feeling a little nauseous,' I lied. 'I had to stop for some air.'

'Are you pregnant?'

'God, no!'

'Oh, well!' she said, cheerfully. 'Sugar in your tea?'

'Please.'

'Let's go into the snug, darling. I've put on a fire. And there's something on the mantelpiece, for you – you go first.'

On the mantelpiece was a cream envelope with 'Morwenna Venton' written on it in Mum's most exuberant fountain-penned italics. I put my mug on the coffee table, sat back in the charcoal-felt Italian sofa, pulled my feet under me and slipped my thumb under the flap of the envelope to open it.

Mum said, 'It's just that all the legal ins and outs took so long, and then Corwin has never been home for more than two seconds and now that he's finally back for at least a while we thought better late than never!'

There was a thick-laid card inside, embossed print: *Robert Marsden and Valerie Venton request the pleasure of your company on the occasion of their marriage.*

'You will come, won't you, darling?'

She was gabbling a little – it wasn't like her. Oh! I thought. She's a tiny bit scared of me. That had never occurred to me.

'Of course I will,' I said expansively, and thought about leaping from the sofa to give Mum a forgiving hug, but my awkwardly folded feet stalled me and it was already too late. Instead I gushed, 'Of course! It's time. You know, I'd sort of forgotten that you weren't married and, you know, it's nice that you still want to be married.' Now I was gabbling. Thank God, I managed to shut up before I said 'at your age'. I would make them a beautiful wedding present – a photo album, bound in cream silk. (Actually, no, that was a little too virgin-bride. Leather would be better.) And with their names and the date debossed into the cover.

I took refuge in the sweet tea and tried again. 'I've been thinking a lot about Dad recently. I've been wondering if he was happy.'

'Happy?'

'Oh, never mind! I didn't mean to bring him into the conversation, just when you and Bob are announcing your wedding!'

'What do you mean by "happy"?'

There was that word, deceptively innocuous, unleashed. I suddenly discerned its full load of implicit rights and responsibilities, incurred and failed duties.

'I don't mean anything by it – I just mean that I've been trying to remember things. How Dad was. How you were as a couple.'

'And how do you remember it?'

'Not happy. At least . . . I remember you as not being happy. And I don't remember being able to tell if Dad was happy or not.'

'Well, darling. You've just described your father!' The cup in Mum's hand circled gently; a slice of lemon bobbed at the surface of her tea. 'What brought all this on?'

'Oh, nothing, really. Have you seen much of Corwin?'

'Yes. A fair bit, actually. He's been bonding with Bob.'

'He has?'

'Yes.' She scrutinized me – with a mother's forensic gaze. 'What do you think that's all about?'

'Oh, you know Corwin. He's big on appeasement. He can't bear not to get on with anyone. Please don't tell me they've been playing golf.'

'No, darling. That would be overdoing it. They've just been on a couple of walks together. Pint at the pub. That sort of thing.'

'Oh. Well, that's nice, I suppose.'

'"Nice"?'

No word was safe with my mother. I stayed silent.

'Are you and Corwin up to something?'

'I've hardly seen Corwin!'

'So – yes?'

'No.'

Mum drank up her tea. 'How do you find Corwin?'

'Different,' I said. Sorrow tugged at my throat. 'Brooding.'

'Yes,' said Mum, reaching into the bottom of her cup and taking out the lemon slice between finger and thumb, 'there's a touch of Heathcliff about him, these days. Well, it's hardly surprising. God knows where he's been!' She ripped at the crescent of tea-stained lemon with her teeth, and dropped the rind into the bottom of her cup.

'What are you going to wear?' I asked.

'Oh, I don't know. It's so difficult. At this stage in life, you're caught between mother-of-the-bride and mutton-dressed-as-lamb. I'm thinking a very pale silver silk and a quiet bouquet – and at my age a piece of Interesting Jewellery is compulsory. It will probably rain, of course. Am I allowed to choose a dress for you?'

'You haven't already?'

'Well, I have. Will you wear it?'

'Yes, Mum. Of course. Will I like it?'

'Possibly. And will you bring Ed?'

'Possibly.'

'You should, darling. After all, you are nearly thirty-five.'

At Thornton, I raged through the house looking for Corwin, but he was out. Matthew was off somewhere, meandering through his visions. Sandra, who was turning the compost, said, 'Crow said to tell you he's gone climbing. Be back teatime.'

'Did he say "tea" or "supper"?'

'He said,' she stabbed her fork into the pile of steaming decay, '"*tea*".'

'Sorry.'

'That's OK,' said Sandra, indifferently. 'You can't help yourself.'

Back in the house, I watched Sandra from the landing. She felt me staring at her and turned to look up at where I stood in the window. Slowly, I raised my hand. Sandra turned back to her forking and I remained at the window, hand raised, like an imprint of myself left upon the house. Indulging in the sensation of insubstantiality, of transparency, I wandered aimlessly, imagining my real self underground, richly mouldering. I searched the rooms for other ghosts, but met only mute objects. I ended up lying on Corwin's mattress. There was a pile of periwinkle-blue books stacked in the corner of the room. I fell asleep and then woke – I could not tell how much later – to the sound of a heavy, limping footfall below and the slamming of the fridge door. I went downstairs and found Corwin in the kitchen with his bare left foot resting on a chair and an ice pack around his ankle. Covering his skin and his clothes was a fine layer of silt, as though he had been uprooted from the damp soil. He smiled to see me. 'How are you?' he asked.

'What's going on?'

'Nothing. I just slipped and twisted my ankle. I seem to have lost all my upper-body strength. But, God, it was great to be out there! I'd forgotten how good it feels. There's nothing like a good climb for returning a sense of proportion to your existence.'

'So you always say.'

'Yes, but it's true. There's the rock face. It has taken millennia to shape, and there's you, clinging to it, for a fraction of time so infinitesimal that the earth never even knows you were there. But still you cling. And you feel time pass.'

'You're talking a lot again.'

'Be nice and run me a bath?'

The ankle was already badly swollen. I repressed the urge to kick the chair from under it.

'With bubbles,' added Corwin. 'I think we've got some bubbles? And a cold beer. We definitely have beer.'

'Have you ever slept with Sandra?'

'Where did that question come from?'

'Oh, I don't know. I just remembered to ask.'

'I'm not her type,' said Corwin, laughing. 'We all fancied her like mad in Juniors, though. She was the only one with breasts. Why did you think I did?'

'You seem rather conspiratorial.'

'You're just making that up.' Corwin leaned forward to adjust the bag of ice around his ankle. 'I always liked Sandra. We used to trade marbles.'

'I don't remember that.'

'Yes, you do. She used to come over with her dad.'

'No. I don't.'

'You must do. Her granddad used to bring the crabs over and we played marbles with Sandra while he gossiped with Matthew.'

'I remember the Crab Man,' I conceded.

'Well, then.'

I remembered the cuffed crabs, scrambling over each other in the bucket, and the man himself, red still glinting in his grey beard, yellow oilskins, but not the marbles and not Sandra.

'You had a huge scrap with her over your favourite blue fiver. I had to split you up!'

'No,' I said. 'Gone.'

Corwin put his hands around his lower leg and lifted his foot gently off the chair, then gripped the kitchen table to haul himself to standing. He hopped over to me and put his arms around me and pulled me close, grazing my cheek with grit from his face and murmuring sadly, 'You've forgotten all the best bits!' When he let me go I could taste sea salt on the corner of my mouth.

'Help me up the stairs,' he said. 'Oh, and don't forget the beer.'

Corwin accepted a glass of wine when he came down. He said, 'I've got a present for you. There, on the mantelpiece.'

Five bleached bird skulls were laid neatly in a row. 'I was out walking last week, up by the pig farm. Someone had shot a bunch of crows and smeared them on the fence and the road. It was a mess! Anyway, I brought back the heads and boiled them off for you.'

'They're beautiful,' I said. 'Thanks.' I picked them up one by one and balanced them on the flat of my palm. They were so delicate. They looked as though they would disintegrate with a gentle calcium crunch if I closed my hand on them.

Corwin asked me to give him a haircut. 'Really short,' he said. I laid out newspaper and he sat on a chair in front of the fire and I began to comb through his hair. He smelt incongruously of lavender. Snippets fell onto the newspaper at his bare feet. The swelling had spread into the top of his left foot. A curl landed on the surface of his wine, and floated there, black on red. He picked it out. 'Not short enough!'

'You look even more like a hostage when you cut it too short!'

'Or a monk,' said Corwin. 'A hermit! That's the effect I want to go for. Give me a hermit haircut.'

'I thought hermits let their hair grow long.'

'Who knows?' said Corwin. 'Just make it ascetic. And don't drink any more until it's finished. You'll have my ears off.'

I tilted his head to one side and began to snip around the curve of bone behind his ear. 'What are you up to, Corwin?'

'Thinking,' he said. 'I'm thinking. How did you find Mum, by the way?'

'She asked me how I found you.'

'What did you say?'

'She said you'd been cosying up to Bob.'

'You'll never forgive them, will you?'

'No. But I do give in.' I manipulated his head between my palms. He was pure trust within my hands. 'How do you find Bob?'

'Interesting.'

'Interesting?'

'Very.'

'Isn't it time you went back to work?'

'I'm giving myself a sabbatical.'

I handed him the mirror. He checked his reflection. 'That's better!' I had my hands on his bare shoulders. 'Can't you drop this?' He met my eyes in the mirror, reached back to take my left hand. 'No. I'm sorry.' He kissed my palm. 'I need you to do something for me.'

'What?'

'We need to track down the others.'

'The others?'

'The others who were at the beach the night Dad died. Mickey, Willow and Oliver.'

'Why?'

'Because they were there. Because *we* weren't *paying attention* – perhaps they were. I've already found Mickey – he's here at The Sands. We're meeting him tomorrow. You can work on Willow and Oliver.'

'I don't want to! Absolutely no fucking way!'

'Why not? It'll be fun!'

'It's not fun – it's weird and morbid.'

He still had my hand. He gripped it tighter and locked eyes with me in the mirror. 'This is non-negotiable,' he said.

'I've missed a bit behind your ear,' I said. He let go of my hand and I picked up the scissors and tilted his head to the side and, very carefully with the tip of the scissors, I snipped at the skin behind his right earlobe. He jumped, but he didn't make a sound. He had known I would do that. A shining bead of blood formed.

'So,' he laughed, wiping it away, 'you're pissed off! That's fine. But it doesn't change anything.'

On the mantelpiece was a grey stone that I had found at Thornton Mouth. It was about the size of my two fists. At its centre was a perforation – it went almost all the way through, but not quite, because within this stone was another, a tiny foreign flint, black and ruthless, which had bored its way with the help of the sea and the centuries into its host. Nothing could dislodge it.

137

'I don't understand what you're trying to achieve.'

Corwin looked regretful, then. He hadn't explained himself properly. Standing up, he put his T-shirt back on. He had filled out a bit, but still his belly was concave. His hip bones jutted above the waistband of his jeans. He was showing the first signs of the Venton sag. He said, 'You remember, when Dad fell, you always said there was something wrong with us and I always dismissed it?'

Outside it was spring – cold evening sun, a frenzy of birds.

'I think perhaps you were right and I was wrong. We were in such a hurry to leave.'

I said, 'Ed asked me what Dad was like, and I couldn't tell him. I can't remember him.'

'You see!' said Corwin, smiling encouragingly – as if I had asked him for help. 'We have erased him, somehow.'

Our father in faint outline – the leavings of lead in the paper's grain. I said, 'He's dead, Corwin. Why does it matter so much now all of a sudden?'

'Mum calls us her "cuckoo children". Don't you think that's terrible?'

When Mum really hated us, she called us her 'beautiful cuckoo children'. We had squeezed her out of her own nest.

'Yes,' I said. 'I do.'

17.

Corwin had arranged to meet Mickey on the seafront. The stretch of beach in front of the café was now the dog walkers' beach and a little pile of plastic-wrapped dog shit had accumulated on the ground next to the Wall's ice-cream board.

'I haven't been here in years!' said Corwin, happily, queuing up with his brown plastic tray. A man with naval tattoos shot a hiss of water onto the stewed tea-bags in a huge metal teapot.

'Sugar,' I said. 'I need sugar.' And then, looking around, 'No. Me neither.' There was a reason that Corwin had chosen this place, but I didn't know what it was, and was not going to ask. The café hadn't changed – even the people looked exactly the same as they had seventeen years ago: grey-haired, anoraked and dog-loving. The floor swarmed with damp, panting fur. Corwin was ordering sausages, chips and baked beans, in an ecstasy of nostalgia. We slid into the moulded red plastic benches, and looked out on the desultory brown tide.

'So,' said Corwin. 'Tell me what you're thinking.'

'I'm thinking I'm being choreographed,' I said. 'And I don't like it.'

Corwin smiled, sliced into his sausage and used a piece of it to scoop up some beans. 'I've had dreams about this,' he said. 'I'm not joking. Whole dreams about sausages, chips and baked beans.'

I didn't recognize Mickey at first. He came in with his hands in the pockets of his denim jacket, his head and face hidden by a beanie and a beard. He looked suspicious and defensive. I stood up to administer a social kiss, but came up short against our lost familiarity. It was as if there had been a mutual betrayal. Our cheeks bumped awkwardly. Corwin stood up and shook his hand. Mickey said, 'Shit, Crow! You are thin! And what's with the hair? You look like a fucking suicide bomber or something!'

Corwin laughed. 'Dysentery,' he said. 'My intestines are a war zone.'

I had to assume this was true. I said, 'He made me cut his hair like that!'

Mickey sat down, keeping on his hat and jacket. 'How long are you home for?'

'Indefinitely,' said Corwin.

'Just the weekend,' I said, although I hadn't been asked. 'Would you like me to get you a cup of tea or a coffee or something?'

'We're not staying here, are we?'

'Why not? I love this place. Old times' sake and all of that,' said Corwin.

'Whatever,' said Mickey. 'But I could do with a beer.'

'When did you move back?' I asked.

Mickey looked offended; it sounded retrograde. 'You still in London?'

'Yes.'

'Just home for Crow?'

'Not exactly.' I drained my tea. I realized that every conversation I had ever had with Mickey had been triangular, held either through Corwin or through Willow. Our only direct communication had been one anomalous secret kiss, some time in the fifth year, lying in the trysting cave at Thornton Mouth at low tide, with the dank smell of seaweed and the sandhoppers tickling our ankles where our feet had disturbed the sand.

Corwin said, 'It's good to see you. I've been away too long! Come on, then. I'll buy you that beer.'

'I should let you two catch up,' I said.

'Not at all,' said Corwin, firmly.

I walked behind them and measured time against their altered bodies, their lost lithe boyhood: Corwin was limping and brittle;

Mickey had inflated, but at the same time gave the impression of having lost a little air. I expected Corwin to turn off into town, but he kept on along the seafront, in the direction of the harbour.

'Where are you taking us?' I called, suspicious, from my ten feet behind.

'The Lighter.'

I thought: I know what you're doing, you bastard. But his little reconstruction experiment was spoiled: the red nylon carpet was long gone – exposed floorboards, mismatched tables and chairs, and a chalked-up menu extolling the local produce declared the Lighter a gastropub. Serves you right, I thought. My father would not have recognized this as a pub; this smokeless echoing room with piped, whingeing music. I imagined his crab-stripped bones twitching with disgust on the sea bed.

'Well,' said Corwin, 'this is a change!'

'Yeah,' said Mickey, leaning up at the bar. 'The old place turned into a real dive. They put the landlord away for running coke in from the continent.'

'It all happens around here, doesn't it?' I said. 'Lost your supplier, then, did you?'

'*No*. I don't do that shit!'

'Only joking,' I said unconvincingly. 'What's everyone having?'

Corwin was laughing. 'What's so funny?' I snapped.

'You, my lovely Morwenna,' he said. 'And your beautiful tactlessness. I'll have a pint of the *organic bitter*.'

'You two are still at it, then?' said Mickey.

'What?' I asked.

'All that secret sarcastic twin stuff.'

'What's your pint, Mickey?'

'I'll have what Crow's having.'

'Three pints of the organic, please,' I said to the barmaid, who looked vaguely familiar. I wondered if we had been at school together.

So we sat, sipping politically correct bitter, and inexplicably

141

disliking one another – apart from Corwin, of course, who found *everyone* lovable, each in their individual way. Corwin waited until Mickey was three pints down and four cigarettes smoked outside in the cold before he moved to his purpose. In the meantime we discovered that Mickey had dropped out of college, fathered two children, neither of whom lived with him, had a stint as a shipbuilder working out of Plymouth and returned to The Sands to set up an outdoor-pursuits shop franchise. He offered us a discount.

'It's so good to see you, Mickey,' said Corwin, bringing the fourth round from the bar. 'I've been away so long. I've lost touch with all my old friends.'

'Yeah,' said Mickey. Alcohol had always made him sentimental. 'How long's it been since we had a drink together? At least ten years, I reckon.'

'At least,' said Corwin.

'Fourteen,' I said.

They both looked at me. 'If you say so,' said Mickey, who had temporarily stopped disliking me.

'I remember these things,' I said.

'So,' said Corwin, 'are you in touch with anyone? Where did Willow end up?'

'London,' he said curtly. 'We don't keep in touch.'

'And Oliver?'

'No idea. Completely disappeared! Never really saw him after the sixth form – he used to come and visit his mother, but she died a couple of years back, and last thing I heard, he and his father hadn't spoken to each other since he came out, so I'm guessing he doesn't visit any more.'

'I miss Oliver,' said Corwin. 'Do you remember the night we made that enormous fire?'

'And he wanted us all to become vegetarians,' laughed Mickey.

'I did become a vegetarian!'

'You're joking!'

'No, I did – I am.'

Mickey looked incredulous, and then recollected: 'You were just eating sausages at the caff!'

'I lapse, occasionally,' admitted Corwin.

'Seems like a lifetime ago,' said Mickey.

'It was – for us, at least. Our whole adult lifetime. I always think of that night as the end of childhood.'

Mickey remembered. 'Sorry, mate. I'd forgotten that that was the same night.'

My dark-eyed brother Corwin! Well, well, I thought, there is malice in you after all. You could not be so manipulative without it. I was still only halfway through the third pint. I couldn't keep up with them. They were beginning to slump – drunks always seem to melt towards each other.

Suddenly furious, I said, 'Corwin has got it into his head that Dad committed suicide.'

Corwin, I noticed, didn't move – he was irritated. This was a failure of subtlety. Mickey roused himself. On his face were, as I might have expected, embarrassment but also, as I didn't expect, surprise – at me. 'Well, we did wonder,' he said.

'You did? Well, I didn't. Why? Why did you wonder?'

He began to retreat. 'Just what people said, you know, about how your dad was the last person anyone would expect to . . .'

'. . . to fall off a cliff. It's OK, you can say it,' said Corwin, generously.

'He was drunk!' I protested.

'Yes. I know. But your dad, let's face it, he was a bit of a dark horse, wasn't he? Kept his own counsel and all that.'

My bladder was burning. I left them at the table and went out into the backyard. The cold air and the rain on my face woke me, and I realized that I was not going to go back in. Instead I walked, as I had last done the night of my father's death, all along the seafront, up the steps and onto the coast path, along the ridge to Brock Tor, where I didn't pause, down into Thornton Mouth, and from there up past the mill, over the leat, through the church-yard and home. The bright yellow gorse released waves of the scent of freshly baked vanilla biscuits, but the sky and sea were pewter grey.

Matthew was asleep in his armchair when I arrived. I stoked up the fire and sat opposite him to examine him for signs of the illness that we were to believe he was harbouring. He did seem thinner. The V of his jumper fell away from his shirt; the collar was loose around his neck. Was he waiting for us to ask? I wondered. Would it be better to know and to incubate his death with care and warmth, or would he be doing us, or himself, a favour, by permitting death to jump him from behind? Were these the questions my father had asked himself? I wondered about Oliver's mother – she must still have been young, in her fifties only. I had forgotten to ask how it was that she died.

Later, when I went to bed, I found that Corwin had placed a book on my bedside table. It was one of the ones I had bound for him – the most recent: *A Coastal Curacy*. I opened it, but already I was bored by it. On the title page were pencilled the words:

> *John Venton.*
> *His book.*
> *1960.*

Matthew, I thought. Matthew had taught him to do that. Matthew and his anachronisms – he plants us with them. And I also thought, This is what Corwin wants me to know about this book: that it belonged to our father. And I put it aside. And I slept. And when I went back to London the following day, leaving before dawn to make it to work in time, I left the book lying there.

18.

Willow was easy to find. I told myself I was looking for her because I'd been bullied into it by Corwin, but perhaps I needed to find out more, if only to shut Corwin up. She popped up on Google with her own PR firm. The girl I had known had disappeared, the one in the Edwardian camisoles and the patched jeans with the criss-crossed shoelace in place of a zip. Her website photo showed her as Cleopatra – sharp black fringe, kohled eyes. Intimidated by her powers of self-reinvention, I looked at myself in the mirror. Seventeen years but, still, it was me. Greenish eyes, brownish hair, freckles, a jumper with too-long sleeves.

'Look at her,' I said to Corwin on the phone. 'That's someone else. How can you expect that person to remember anything for us?'

But then she was on the phone. 'Morwenna! Oh, my God! How are you?' Her speech had always been full of exclamation marks. It had been like being in a room of bursting balloons. 'We must have lunch!' she shouted. I remembered to ask if she was still in touch with Oliver, but she hadn't seen or heard from him since school.

Oliver didn't show up on the web. I phoned his father's number. It rang and rang. There was no answer.

I googled Corwin. He was quoted in a couple of newspaper articles. His was a world of *plight*. Poor Corwin. I wanted to say to him: I know I'm bad at this, the soothing, caressing thing that women do. But look – the box is not empty. Look: that little unhoused mollusc in the bottom there – that's Hope!

I googled myself. I was not there.

Oliver and me, I thought. We do not appear.

Summer loomed. It's so ruthless – either relentless light or unwelcome rain. It's such a relief to reach autumn. And this summer would be full of trials: Mum's wedding, Matthew's decline.

I prepared myself in the only sensible way: I pretended that nothing was happening and left Corwin to himself. He said he'd been climbing a couple of times with Mickey. He didn't mention our father, and it was easy for me, so far from the coast, and with so much daylight, to ignore what I preferred to think of as Corwin's affliction. Corwin said that Matthew was much the same – he would let me know if anything changed. Mum called regularly to discuss arrangements. She had got it into her head that it was important Corwin and I were happy with the details of her wedding – perhaps because we could be at best only indifferent to the fact of her marriage.

As I worked on Mum's wedding present, I was forced to think about her. I made choices for her: the palest of grey leathers rather than silk damask or printed Indian cotton; plain endpapers, but with a subtle shimmer to reflect the occasion. I considered tooling flowers into the leather, but felt that she would prefer it unembellished. In the end, it was a straightforward, elegant object that ought not to be exposed to dirt. On the front, in a simple unserifed font, it said, in silvered-blue lettering: *Robert and Valerie, 19 June 2005*. There, I thought, pushing away the memory of that other wedding album at the bottom of a cardboard box: that's that.

That was May. I allowed myself to wish Mum well and was at peace with myself. At the bindery we worked on a huge order of journals that were to be party favours at some celebrity feast. It was soothingly repetitive. I was lulled.

I tried on the outfit that Mum had asked me to wear: an oyster chiffon concoction with very little stride-room. It was a while since I had worn a dress and heels. Ed said that I scrubbed up well, but wondered why women did that to their feet, and waited for me to ask him to join me for the wedding. Eventually I did. I thought it would be good to have a buffer.

I met Willow in the week before the wedding. She threw her arms around me. 'Oh, my God! Look at you!' Her hands waved as she talked. Her fingernails were painted pillar-box red.

'How's Crow?' she asked. 'Is he still gorgeous?'

'I don't know,' I said. 'He's my brother. Was he?'

'God, yes! You must have noticed! You two were always so . . .'

'What?'

She settled on '. . . close.' But that wasn't what she had been intending to say.

'He's very thin,' I said.

'Ah! Poor love. Well, it's hardly surprising, considering. Is he back for good?'

'I don't know. He's having a bit of a mid-life crisis.'

'Aren't we all, sweetie! Aren't we all!'

'I'm not.'

'Are you sure?' she asked. She contemplated me for a moment. 'Well, perhaps not. You always were Little Miss Contrary.'

'He's got compassion fatigue,' I said, not prepared to pretend to talk about myself. It seemed to me that reunions only reminded you of all the things you hadn't liked about a person. I knew that once I had felt towards Willow something approximating love, but now I couldn't remember why. 'And he's got it into his head that Dad committed suicide and he wants to know what happened. That's why he's pretending to be all nostalgic. He thinks you might have noticed something back then.'

Willow's wine glass stopped halfway to her mouth. She put it down again. 'God!' she said. 'I'd forgotten how harsh you can be.'

'Sorry,' I said.

We sat in silence for a minute or so. The food was Asian fusion – there were artistic crispy noodles, which were complicated to eat when you were embarrassed. A coffee machine hissed expensively.

I relented a little. 'I'm sure Corwin genuinely wanted to catch up as well,' I said.

'But *you* don't. Well, thanks a million!'

'That's not what I meant.'

Willow was doing her best not to sulk.

'How's your mum?' I asked.

'Oh. You know. She's moved to Totnes.'

'Where old hippies go to die!' It was an old sixth-form joke.

She laughed. Willow had never held grudges – life was too short. She would much rather enjoy herself. 'So,' she said, in a tone of intrigue, deciding that there was something to be rescued from the meeting, after all. 'Tell me all about it!'

'Well,' I said, 'Corwin's got this idea that Dad committed suicide. He thinks we missed something.' Saying this made me feel very tired. 'He's *combing the past*,' I said, and ran out of words.

'Why now?' asked Willow.

'I don't know. It never occurred to us before, and then it occurred to Corwin, and here we are.'

'Oh, Morwenna! Really? You must have thought about it!'

'No! People keep saying that. I never did. Is there any reason I should have?'

'What would I know about fathers?'

'Honestly, Willow,' I said, suddenly wanting to confide, 'I don't know what to do. Corwin's become completely obsessive about this. I'm worried about him.'

'And I thought we'd spend lunch talking about house prices and soft furnishings!'

'Sorry,' I said again. 'But Corwin's not going to get off my back until I've had this conversation with you. And then . . . I never thought I'd hear myself say this, but hopefully he'll piss off back to Sudan.'

'You don't mean that,' said Willow, correctly. 'So? Why does he think all of a sudden your dad committed suicide?'

'I don't know. He won't say. He wants me to draw my own conclusions.'

'The little shit! He always was a didactic bugger!'

'I've been missing and missing him for a decade and a half, and now there he is, at Thornton, filling the house with dour frowns and deep silences.'

Willow was framing her thoughts. 'I'm not sure I'm qualified for this,' she said, and beckoned the waiter over to order coffee. Then she leaned forward and said, 'OK! So! Are you ready?'

I nodded.

'Well,' she said, 'when your dad died, we all talked about it, obviously. You know – Ooh! How weird! One minute there he was playing his fiddle and the next minute he's falling off a cliff and we were so close and we didn't even know.'

I must have flinched, or something, because she stopped, and said, 'Sorry – that came out wrong. But you know what I mean.'

'I know what you mean.'

'And everyone said how your father was the last person anyone would expect to have an accident like that. You know. He was so . . . grounded. '

She paused again. 'Are you all right with this?'

'Yes. I'm fine. Go ahead.'

'Well, there had been some gossip . . .'

'About?'

'About . . . your mum and Bob. They seemed . . . intimate. People thought that perhaps they'd been having an affair and your dad had found out about it. Especially, later, when, you know . . .'

I did know. I was flooded with a sense of self-disgust that I should have been so naïve. Willow's expression was full of concern for me.

She said, 'Mickey and I saw them once, your mum and Bob, having a cup of tea together at The Sands. They were just sitting opposite each other drinking tea, chatting. They weren't doing anything, not touching or anything. It just looked – wrong, somehow. You know. Comfortable. Together. Like a couple. We talked about it afterwards. We wondered.'

She put her hand on mine. 'I've upset you,' she said.

'No, it's OK.' Then I said, 'Sorry,' for the third time, aware that since Corwin had come home my life was full of apologies. I wanted my unapologetic life back.

The coffee arrived. I looked at my watch. 'Oh, God, I have to go!' I said. 'My boss is really strict about lunch breaks.'

It wasn't an excuse. I did have to go. I wanted to stay and show her that I was grateful – she had liberated me.

I said, 'Thanks, Willow. Really.' I dropped a kiss on her cheek. 'And it is good to see you. Honestly. I'm just . . . you know.'

'I know, sweetie!' she said. 'Off you go! Give Crow a kiss from me.'

All afternoon I stitched away, glowing with self-righteousness. But when I got home and was about to call Corwin, something else struck me: a detail of my conversation with Willow. And when he picked up the phone the first thing I said was, 'Corwin, what happened to Dad's fiddle?'

19.

Ed was silent as we approached Thornton. He had seen photographs, of course, but I had underestimated the effect of that first view, when the hedgerows shoot you out at the top of the combe and you look down on the scattering of houses above the church and the solitary mill perching just where the sea presses the land, which was all velvety with the lush green of June. Ed gasped, and looked at me. He said, 'You don't do it justice.'

'I've forgotten how to see it,' I said.

I stood in the hall and shouted but no one answered.

'What do you want to see first?' I asked.

'The beach, of course.'

We took our bags up to my room, and I had the sensation that Ed was observing everything and attaching the new information to what he already knew about me. I didn't like the idea that I could be explained by Thornton and began to regret bringing him.

I paused as we went downstairs. Something had altered. It had flickered in the corner of my eye. I looked back to see what it was. The key was in the door of my parents' room.

We went for a long, long walk, which looped up through the woods and came out onto the high cliffs and down into Thornton Mouth, where we paused for tea in the cabin. I could see that Ed was love-struck.

'It is beautiful,' I said. 'But there is a "but" – same as anywhere.'

Ed didn't believe me. He had a glazed look in his eye. He was staring at the photo hanging on a nail in its broken frame – the one of Great-grandfather James standing before the wreck of the *Constantia*.

'Who's that?'

'James Venton. Matthew's father,' I said. 'He was the one who built the cabin.' I pointed to his boots. 'He always wanted to go to America. He had these boots made especially.' I pointed to the beached ship. 'And this is the last sailing ship to wreck off The Sands – the *Constantia*. Look,' I traced the twisted sails. 'Her masts are swinging against each other in opposing arcs. They're wrenching at her hull and any minute now she'll split open and spill her cargo of pit props onto the water and they'll roll to the shore on the waves and James will buy a lot or two at the salvage sale and build this cabin from them and pretend he's on Cape Cod, or somewhere like that. That's why that stag's head is hanging over the stove. He never hunted in his life, but it adds to the illusion.'

It had always bothered me, that photo. Everyone else has their backs to the camera and is watching the death of the ship. But James is caught looking inshore, past the camera – he has been caught by accident, hunched up in his heavy pea-coat. I will always wonder what could possibly have turned his gaze.

When we returned to the house we found Corwin helping Sandra in the kitchen garden. They were tying peas and beans to their supports of hazel tents. I had a sudden memory of being very small and chatting away to my father while snapping pea pods from their tendrils and popping them open, the sweet green taste of them. I remembered the hazel branches, cut too late in the season, taking to leaf.

Corwin shook Ed's hand. I hoped that Ed would continue to resist his charm, but already he seemed to be softening. His idea of Corwin was improved by the setting, and, what was more, here was an opportunity for Ed to help out. I left him playing with balls of string and went to unpack.

The key was gone from my parents' bedroom door. I carried on upstairs and hung up Ed's suit and my dress, then went to the kitchen to see if the key was where it should be, but the hook was empty.

As I closed the key-cupboard door, I heard Matthew's shuffle in the back porch. I found him sitting on the bench, removing his walking boots. He didn't hear me, and I watched him for a while. I could see now that he was ill. Each movement required planning. He rocked himself forward incrementally, each ratcheting motion taking him a little closer to his foot. Once he arrived at his shoe, he pulled first one end of the lace and then the other. At last I recollected myself and said, 'Matthew, let me help.'

He looked up and smiled, but had no breath for speech. He straightened up again, almost as slowly as he had bent forward. I knelt down and loosened the laces and pulled off first one boot, then the second. I slid his slippers onto his feet.

I said, 'I worry about you, on your walks.'

'Ah, Morwenna,' he said. 'You mustn't worry.'

That night, I didn't hear Corwin come to bed and, after Ed had fallen asleep, I left my own bed and went downstairs. There was light under the door of our parents' room. The key was in the keyhole.

I placed my hand on the doorknob. I knew I would find Corwin in there, but at that moment I half expected to surprise him in another form, one that I never saw – something fanged and clawed. I was just about to turn the knob when the door opened and he stood there.

For a moment I did recoil. There was something wrong with his face. He was pink – as though he had been peeled. I thought: His skin has been flayed! Then I realized that he had shaved off his beard.

'What are you doing?' he said. 'Are you coming in, or what?'

I hadn't been inside that room for over ten years. I remembered a junk room, everything covered with dust. But now it had been ordered. The furniture was neatly stacked to one side, and next to the bed was a pile of boxes. The bed was covered with papers.

'What's going on?'

'I'm looking for Dad's fiddle.'

'No, you're not.'

'Well, I am, actually – among other things.'

'Why don't you just ask Mum, or Matthew?'

'I have. They can't remember what happened to it. And I asked Bob too, but he can't remember anything much.'

'Dad was probably holding it.'

'Not if he was taking a piss, he wasn't.'

'Can't we do this after the wedding?'

'Aren't you curious? Some of this is really interesting. These are all his old school reports,' he said, pointing to a pile of papers on the corner of the bed. 'He was a crap pupil, apparently.'

'Well, he hated it there,' I said. Corwin handed me a pile of papers. The reports read: 'Disappointing. Distracted. Day-dreamer.'

My father's letters home were bland, unilluminating – cen-sored, probably. He had written: 'It is very flat here. I miss the sea.'

Homesick, I thought. Poor homesick boy.

There were letters from my father to my mother – I placed them aside. I did not have Mum's permission to read them. Corwin had no such scruples. He read out snatches to me: '"Let's have our babies in winter, when Thornton is asleep and we have time to gaze at them. We'll lay them by the fire and tweak their toes and I will find you all the more beautiful by firelight."'

'He was in love with her!' I said.

'Of course he was. Why would you think that he wasn't?'

'Why didn't she keep the letters?'

'Why don't you ask her?'

'They didn't have their babies in winter,' I said.

They'd had their babies in summer, and they had too many at

154

once, and the babies didn't gaze back at their parents. They only gazed at each other.

'What else have you asked Bob?' I asked.

'I'll tell you after the wedding.'

'What are you really looking for?'

'Proof. An explanation.'

'Do you think,' I asked idly, 'that Bob pushed him off so that he could have Mum? Perhaps they planned it together!'

'No! Don't even go there. That's not fair!'

'You started it! And, anyway, it would be a good story. I think I might work on it. It makes more sense than suicide.'

'You need to read that book. I keep asking you to.'

'Stop nagging. I left it here. I'll read it after the wedding.'

'You will be good tomorrow, won't you? Don't spoil things for Mum.'

'I'll be a perfect angel.'

'It's nothing to do with Bob – I swear.'

'Mum and Bob were having an affair, and you say it was nothing to do with Bob! OK. Whatever! Good night!'

'Good night.' He called after me: 'And remember. You promised.'

20

Mum and Bob's wedding was in a manor house turned boutique hotel, which was attempting to evoke Provence. There were lavender and oleander in stone troughs. The ceremony itself was to be in 'the Orangerie'.

Matthew, Ed and I arrived early, so that Matthew shouldn't be anxious about being late. The chairs were dressed in white cotton and tied about with silver ribbons. There were pale flowers arranged in silvery foliage. We weren't meant to be there yet – the room wasn't ready for us.

Eventually guests began to drift in. They assumed that I was there to receive them, and it was too late to correct the impression. They seemed to know me, but I couldn't remember, or had never met, most of them. The guests moved from me to Ed with an expression of curiosity and delight, as though he was being introduced as my intended. He took to the role immediately. Matthew stayed seated, and people went over to greet him, and to lay their hands on his shoulder in a comforting gesture – subconsciously, probably, I thought. And comforting him for what? That he was dying? Or that his son's unfaithful widow was marrying her lover, his son's best friend and dispatcher to the depths of the sea?

Aunt Jane arrived, moved her cheek to within three millimetres of mine, wafted some perfume in my direction, expressed her approval of Ed, then took over as Receiver of Guests. I returned to my place beside Matthew. He took my hand and whispered, 'You stay here, where it's safe.'

In the rows behind us there was a heightening of excitement as Bob arrived. He came over to us, and I stood, kissed his cheek, introduced him to Ed. I wasn't listening, but seeing him, some-how. He was still vain: he wanted you to notice that he was keeping himself in good shape. What, I thought, do you have to do with my father? I answered myself: Nothing – you have noth-ing in common. But still you are connected – by his death, and because you are marrying my mother. He was happy to be marrying my mother – I could see that. Pure joy, untarnished by the many years they had already spent together. It was, after all, love. And it outshone even his vanity.

I hadn't been able to dissuade Mum from walking down the aisle on Corwin's arm. I said, 'She'll be making a spectacle of herself.'

'It's important to her – let her have it.'

'Our stamp of approval?'

'*My* stamp of approval – if you insist on characterizing it like that,' he said.

So walk down the aisle she did, to a Bach orchestral piece sug-gested by the Classic FM website, looking very elegant, but leaning in a little on Corwin, because she had underestimated the height of her heels. She smiled and smiled and smiled, and when she reached Bob they held hands and interlocked their fingers.

Bob's brother stood up and read, with appropriate irony, the lyrics to 'When I'm Sixty-Four', and then I stood up and read, without any irony whatsoever, 'A Red, Red Rose'. I read it very well, and as I sat down again I congratulated myself on my mon-umental impassiveness.

Afterwards there was champagne on the lawn. We drank within a circle of coral and cream roses. I drank a lot. Ed was too busy ingratiating himself, and Corwin too busy being charming for either of them to notice. I cornered Mark Luscombe. 'Can we talk about Matthew?' I asked.

'I'm not sure that this is the time or place, Morwenna,' said Mark, moving away from me.

Matthew seemed to be enjoying himself immensely, sitting at

a table and surrounded by the parish widows. I went and hovered near them, but they didn't want me there, so I wandered away again. Corwin banged on his glass and gave a speech about how well Bob had looked after Mum for the last however many years, and made some better-late-than-never jokes. The women especially laughed; he looked so very handsome in a suit. Then everyone launched themselves on the buffet.

I think I was sober by the time the guests had all gone. I had realized by lunch that I needed to stop drinking, and touched only water for the rest of the afternoon. Mum said goodbye to the last guest, then turned to us and said, 'That all went rather well, didn't it?'

It did, actually. Even I had been warmed by all that radiant goodwill. Corwin put his arms around her and gave her a hug. 'It was a great day, Mum. Well done.'

'You will come back with us, won't you? You'll need some supper.'

'Of course,' said Corwin.

Matthew had already been delivered home by one of his old ladies. Jane went back with Mum and Bob, and Corwin drove me and Ed. It was about six o'clock. The evening sea pushed back the cloud, the sky cleared. I wasn't having any dark thoughts. I felt fine. I was glad it was over.

At the house, Bob opened a bottle of champagne that he had been saving. The cork soared up into the beautiful void within the timber frames and we laughed and we drank to Mum and Bob's happiness. Then Mum took Ed by the elbow and steered him to sit next to her on one of the sofas that faced each other in front of the fireplace.

'You know, Ed,' she said, 'Morwenna still hasn't been able to explain to me what it is that you do.'

'I teach maths,' said Ed.

'Oh, she made it sound a lot more romantic than that!'

'Did she?' Ed looked surprised and pleased.

'Yes,' said Mum. 'She said you're a sort of mathematical Don Quixote.'

Ed looked less pleased. 'I'm not sure what that means,' he said. 'I teach maths. I work with other mathematicians, but maths is a young man's game – making breakthroughs, that is. Perhaps that's what she meant. I'm always hoping that the next mathematical genius will turn up in one of my seminars and unlock my mind.'

'You see?' I said, to Ed as much as to my mother. 'He's a poet!'

'He's an idealist!' pronounced Mum. 'Morwenna's father was an idealist,' she added. 'So it follows.'

'So how come you're not rich?' asked Bob. 'I thought you maths brains all went and made millions from hedge funds.'

'That doesn't really interest me,' said Ed, as tactfully as he could.

'I told you,' I said stubbornly. 'Ed's a poet.' And then, unnecessarily, 'He has integrity.'

Jane snorted. She didn't trust people with integrity. She couldn't see how they pulled it off.

I remember thinking: I don't care. Let her snort. So I can't even blame Jane for what I said next. I still have no idea why it came out right there and then. I had intended to ask, but not in the way that I did. I can only ascribe it to relief and exhaustion now that the wedding was over – I was falling on the descent.

'So, Mum,' I said, 'just out of curiosity. Were you fucking Bob before Dad died?'

Too late, my skin gave me the alarm. Every cell began to swell with blood – I felt it rise to fill my ears and lift me while everyone else in the room disappeared and all I could see was Mum. She had taken off her shoes and there was a hole in the toe of her tights. She had still been talking to Ed, and her hand, with its new wedding ring, was on his sleeve (I found myself wondering what she had done with the old one), and she turned and she was *smiling*.

She said slowly – I saw her mouth form each syllable, 'No, Morwenna, I was not, as you so charmingly put it, "fucking Bob" before your father died. What makes you ask?'

I could see quite clearly now that this smile of hers was toxic – that her toxic smile had been with my father at the edge of the cliff, and that Bob, even if he hadn't pushed him, had been too present that night. His drunken laughter had been sufficient mockery to induce my father to jump.

'We were just wondering,' I said, 'what it was that might have encouraged Dad to throw himself off a cliff.'

I sensed Corwin move. He was about to intervene. But Mum held up her hand to stop him. 'You think your father committed suicide?'

'Yes!' I said. But already I could see what I had done. I saw their faces: Bob's, Jane's, Corwin's. Most of all I saw the repulsion on Ed's.

'But why are you asking me this *now*?'

'It has only just occurred to us.'

Mum laughed. 'Really? Surely, darling, it must have occurred to you both at the time.'

'No!' I yelled. 'It didn't. It never occurred to me that he had any reason to commit suicide! Now I see that he did have!'

Strangely, Mum was putting her shoes on, quite calmly. She didn't want to continue the altercation in bare feet. She wriggled her heels into her pumps, first one, then the other, and stood.

'Darling,' she said calmly. 'You're being hysterical. What can I say? It did occur to me that your father had committed suicide, and it had nothing to do with Bob. *If* your father did throw himself off, and *if* it was because anyone was fucking anyone, it's much more likely to be because he thought that *you* were fucking your brother.'

Something dislodged from my belly and flopped between us – a hideous translucent jellied thing. She and I had made it together. Every gibe against Bob had been caught up and fed to it. Mum was smiling the indulgent smile of the new mother.

'He saw you both, the week before he died,' she said. 'He was very upset. So upset, in fact, that he deigned to discuss it with me.'

'Saw us both? What do you mean, he saw us both?'

But already a memory was forming.

'He went up to wake you for work and saw you in bed together.'

'But we often shared a bed. You know that. Dad knew that.'

'What we knew was that your behaviour was disturbing. You were eighteen and in bed together and naked!'

Corwin was standing. He was saying, 'It's time to go.'

'Yes,' said Mum. 'I think it is.'

Corwin was pulling me from the sofa and saying, 'Ed. Get up. We're leaving.'

Mum was still smiling. She said, 'Look at you both – you've only ever needed each other. And you have the gall to begrudge me Bob!'

Outside, at the car door, Corwin slapped me hard. 'You stupid bitch!' he yelled, and pushed me into the back seat.

'Ed,' he said, 'you can sit in the front.'

21.

At Thornton, Corwin got out of the car. Ed sat in the passenger seat, waiting for me to offer something in mitigation of my behaviour, but I couldn't speak. Finally, he said, 'Aren't you even going to try to explain that?'

'I can't,' I said. 'I can't explain.'

'Well, that's not going to work for me this time.' He was gripping the door handle. As he opened the door, he said, 'You know, when I first met you what I liked about you was that you made beautiful things. I don't understand how that's possible when your thoughts are so ugly.'

I sat in the car a little longer, then roused myself and went round to the boot room and changed out of my stupid uncomfortable shoes, then walked down to the cabin in the floaty dress I had worn to please my mother on her wedding day.

I felt calm – shock, I suppose. I knew that Mum and I could never forgive each other. We would never argue again; we would never again have that intimacy. I wasn't angry with her, or even with myself, for that matter. I wasn't thinking about Mum's accusation or about my father's suicide. I felt bad about Ed, but from a great distance. Mainly, I had the buoyant sensation of having set down a great burden and walked on. It was still light. There was a scattering of summer colour on the fields.

At the cabin I took a blanket and wrapped it around myself and sat on the steps and watched the stars appear and waited for the moon to rise and for Corwin to come. He would know what to do next. The moon was almost full – a gibbous moon. Matthew had given me 'gibbous'. It was one of his uncountable gifts to me. I had always been able to receive them without rancour. I wondered why I had been unable to do the same for my parents.

The tide was gentle and quiet. Eventually I heard Corwin's steps on the shingle. He sat down next to me. We watched the moon. I had matters back in proportion: the Atlantic, the blind cliffs, my self set against them.

'I'm sorry,' said Corwin. 'That was my fault.'

I draped the blanket around us both. 'Has Ed gone?'

'Yes. Will you be able to explain it to him?'

'Probably not.'

After a while I said, 'Do you think she was right? Do you think Dad really thought that?'

The memory was clear. It had been so hot that summer. We had fallen asleep, talking, and some time in the night I had freed myself from the irritation of clothes, half asleep. I remembered the comfort of spooning into Corwin's skin. His chest and legs had been smooth then. It had not been the first time although perhaps it had been the last.

'She's just punishing you.' Corwin picked up a pebble and threw it towards the approaching water. 'Actually,' he said, still staring after the pebble, 'Dad asked me about it.'

'What? When?'

'A couple of days before he fell.'

'So it *was* to do with us! How did he ask? What did he say?' I felt a spasm of remorse. My poor private father, asking out loud if his son was having sex with his daughter.

'He brought me down here and we sat like this. And he said something about our "affinity" – yours and mine. How you and I had always been close, but he was worried that we'd become too close.'

'Affinity,' I echoed. At that moment I felt it very important to be accurate – honest. I had just broken with my mother and it seemed to me that in that there was something far more unnatural than any distortion of love there might or might not be between me and Corwin. I thought of my father, standing in the doorway, watching us sleep, not understanding us. I was ashamed. I acknowledged how lonely we had made him – him and Mum.

I said, 'Look at me. Let me see your face.' He turned to me and I looked at him properly for the first time in years. 'Did he see anything, do you think? In us? Anything that we didn't see at the time?'

'I've thought about that a lot,' said Corwin; he sounded very, very sad. I thought: He's weary. He's almost reached the end. But the end of what? 'Dad said that we were "in danger of violating the laws of nature". I was so angry – I just wanted to hit him, but I didn't. I remember that quite clearly – the sensation of having stopped myself from hitting him. He wanted my assurance that my feelings towards you were "chaste". I laughed at that. That word, *chaste*. He said it was a good thing we were going to be separated for a while. I said I couldn't believe that he would think that of me – of us. That he offended us in asking.'

'Did he believe you?'

'I think so. Yes – I'm sure he did.'

'He should have talked to me about it.'

'He was going to – he told me he would talk to you too.'

'Why didn't you tell me?'

'Well – events were superseded somewhat, don't you think?'

That was when I remembered my father standing in the doorway with a cup of tea. So that was what he had wanted to talk about! It had been too difficult. He had not had the courage. What would I have said, if he'd asked me? I would have shouted. I would have thrown something. And I had not been wearing pyjamas – he had misjudged the setting. It was all wrong for an accusation of incest. Poor Dad! How unpleasant it must have been for him.

'Dad wasn't the only person who asked me,' Corwin said suddenly, as if he'd just decided not to hold anything back.

'Who else?'

'Mickey.'

I was beginning now to feel laid out to view; pried open.

'He said we were freaking everyone out. He asked me if I'd ever thought about it.'

'And had you?' I asked.

'What?'

'Had you ever thought about it?'

'Christ! I don't know. I don't think so – but you really don't want to know what goes on in the minds of adolescent boys. Dad did know. That's why he talked to me first – me "in particular, being male and therefore less in control of my appetites".'

'Well, that was one of his longer sentences,' I said. There was acid in my mouth.

'Oliver did his wise-old-man thing and said, "All kinds of love are possible."'

'Oh, Oliver too! Oh, good!'

We said nothing for a while. Corwin threw pebbles, his arm protruding from the gap in the blanket. The tide was now close enough to receive them. *Plop! Plop! Plop!*

'We humiliated him,' I said. 'You see? She was right. It was us!'

I leaned my head on his shoulder. 'Have you noticed how we've been talking in euphemisms? I have no vocabulary for this.'

'No.'

'Do you think we love each other too much?'

'What's too much?'

'I don't know.'

'So,' I said, 'are you finally going to tell me what you've been doing for the last five months?'

'Better than that. I'm going to show you.'

He stood and reached out his hand to help me up to standing. Then he pulled shut the door of the cabin and returned the key to its hiding place. I kept the blanket around my shoulders as we held hands and walked along the beach. Then I followed

165

him up onto the cliff path and zigzagged up to the ridge where the lighthouse flash up-coast beckoned us on. As I walked behind Corwin I thought of seven-league boots. Each of our steps was taking us a great distance. There might not be a way back.

Just before Brock Tor we turned into the hidden path between the furze bushes, which caught on the delicate fabric of my dress and scratched at my legs. We came out above the chine. 'It's OK,' said Corwin. 'I'm not going to make you stand too close.' I moved as close to the edge as I dared until I could just see the glitter of the waterfall.

'Now,' said Corwin, 'where do you think Dad was when he fell?'

I pointed ahead of me, over the falling stream, to where I had thrown in the box of secrets. But Corwin shook his head. 'That was the assumption, wasn't it? That he went over there?' I thought of the great shards of granite below; of my father, sliced.

'I brought Bob up here,' said Corwin. 'He wasn't that pleased about it, but I think he thought he owed it to me. Bob said he pissed over the waterfall, but Dad walked around.'

He took my hand again and started to lead me around the horseshoe curve of the cliff. 'So Dad walked around, and Bob started to go after him. Then Bob gave up about here, and sat down and watched Dad walk around a bit further.

'Here,' said Corwin. 'Bob said that he remembered Dad being about here.' He pulled something out of his jacket pocket and handed it to me. 'This is the book you sent me,' he said. 'I want you to read it – I've marked the passage.' He took his jacket off. 'You're freezing,' he said. 'Put this on.' He pulled the blanket from my shoulders and held it while I put on his jacket. Then he wrapped me up again and stepped away from me.

'Corwin,' I said. 'You're getting too close to the edge. You're making me dizzy.'

'Wait for me at the cabin,' he said. 'If I'm not there in six hours, do whatever you think is right.'

Then he turned and spread out his arms. Crow, I thought. Crow: about to take flight.

And then he tipped himself forward into the deep black air.

PART THREE

22.

Corwin dropped into the blinding dark. Something ripped from my chest as I lurched after him – my voice: it was gone, falling with him. He himself made no sound. I thought: I should have heard him hit the water by now. Or the rocks; I would have heard him cry out if he had hit the rocks. I crawled towards the cliff edge, but he had fallen into the black hiss of the sea and the whispering of the grass. The lighthouse flashed, and then flashed, and then flashed.

I found that I was curled on the ground and that I was very cold and that something like thought nuzzled at my brain. I held something hard to my chest. It was the book. I raised myself up and started to walk, and then my legs began to run and they ran me back along the cliff and down towards the glowing shingle and splashed me through the edge of the tide. It didn't occur to me to disobey Corwin and go for help. I had only one instinct: to get to the cabin and to warm myself so that I might think.

The skirt of my dress was soaked and clung in gorse-torn shreds around my calves. I undressed to my underwear and put Corwin's jacket back on and fired up the stove and filled the kettle and placed it on the hob. Then I pulled the great-aunts' bedspread from the bunk and wrapped myself in it and sat next to the stove and watched the kettle, fiercely. This kettle-watching required an enormous amount of willpower and concentration. It took a very, very long time to boil. I thought of watched kettles. I thought that I would never speak again, that Corwin had silenced me. I resented him for it. Corwin might be dead and bumping about on the tide leaking blood onto the water. I hoped he was. Then I made tea.

The book lay on my lap in its periwinkle-blue binding. *A Coastal Curacy*. I didn't need to read it to know what it was: the country memoir of a well-educated Victorian. It would contain observations on flora and fauna and on the architecture of churches and stately homes: the gentle pursuits of the English. It was a conventional book with nice enough engravings. I opened it at Corwin's marker and tried to read, but my mind would not receive the words so I put it down again and fed the fire and sat some more. I pulled the bedspread closer around me and thought of the great-aunts making it. I thought of them pulling apart old socks and jumpers and winding the wool around cards and steaming it with a damp cloth and a heavy old iron and then unwinding the wool around hands held apart and rewinding the skeins into neat compact balls. I thought of them sitting and cro-cheting. I wondered what they had talked about. I wondered if they had laughed.

I had no way to measure time but the sound of the tide edged further and further away off the shingle until it was silenced by the soft sand. I slept, open-eyed, starting awake over and over again into the nightmare of Corwin's madness. Night began to lift. I stood and went to the cabin steps to feel the sunrise. I found that I was crying. That's interesting! I thought. I licked at my tears and went back inside to look at myself in the cracked mirror on the shelf above the photo of Great-grandfather James. My face cried at me. I disliked the sensation and made myself stop.

I refilled the kettle. He will be here soon, I thought. And then I noticed the conviction I had that he was alive. If he were dead I would know. We were conjoined at some point of the soul. It was a terrible epiphany. Combined, we made a monster. Somewhere I had read that in a case of conjoined twins one tends to be stronger, sapping the other's blood and organs. I wondered which of us was the parasite.

The sea glinted a mackerel silver. I went to stand on the steps again and watched for Corwin. The tide was right out. The sun had breached the horizon and the blush evaporated from the sky. At the end of the tumble of rocks that spilled onto the beach dividing Thornton Mouth and the cove below Brock Tor, I caught a scribble of movement on the dark granite. I watched hard. It was Corwin, climbing down the jagged slabs. I watched him reach the sand. I went back into the cabin. I knew that now I would be able to read.

Corwin limped in through the door clutching his shoulder and fell on the bunk, turned on his back and closed his eyes. He was shivering, a trembling right through every muscle of his body. I drank my tea.

Eventually he said, 'Did you read it?'

'Yes.'

'And? What do you think?'

'I'm not thinking. I'm too exhausted.' I held my cup out. 'Tea?'

He propped himself up to drink; the tea shuddered in the cup. 'I think I may have dislocated my shoulder. It really hurts!'

'That'll teach you!' I said. 'So? Apart from any physical damage you may have done to yourself, do you feel better now?'

Corwin looked a little surprised. 'Yes!' he said. 'Yes. As a matter of fact I do. I feel better. It was amazing, actually.' The words stuttered in his mouth, his teeth were chattering so much. 'The jump, I mean. The rest was a little hairy. But I do. I feel better. My head is clear now.'

'Oh, good! That must be nice for you. Better than being dead.'

'I knew I'd be OK.'

'You did? Well, I didn't.'

He was trying to take off his wet clothes, but couldn't raise his arm. I helped him ease his T-shirt over his shoulder and take off his trousers. I draped them over the drying rack and placed it close to the stove. His skin was white and blue, his lips almost black. He had lost his shoes. His socks were shredded and his feet grazed and bleeding. When I touched his skin it was so cold that I was shocked out of my numbness and suddenly I felt anxiety for him. I stoked up the fire, then lay down next to him and cocooned us both in the bedspread, trying to give him some of my warmth. I pulled his hands between my thighs and took his feet between my own. His jaw vibrated at my temple. After a long while, the shivering stopped and the warmth returned to his hands and feet; the red returned to his mouth.

'So you read it?' he said.

'Yes.'

'And?'

'I can see what you're thinking.'

'Did you see the pencil marks?'

'Yes.'

'I never realized that you didn't read the books,' said Corwin. 'I wondered at how bad some of them were! I read them all, looking for hidden messages. I thought I'd finally found one.'

'No,' I said. 'There were no messages. Or, rather, there was just one message. You missed it.'

After a pause I said, 'I never realized that you did read them.'

'Well,' said Corwin, 'there are only so many times you can play Trivial Pursuit. Especially with people who don't have the cultural references.'

'You are cruel,' I said. 'Cruel and flippant.'

'Yes, I suppose so. I've had to think a lot about that – can I be that cruel? But I had to be. Can I have some more tea?'

I made more tea. He took the chair next to the stove and warmed himself there.

'So,' I said, 'are you going to explain yourself?'

'OK,' he said. 'Well, I had this friend, when I was working in Congo. He was called François. He'd been a teacher in Rwanda and he was very articulate – good company. He spoke really good English and acted as my interpreter for a while. He had this incredibly deep voice. It was like the rumble of the earth. He could have said anything and it would have sounded wise. We played chess together in the evenings.'

'Is that what you've been doing for the last decade?' I snapped. 'Playing board games?'

'Don't interrupt!' said Corwin. 'This is important.

'Anyway, François was my interpreter for about four months and I learned so much from him. We talked about Africa mostly – about the genocide, obviously. About the future for Africa. But he never told me anything about his family. And I never asked, because – who knew? – he might be a mass murderer, or his family might have been wiped out, or he might have been forced at gunpoint to rape his mother . . .'

'Jesus, Corwin!'

'Oh, don't be so precious! The one time I put an unpleasant image into your head you split my lip!'

'*Unpleasant image!* What a nice little euphemism! The way you wallow in the excrement of humanity is perverse!'

'Just shut up and listen! One evening, François comes over and says he's sorry but he has to leave. He says he's seen someone from his village and he doesn't want to be recognized and he begs my forgiveness. He says his name's not François. He says his family thinks he's dead and he wants it to stay that way. And then he says, "I want to reassure you that it was nothing that I did, I was not a participant. It was simply that I was presented with the opportunity to be dead and I took it. And afterwards, when so many were returning from the dead and I might have resurrected myself, I found that I did not wish to."'

'What – in those exact words?'

'That was how he talked. He spoke slowly, always. His sentences came out fully crafted. It's a form of courtesy. Not all cultures encourage the idea that every connection of the synapses should be inflicted on other people.'

Corwin leaned over and took my hand gently. 'And then he said, "Sometimes it's lonely being dead, but it suits me well."'

'No!' I flinched. 'It's all just coincidence.'

'I thought about that conversation a lot over the years. And then you sent me that book.'

We sat in silence for a while. I imagined François walking out into the dark, into the vastness of Africa. I thought of the sweeping arrows on historical maps that represent the mass movements of peoples after wars and of his feet moving along them.

'You think Dad didn't die. You think . . . what? He jumped off a cliff and then just walked off into a new life somewhere?'

'Yesterday I still thought that. Now I *know* it.'

'That's not true! You don't know!'

He was looking at me with enormous pity. His was the face of the torturer, the face that says, This is going to hurt me more than it will hurt you.

'I don't understand why you had to jump. Why couldn't you just tell me what you were thinking?'

'Because I thought I was going crazy. I wanted to see if you'd get to the same place without me. But you were being so obtuse. And in the meantime, I was going over and over the cliff, trying to work out how he did it. I got Mickey to show me all the tombstoning spots – he knows all those extreme sports types – and I knew it could be done here. It's simple in the end – once you know where to jump. It's a bowl. You just need a high enough tide so that you have enough depth and so that the tide pulls back far enough to give you enough beach at low tide to get out to the end of the rocks to climb over. The worst thing was the cold and the waiting. I was planning for a better tide, actually. But things came to a head.'

'Were you waiting in the water? All that time?'

'No. I got up onto the rocks – which wasn't easy. In fact, it was fucking scary. I sort of tucked in while the tide went out. Then I climbed down, but that was hard because I'd hurt my shoulder, and then I walked out and made the climb.'

'I still don't understand why you had to jump.'

'Because that's what he did. Why jump off a cliff – why not just leave? I had to know. I'd rather die than not know.'

I thought that I would rather not know. I said, 'It might be possible in Africa, but it's not so easy to make the better-off-dead lifestyle choice here. What's he supposed to be doing? Hanging out with Essex gangsters on the Costa del Sol?'

'Of course not,' said Corwin, firmly. 'You're right. It would be harder here. But not impossible.'

I didn't want to believe him. I wanted to believe that he was unwell, that these were delusions. My father grew things. He had been training a peach tree into a fan against the southern wall of the kitchen garden. He kept telling us it was a ten-year project. A man like that didn't fake his own death – but, then, a man like that didn't commit suicide either.

'Corwin,' I said. 'Please stop. You're driving yourself mad – you're driving us both mad. You don't *know* anything. All you have is a strong hunch and a lucky escape. After all this, we're still where we began. The original explanation is still the most likely.'

'I do know.'

'So you know,' I said. 'So what's the answer to your own question? Why jump off a cliff?'

'Don't you see? It had to be one thing or the other – life or death. It was a gamble with fate. Like Russian roulette, or something.'

'So where is he? What's he doing? What's he living off?'

'That I *don't* know. We have to find him.'

'You need help!'

'Morwenna!' He took my face in his hands and looked hard at me. 'We have to find him!'

He let go, sat back on the chair and warmed the palms of his hands against the stove. 'And then,' he said, 'I don't know.'

Steam was rising from our wet clothes. They had already dried in patches. The cabin smelt of scorched cloth, of seawater, of hot stove metal. Corwin stared at his hands. 'I really don't know.

Then I have to stop and consider what to do. Because right now if I saw him, I think I might have to kill him.'

Quietly, coaxingly, I said, 'But how, Corwin? How would we even start?'

Corwin looked at me, incredulous. 'With Matthew, of course. How do you think? If I'm right, then *he* certainly knows, the old bugger. He has to.'

23

The following Sunday I determined to visit Thornton in order to worship there at the pretty Norman church, which was famous locally, so I had been informed, for its pew carvings.

I set out on foot, taking a steep climb to the top of the cliffs, after which the walking was easy and pleasant along the ridge and I eventually began to descend around a high granitic outcrop beneath which a stream flung itself into the sea over a sheer slab of rock. A lonely mill soon came into view, pressed up against the sea, and, further along the beach, tucked into the lee of the cliff, a dwelling on the foreshore. I was surprised to see a fishing boat pulled up beside it. It is rare to find safe landing for a boat along that stretch of coast, but the cove, I surmised, was protected from the battering of the sea by a long sheltering cliff wall.

The hamlet lay in a deep combe, which now, in spring, was white with hawthorn. Uphill of the mill was a scattering of houses and cottages around the church spire. My path led me past the mill and over a small footbridge along a twisting stream, which disappeared, at times, beneath cascades of tumbling thorn, which soon turned to ancient dwarf oak, laden with moss. The church itself was guarded by two enormous cedars, which, as I later observed, appeared when viewed uphill of the hamlet to form a gateway to the sea.

I arrived while the church was empty, in order to make some sketches of the pew carvings. I had copied into my sketchbook an intricately scaled mermaid and the profile of a Red Indian in fine feather head-dress when the bell-ringers arrived. They were curious to see my work, and one, an old man who could barely climb the ladder to the bell tower, declared it 'as good as any I've seen', for they were used to visitors with sketchbooks and had tales at the ready about the smuggling days when the church had been used to hide contraband. Such tales are told up and down the coast, but, having seen the landing down at Thornton Mouth, I could well believe that this spot had been indeed a favoured haunt for smugglers.

It was a lively service. The congregation had descended from the surrounding farms to hear the old rector, who was more ancient still than my approving bell-ringer, and who was of the fire and brimstone variety, to the obvious satisfaction of his flock. Upon hearing that I was the new curate at St Peter's, he invited me to take lunch with him at the rectory, which invitation I gladly accepted, and while we were at table he regaled me with the story of Thornton's Devil Stone.

The church at Thornton had taken many years to build. This was not the fault of the workmen, who were diligent and skilled. But each morning, when they returned to work, they discovered that their tools and materials had been removed a mile away and thrown to the foot of the cliffs at Thornton Mouth, and each morning, before the work could continue, the workmen must move it all back up the hill to the site of the church.

One night, the youngest of the builders hid in a tree and waited for the culprit to reveal himself. At midnight he was assailed by a terrible smell of sulphur, and he thought he might faint and fall out of the tree, but he held fast and soon he heard voices. He climbed up higher into the tree and looked down upon a troop of demons who were being overseen by the Devil himself, and he watched as they marched down the combe carrying on their shoulders the builders' bricks and tools.

The next day, the young builder told his fellows what he had seen, and they sought the advice of their priest, who told them to pray to St Michael, for it was he who always knew how to get the better of the Devil. Thereupon they prayed, and the very next night they watched for the Devil, and when he and his demons were gathered a great light appeared in the sky and St Michael came down and grabbed the Devil by his forked tail and flung him over the parish boundary, then picked up a great boulder and hurled it after him, pinning the Devil beneath it. And there the Devil was stuck, his demons all scattered, until such time as the building of the church was completed and could be consecrated, whereupon the grateful worshippers of Thornton dedicated their church to their protector, St Michael.

The rector rounded off his story with a spirited quotation from Revelation, Chapter 20: '"And I saw an angel come down from heaven, having the key of the bottomless pit and a great chain in his hand. And he laid hold on the dragon, that old serpent, which is the Devil and Satan, and bound him a thousand years, and cast him into the bottomless pit." Yes,' said the rector, 'the Devil likes it here. The sea entices him. He hopes one day to bounce off her belly back into the middle atmosphere, out of which he was cast into the earth. Above all else,' he warned, 'the Devil is an optimist.'

As I took my leave of the rector, I thought to enquire about the strange dwelling on the beach. 'Ah!' said he. 'Now there's an interesting fellow. You must drop in on your way home and see for yourself. He enjoys a bit of Christian company, and his mortal soul is much in need of it!'

It was upon this advice that I approached the hut at Thornton Mouth, although I hesitate to dignify it with that designation, the 'hut' resembling an upturned boat, being a precarious clinker-built pile of old ships' bones with portholes for windows. As I approached I observed that it was garlanded about with glass fishing floats and strings of perforated pebbles and was buttressed by coils of thick, tarred rope. Before the entrance were piled crab pots and driftwood. Smoke issued from a stovepipe that protruded from the roof.

I hesitated to knock at the door, and instead attempted to peer discreetly through an open porthole, but before I could so much as glimpse its occupant, a voice called out from within: 'If you're from the dead, be off with you. Unless you come to take me with you!'

I was so taken aback that I believe that I turned my head to look about for a ghost, and only then understood that the voice spoke to me. I returned that, indeed no, I was alive and well, and stated my business: that the rector had sent me with his greetings.

'In that case,' said the voice, 'you'd do better to come round by the door.'

Bending to enter, I was met by the stench of damp rope, tar, smoke and stale fish. The walls were piled high with insulating coils of rope, and a hammock stitched from sailcloth hung from a beam formed from a broken mast. A crate served as a table, and crude shelves and benches sawn from ship's planks made up the remaining furniture. A driftwood fire smouldered in a stove, which stood on a pile of sand in the middle of the floor.

The man sitting there might have been old, or he might not have been more than forty. He had that look of the sea, which disguises age. His forearms bore the inkings of a mariner. He sat on a bench, working at his nets. As I entered he looked up and said, 'Take your place by the fire and be welcome.'

His speech bore some trace that was not of the West Country. 'No,' he acknowledged. 'I'm not from these parts.' I asked from where he hailed, but he would not say. 'They all ask me that,' he said. 'But I never tell.'

He stood to take from the shelf a bottle and two pewter mugs. 'If the rector sent you,' he said, 'you must drink with me.'

I was apprehensive of the concoction that the proffered glass must contain, but was surprised by the taste of a good brandy. Noting my surprise, my host laughed and, waving the bottle, said, 'This is how I'm paid for my services.'

'And what might those services be?' I enquired.

'Well,' he replied, 'I serve as sexton to this cove, here.'

Naturally, I sought to understand what he meant by this. 'Well,' he explained, 'you know how it is. This is a bad stretch of coast. The dead wash ashore, for the sea don't always want them. And I bring them home, to their final resting place, to the church. The rector and I used to share the work, but he's too old for the climb now.'

'Are there no survivors?' I asked, thinking with a shudder of the tales of murderous wreckers with their lanterns and their knives.

'Only me,' he said. 'I'm the only one ever washed up alive on this beach.'

This I recognized to be a cue for a tale, and so I permitted him to refill my glass and settled in to hear what he had to say.

'As you so rightly observed,' he began, 'I'm not from these parts. And I took to sea when I was a lad and stayed afloat until I was a young man. I didn't much take to the life. All the hours they let a man call his own, and he believes it: needle and ink, whittling at whalebone. I spent days put together over a fine waistcoat, but what for? Who was ever to see me wear it? So I was the quarrelsome sort. And one day we were harboured up for repairs and I took off. And they took after me, for I had enemies aboard and they were only too glad to hunt me down. And I ran for three days and they came after me and I found myself up on these cliffs and there was a big pile of rock sticking out over the sea and I went around it to hide. Now my enemies had caught up with me, and I found myself looking down into the water, and I thought to myself: Jump or you are lost. So I jumped, right off the edge of that cliff and into the sea.

'Well, when I hit the water I felt pain all over, like a thousand slaps with the back of the hand, it was. And I went down, down, down. And when I popped back up, who should be waiting for me in the water, but the Devil himself, red eyes, jack-o'-lantern grin, horns and all. And he said my name, and he said, "You're coming with me." And I said, "No, I'm not. Not if I can help it." And he leaped at me off the top of a wave, and I fought with him right there in the water. He thrashed like a conger, but I caught hold of him by the tail and twisted him over and over until at last I *climbed up onto his back and I rode him through the waves till he was tired and spent, and he shot off into the sky, shouting and cursing.*

'Next thing I knew, I was lying on this shore, all betangled with seaweed and spewing like a baby. I thought I must be dead, but when I looked down I saw that my leg was bleeding, and so I told myself that if my blood was running I must be alive still. And I lay there until the rector found me, and he took me with him and nursed me. And I believe that my enemies must have thought me dead, because they saw me fall. So then I thought to myself: No one knows me here. My enemies think me dead, and only the Devil knows my name, so he may have it, and I will take another one.'

Twilight was now upon us, so I thanked my strange host and took my leave. I had twice encountered the Devil during my short stay at Thornton, and had no wish for a third meeting, and I hurried back along the cliffs to return to The Sands before dark fell.

24.

Underneath the sentence 'only the Devil knows my name, so he may have it, and I will take another one' was a faint pencilled line – drawn lightly, neatly. In the margin was written the name 'John Greenaway'. I recognized the tiny pedantic handwriting, but I could not tell if it belonged to my father or to Matthew.

At the hospital we had said that Corwin had slipped on the rocks, which was almost true. They patched him up and gave him some strong painkillers. It was around midnight by the time we returned to Thornton. The ghosts were active. We passed the memorial cross and I thought of Matthew, who never passed it without saying the names out loud. He always appeared to read them from the plaque, but even I, by the age of eight, knew them off by heart. I can recite them still: from Arthur Cornish all the way down to Peter Thompson.

Once, in winter, I told Matthew that I was frightened to be calling out the names of the dead on such a dark night, and Matthew said, 'What do you think those poor boys could possibly want with you? The dead aren't to be feared, only the living.'

And I trusted him, and was persuaded, and have never since feared the dead. But now Corwin and I had allowed ourselves to imagine a different kind of haunting, by the shade of a living being. We didn't even have a name for such a terrifying spirit.

I was frightened to leave Corwin. 'You have to promise!' I said. 'Promise me. No further action until I get back. I don't even want you going into Mum and Dad's room.'

I said, 'Patience, Corwin. Without patience, we'll just go mad.' I had patience, I suddenly realized. I had a virtue. I had patience for things that no one else noticed. I could spend days standing at a vice, sanding spine papers until they were smooth as silk. I could pare leather until it was as thin as tissue. I could take as long as it took. Corwin, on the other hand, was skittish. I didn't trust him alone with Matthew.

The book came back to London with me. On the long train journey I turned it in my hands: *A Coastal Curacy*, by Ambrose Pearce, published by some long-forgotten house in 1887. On the frontispiece the words: *John Venton. His Book*. I must have noticed at the time, and then immediately forgotten it, this conventional book, with nice enough engravings that I had spent precious hours of my short life in rescuing, that I had carefully teased apart and restitched and pasted and pampered, when it was just a molecule in a mountain of vanity and self-regard and utterly deserved to be forgotten and left to decompose.

I put the book back into my bag and listened to my messages. There was nothing from Ed. There were two messages from the bindery. One from a colleague confirming that they'd received my message saying I'd be a day late getting back, and one from Ana saying that she would like me to keep my lunch-break free so that we could have a chat. In fourteen years I'd never had lunch alone with Ana. I assumed that she was going to fire me.

The green hills end long before London begins. I looked out on the rainy suburbs. I was altered, irrevocably, by the last forty-eight hours. A mutation had occurred in my soul or, perhaps, it had simply completed. Maybe it had started with the imaginary falling man, or before, with the simple act of removing my T-shirt in the middle of a hot night. The words from that song in *Oliver!* leaped incongruously into my head: 'I am re-*view*-ing the situation . . .' Corwin and I used to love that film. I found myself irritated by the exclamation mark. Why was it *Oliver!*, not simply *Oliver*? It was a very annoying piece of punctuation.

Fagin and the Artful Dodger clowned off into an East End sunset. They sang in my head: 'I think I'd better think it out again.'

When I returned to the bindery, there was a stranger working at my stool. 'That's Birgit,' said Ana. 'She's going to be here for a few weeks. You can help out on repairs while she's with us.'

Birgit looked up and smiled at me, from behind owlish glasses. She was wearing a black waistcoat, embroidered all over with what looked like birds in flight. Meekly, I set myself up at another bench and began to take apart a book that had been brought in for repair. It was a beautiful book, badly damaged. An eighteenth-century copy of *Gulliver's Travels*. It would take time to restore. I watched Birgit from the corner of my eye. On closer examination, I saw that the waistcoat was not covered with birds: they were books. Their pages fluttered like the wings of parrots and birds of paradise.

Ana suggested that, as the weather was so warm, we take some sandwiches to the Priory Church Garden. I was terrified of Ana. She had been perched on the edge of my life for all those years like a beautiful hawk, black-feathered with a red beak and bright collar, watchful and indifferent. I had never heard her say anything foolish or unguarded so my respect for her was boundless. I feared her disapproval more than Matthew's.

We sat on a bench. Angels looked down on Christ hanging from the cross. I had always thought that Ana came from Argentina. 'No,' she corrected. 'But close. Chile. How strange that you don't know that after all these years, Morwenna.'

I didn't try to defend myself. It was true. It was strange. She said, 'You seem troubled, Morwenna. And it's beginning to affect your work.'

'Do I? Well, yes. Everything's falling apart a bit. I'm sorry.'

'Are you?'

'Am I what?'

'Are you sorry? I never know what English people mean when they say that.'

'Oh.' I had to stop to think. 'Yes. I mean, I am sorry. I regret my unreliability. I am racked with guilt,' I added.

Ana sniffed, annoyed, and lit a cigarette. She smoked in the way that people smoked before they knew it killed them: with panache. 'That,' she said, 'is another word you English throw around. You say things like "I feel so guilty because I haven't washed the dishes for two days." Guilt arises out of sin. Whether or not to wash the dishes is simply a matter of choice.'

'Oh,' I said. 'I see what you mean.'

We ate our sandwiches silently for a few minutes. Then I said, 'I don't really believe in sin.'

'In that case,' she said, 'you are not racked with guilt.'

'Do you believe in sin?'

'Of course not. It's a patriarchal construct designed mainly for the bullying of women.'

'Oh!' I said.

'In my experience,' she said, 'people are troubled when they are too close to love or death or sex or power. Or they have betrayed someone or themselves – their own ideals. I don't need to know what's going on in your case – it's always complicated to the individual and a little sordid to everyone else.'

'It is complicated,' I said. 'But mainly my grandfather's dying. I ought to be looking after him.' This surprised me a little. I hadn't realized until I said it that, among all my current concerns, Matthew took priority.

'Morwenna. At the moment, you are either absent or tired and distracted. You hurtle off to the end of the country and back as if you are popping out to Tesco. Consequently, you are not much good to me at work at the moment,' she said. 'Would you like to take a short sabbatical?'

'Yes, please,' I said.

'You can have four months.'

'Thanks,' I said.

'Another thing,' she said. 'Birgit is journeying. She did her apprenticeship in Switzerland, and now she is travelling and working for free and needs somewhere to live. Can you put her up for a while?'

I recognized this as a condition of Ana's tolerance. 'Yes, of course,' I said. I didn't mind, I'd be going away. And, anyway, I wanted a chance to hold the waistcoat; see how it was worked.

The smoke streamed from Ana's mouth into the June sunshine. I studied her for uncertainties. I couldn't find any. I said, 'I wouldn't mind doing that – journeying for a while.'

'My grandfather did it,' said Ana. 'On my mother's side. He was German. But I never met him. My grandparents were Nazis. My mother hated them. But that's how I inherited the habit of punctuality.'

'When did you come to London?'

'A long time ago, Morwenna. A long time ago.'

'Were you a binder before you came here?'

'My father had a bindery. He was Italian.'

She smiled at me. 'You know, Morwenna, when I came to London I thought: This is exile, this grey city, these strange people who never say what they mean. But observe this garden, this peace, here in the middle of the city. London is a sanctuary, Morwenna. A sanctuary.'

I packed for four months and handed over my flat to Birgit. I had stayed and worked for the rest of June in a daze, waking every morning with a heart-flutter of panic. I called Ed a couple of times. He didn't answer, so I left a message. I said that I was sorry, really and truly, and that I had to go down to Thornton for the summer, and that when I got back I would like to talk to him, if he would listen.

Corwin was waiting for me at the station, black rings under his eyes. 'You're not sleeping,' I said.

'Matthew's in a lot of pain at night,' he said. But I knew that that wasn't it. I put my hand on the back of his neck as he drove.

'I'll sleep better now that you're here,' he said, smiling.

'Have you heard from Mum?'

'I got a postcard from Bermuda.'

They were on a once-in-a-lifetime round-the-world cruise, but I was still too ashamed of myself to make any snide comments about it.

The Hare and Hounds loomed on the side of the road – a boundary marker. We had entered Matthew's circle.

25.

The following day, when we sat down to coffee, Corwin said, 'Matthew, there's something really important we have to ask you.'

'Yes,' said Matthew, 'of course. It's time.'

But he assumed we were asking about his dying, so he told us. 'Cancer, of course,' he said pleasantly. '*Riddled* with it, apparently. And I really don't want to be poked and prodded and experimented on. At eighty-five I'm far too old for all of that. No. I shall let nature take its course. I have agreed with Mark upon palliative care. They will *make me comfortable* – I think that means industrial doses of morphine. There's this marvellous organization called Hospice at Home, apparently. And I'd really much prefer to die here. I do hope that you won't object?'

We were humbled, then. Each of us utterly alone, and Matthew already beyond reach.

When we were in that time, the summer of Matthew's dying, it seemed like an eternal season of damp mornings, rose petals scattered on the grass by the night's rain. It was as though Matthew's admission that he was dying unleashed his cancer. He gave himself up to it. Almost overnight he became thinner and weaker. We moved his bed down to his study and positioned it so that with the curtains open he could look out over the sea from his pillow. Some days I pushed him to the map in a wheelchair. I had to get it down off the wall so that he could reach it. His hand shook and I had to support his wrist to allow him to paint. He painted bluebells. He said, 'They have always raised my spirits, Morwenna, and I shall never see another bluebell wood – unless

I'm wrong, of course, and there is a heaven. Goodness! How fascinating that would be!'

One day, he painted his own name on his own tombstone, beneath my grandmother's name. 'Matthew!' I said. 'That's perverse!'

'Oh, don't make such a fuss, Morwenna! Every painting must be signed off. If you decide to keep it, by the way, you must remember to varnish it.'

I was still staring at his name on the tombstone when I noticed something else. The top half of a child's face peered out from behind a neighbouring gravestone. 'Who's that?' I asked.

'That's Death,' said Matthew. 'Your grandmother said that Death was a small child. She could hear him calling.'

'When did you put him there?'

'You know,' he said, 'I don't remember.' Suddenly, he was disoriented, distressed. 'I don't remember. I'm very tired all of a sudden, Morwenna. Please, be so kind and help me back to bed.'

His name was the last thing he painted. After that, there were nurses and drips and bedpans and soiled sheets. It was my first death. Not my first bereavement, obviously, but my first acquaintanceship with the business of dying – the routine of it, the maintenance of the failing life-support system. The mess of it. Corwin and I lifted him, turned him, supported his head. We undressed him and washed him. Death moved in with us. Matthew absented himself, fragment by fragment, to spend time with him. They chatted together while I held Matthew's hand. I could almost see his face; the wide, frank stare of a child. He was not so terrifying after all, and so very patient.

I was waiting for Matthew to confess, if that's the right word. I had more faith in him than did Corwin. I kept saying, 'Don't ask him yet. Wait a little longer.' While he slept we sat on the bed in our parents' room and went through boxes looking for clues. Where could our father be? If he was going to run away, where would he run? We put a baby monitor in Matthew's study so that we could hear him if he called. The monitor crackled into life every few seconds as Matthew stirred and moaned.

There were no clues. Everything in my father's life led back to Thornton. When Matthew was lucid, I tried some gentle leading questions.

'Why did Dad hate school so much?'

'Oh,' said Matthew, 'your poor father. He hated to go anywhere. We had to take him out of school, you know. It was too flat for him. He felt exposed to the sky. He said he expected always to be swooped upon and caught up in great talons.' Speech was hard for him now. Each sentence required recovery time, snatched breath. 'And all those *games*! He couldn't think of anything more pointless and soul-destroying than chasing around after a ball. He said that he imagined Hell to be one endless ball game. We couldn't leave him there.'

'Did he ever try to run away?'

'John? No. He was a good boy.'

One morning, Bob appeared in the garden at Matthew's window. He could tell that I had seen him. Neither of us made a gesture; he simply waited until I came out. The garden looked neglected but happy to be left alone. The plants had knitted themselves into each other. Sandra had no time for flowers.

Bob was very tanned and wearing red deck shoes – my eyes kept being drawn to his feet, perhaps because if I met his gaze I was going to have to speak, but he said, 'Can we have a chat?'

'OK.'

I gestured to the bench on the terrace. 'Is this something you and Corwin cooked up?' I asked.

'No. This is all my idea.'

We sat at opposite ends of the bench and stared at the sea.

'When did you get back?' I asked.

'A couple of days ago.'

'Did you have a good time?'

'Yes. It was great.'

'I suppose you want an apology?'

'I don't give a shit. But I think Val deserves one.'

'I'd had too much to drink. I behaved badly.'

'Well, that ought to make you and me even, then.'

I hadn't thought of that. 'Oh,' I said. 'It's not even that any more. It's just decades of habitual dislike – that and the golf club and the Range Rover and the fact that you call Mum "Val".'

'Wow!' said Bob. 'I thought you might have grown out of that by now. But you're still just as much of a snob as ever!' He was laughing. 'Poor Val. A hippie, snob daughter, and a sanctimonious, do-gooding son. What did she ever do to deserve that?' I was laughing too. It was a warm, comfortable feeling to be out in the open with our enmity.

'I'll go and see her,' I said. 'I'm getting the hang of this apology business. Not that she'll care. We don't like each other very much.'

'Mothers don't get off so lightly.'

I supposed not. I stared at his tanned feet.

'I'll be off, then,' he said, standing up. But I followed him to the gate.

'I've been going through Dad's old things,' I said. 'I've never understood why you and Dad were such good friends. Why were you?'

'We grew up together,' he said.

'That doesn't seem enough,' I said.

'Well, it was,' he said, exasperated. Then, relenting: 'We'd known each other for ever, climbed together, played music together. That was enough.'

'Do you think it was us?' I asked. 'Me and Corwin? Was he depressed about us?'

Bob had been reaching for his car keys, but stopped to sigh the sigh of the exasperated stepfather. 'I think you and Corwin

194

are a couple of drama queens. John was pissed. He fell off a cliff. Let it go!'

'I can't reconcile it,' I said.

'What?'

'You used to play music. I can't reconcile that music with this waxed-coat lifestyle.'

He shrugged his shoulders. He'd had enough of me. 'What can I say, Morwenna? I don't need you to.'

'Fair enough,' I said. He climbed into the Range Rover. Through the open window I asked, 'Does the name John Greenaway mean anything to you?'

'No? Why?'

'Just something I came across in something of Dad's.'

Bob raised his hand from the steering wheel as he drew away. It was as though he was thanking me for pulling over.

26.

Corwin said that John Greenaway was a distraction. It was code for an idea. Who or what he had been was an irrelevance. 'Matthew holds the answer,' he said. 'Let me ask him.'

'No,' I said. 'Not yet.' Because I didn't want him to hurt Matthew, and because I didn't want to know, because I remembered now the ache and bewilderment of bereavement and I didn't want to believe that my father could knowingly inflict such pain upon us.

Matthew's body had shrunk. It was nothing more now than the casing of a tired spirit, which escaped from him in curls of vapour. Somewhere inside was an answer, hard and shining: a diamond truth.

'What if the answer is, he doesn't know?' I asked. 'What if the truth is, he doesn't know? What if he believes that Dad fell off a cliff and is dead? What will you do then?'

'There's only one way to find out.'

'Not yet.'

We were whispering. I took a sketchbook from the shelf. I ignored the ones he had kept from his childhood – and took up the one dated 1941, the year of Matthew's Disappointment. 'We look for John Greenaway,' I said. 'Matthew must have put him somewhere. Then we'll know whether he knows or not.'

That was when we started to go through the sketchbooks. We were systematic about it, as Matthew had been; every sketchbook entry had a corresponding cipher on the map. We needed to enter into his way of thinking to work it out. I started in 1941 and worked forwards while Corwin worked backwards from

2005, and we gridded off the map so that we could catalogue the image that corresponded to the sketchbook entry.

As Matthew had told me, he started with the farting Devil. I pictured him returning from his day's walk, spreading the Ordnance Survey map out on the kitchen table, piercing Thornton with the sharp point of his compass and extending it out to meet the mark he had made in the middle of a field twelve miles away and turning the circle. Then scaling it up onto the large canvas, a canvas of undulating lines with a tiny red and black devil at its centre.

Much of it was familiar, and we already knew where to look on the map. On one page, two enormous cedars framed the church and beneath the sketch he had written, 'The Thornton Sentinels'. And then, in an older, smaller hand, 'Lost in the Great Storm of 1959'. Not lost to Matthew's map, though, where they still stood guard. But not all were so literal. At other times, we would find a page full of details, then search and search for its cipher. Matthew had devoted two pages to the story of a Civil War skirmish between cousins. In the sketchbook the exact location was mapped out, but when we looked at the map, we could find no obvious reference to the event. We were tempted to dismiss it and allow ourselves to believe that it was a story Matthew had rejected for inclusion. But we kept going back to it – Matthew was consistent: what appeared in the sketchbooks had a symbol on the map. We kept looking. Eventually I found it by standing back: the family coat of arms was painted into the bark of a trunk of a bifurcated oak tree. Once I knew it was there, it was obvious, but my eye had slid over the image countless times.

By now I had read *A Coastal Curacy* twice; Ambrose Pearce, with his stranger's eye, storm-shocked by both the weather and the poverty. The people of the coast loomed misshapen and lonely out of the mists. He imagined them wild and murderous, the beaches littered with their lantern-lured victims, the fingers hacked off. But there was only one mention of the occupant of the strange cabin at Thornton Mouth.

I went looking for Ambrose Pearce. He was easy to find. He had been curate at St Peter's for three years in the mid-1860s, before returning to the civilized south-east, where he wrote two other books about being the vicar of a land-locked village with a pretty duck pond.

I went looking for John Greenaway in the Thornton Parish Register, starting with the time of Ambrose Pearce's curacy. I looked for him among all the dead children, the bled-out young mothers, the consumptive, the poxed, the drowned, and those who had managed somehow to outlive their teeth. They must have felt a grim sense of achievement, those old women who had laid out God knew how many sons and daughters and grandchildren in sheets fragranced with herbs. I was thirty-four and had never seen a corpse. I thought: It will not be me who lays out Matthew. Someone else will do that. Someone else, whose job it is. Someone who doesn't know him. There will be no lavender or rosemary scattered on his sheets.

Names, names and more names, excised from their stories. John Greenaway was not among them. I went to the churches in The Sands – I found a couple of Greenaways, but no Johns, and no one of the right age.

'He must have moved on and out,' I said to Corwin. I had said 'on and out' as though Matthew's circle were a geographical feature.

'It doesn't matter,' he said. 'He's not important.'

But now, when I went down to the cabin, I thought about John Greenaway living on that spot. I could smell the tarred rope. Here was a ghost that I could grapple with, a good honest ghost, who might be relied upon to rattle a few pebble chains and appear with a warning hand raised, pointing even; he had seen the Devil, after all – he was a ghost to heed. There were ways to dispatch a ghost like him. Matthew knew them all –

they were in the sketchbooks: you could throw churchyard soil at it, or declaim, 'In the name of God, be gone!' Or you could set it an impossible task. If I met John Greenaway's ghost I would banish it from the cabin until it had translated into English each and every scribbled stone at Thornton Mouth. That would keep it occupied for all of eternity.

My life was full of shades: John Greenaway, John Venton, the child, Death. I felt as though I was being called to the Underworld.

I went to visit Mum. She bestowed her forgiveness on the threshold, all graciousness, freshly pedicured – Rouge Noir to go with the tan. 'Tea?' she asked, prescribing my penance. 'Darling,' she said, 'you're the only person I know who still takes sugar in their tea.'

Her tea, I wanted to say. Not *their*. I had apologized, but she hadn't.

'What lovely flowers,' I said, because that was the kind of thing I had to say from now on.

'From your brother,' she said, allowing me to infer the unfavourable comparison. 'How's Matthew?'

'Fading fast.'

'I suppose I'd better come and say my goodbyes.'

'I think he'd like that.'

That night, as I took over the vigil, I pulled a sketchbook from the shelf. It was from 1951, and in the moment that I grasped the spine to slide it out I knew that I had found something. The book felt wrong. I knew how a book should feel, and this one was slightly hollow to my touch. There were pages missing. I didn't need to open it to know this. When I did open it I saw immediately that the stitching was loose. I counted the pages and compared them to the previous sketchbook. Two leaves had been removed. Matthew, surely.

I waited until he opened his eyes. I sat there for two hours watching him, listening to his breath. Eventually, he stirred, looked around in confusion. I took his hand. 'Matthew,' I said, 'it's me, Morwenna.' He recognized my face then and his own relaxed and he made a mewing sound of contentment. I gave him some water through a straw.

'Matthew,' I said, 'what do you know about John Greenaway?'

But I had left it too late. He had no full sentences left, only single words. And, in any case, he showed no sign that he had understood the question.

27

Corwin and I began to take turns to sleep in Matthew's room. We lived within his breathing now. It was the first sound we listened for each time we woke. But at the beginning of August, on our thirty-fifth birthday, Corwin suggested that we ask Sandra to sit with Matthew so that we could go out. Sandra agreed without hesitation, generously. I had to thank her, not so much for the favour but for loving Matthew, which cost me.

We didn't talk much that evening. There had been so much talking. We sat next to each other in the pub, enveloped in a brown leather sofa, and drank beer and ate chips. It was quiz night and we paid up to take part. 'You and me against the world, Morwenna!' Corwin said, clinking his glass against mine. He became quite animated. It had given him something else to think about.

I thought: Why always *against* the world? Most of the quiz questions went over my head – I didn't watch television, had no interest in sport and had given up paying attention to the news. I looked around me, the intense debates over each question, the laughter. Why not *of* the world? I wanted to join in, but I didn't know how.

Corwin did pretty well on the questions. 'All that Trivial Pursuit,' I said spitefully.

'Look at your face!' laughed Corwin. He imitated Matthew, perfectly capturing Matthew's anachronistic upper-crust closed *a*'s: 'Morwenna, I do believe that you are some strange scowling woodland creature that has strayed into the human world by accident!'

'Very funny!' I said. And then I realized something. 'Oh!' I said. 'I'm in there. I'm in the map, after all!'

I had seen it so many times recently, sitting in the branches of the oak in the middle of the cow field, a cross creature with enormous hazel eyes, but hadn't yet decoded it. Matthew must have been waiting decades for me to work it out. I felt forgiven – what for, I couldn't have said.

We walked home through the middle of town. Some teenagers were gathered at the high raised flowerbed that surrounded the shopping-centre clock. It was still the triage point, just as it had been when we were that age. We carried on past the closed-up Boots and WHSmith. A man was walking towards us. He was wearing a denim jacket. I wouldn't have paid him any attention (I was thinking about Matthew, hoping that he hadn't woken up and felt abandoned) except that he made a sudden movement of avoidance, a shoulder-led swerve into the alley that led to the car park, and in the moment of that movement I recognized him and saw that Corwin had too. Corwin began to run after him, shouting his name: 'Oliver! Oliver!'

I followed Corwin into the alley and out into the empty car park, but Oliver had disappeared. Corwin stood in the middle of the tarmac looking wildly around him. Then he threw his head back and yelled one abrupt, despairing 'Fuck!' into the night sky and sat down.

My lungs were hurting from the effort of running. I went over to where Corwin sat and stood over him. 'When was the last time we saw Oliver?' he asked.

'I don't know. All I can remember is him crying at the funeral.'

'Memorial service,' snapped Corwin. 'It wasn't a funeral.' He stood up and grasped my hand and started pulling me along behind him.

'That treacherous little fuck!'

Corwin dragged me across town to what we still thought of as Oliver's house. The cul-de-sac struck me as a vision of pure loneliness, a ring of identical houses lit by a weak orange light from the streetlamps, each emitting a blue flicker from behind the curtains of one or two rooms.

We stole up to the house. There were pots of red geraniums on the front doorstep. We clicked the gate open gently and prowled around to the back, but there was light only in the living room. We tried to peer through a chink in the curtain, but there was nothing to see. We returned to the front door and Corwin put his hand out to ring the bell. 'It's the middle of the night!' I whispered, but it was too late. Corwin's finger pressed the button. *Ding dong* went the bell. It seemed to reverberate right around the circle of houses. 'Ding,' said Corwin, grimly. 'Dong.'

For the longest time, nothing happened. Then we heard a shuffle in the hallway, and a light went on and an old man's voice, suspicious, scared, called out: 'Who is it?'

'Mr Finch? It's Corwin Venton. Sorry to disturb you so late at night.'

There was a pause during which he must have been looking through the peephole to satisfy himself that it was indeed Corwin. Then the door opened on the chain and Oliver's father peered through the crack in the door. 'What do you want?'

'Mr Finch, we thought we just saw Oliver. We thought he might be here, and we'd really like to talk to him.'

The harsh hall light fell across Mr Finch's face. The skin under his eyes was a deep purple, his eyes dark with bitterness. 'He's not here.'

'Have you seen him recently?'

'I told you. He's not here. He's nothing to do with me.'

'But do you know where he is?'

The door moved towards us, but he was simply removing the chain, so that he might open it wider, the better to display his anger.

'I don't know where he is. But I know where he's going,' he said. 'That filthy little sodomite. I told him where he's going. I said, "You, boy, are going straight to Hell!"'

Now that he had us there, he was glad. There was no one else to tell. He pointed his right hand towards the ground to show us how forcefully he had dispatched his son into the flames. He was wearing checked slippers, which made his righteous fury all the more terrifying.

'When did you tell him that, Mr Finch?' Corwin asked calmly.

'He comes round here,' said Mr Finch, 'to tell me the world has moved on! But I asked him, "And God?" I asked him. "Does He move on?"'

'Do you have an address? We really need to speak to him.'

He gave us a fiery look, which told us that we were going the same way as Oliver, and shuffled off into the kitchen, then came back with a piece of paper in his hand. 'Here,' he said. 'I have no use for this!' And he shut the door. The hall light went off, but the blue continued to flicker through the crack in the curtains as we walked away.

I wasn't able to sleep, trying to remember the last time I had spoken to Oliver. I could never get beyond the morning after the memorial service. I revisited desultory evenings in the pub during university term breaks and couldn't picture him there. I must have written to him. At four in the morning I got up to trawl through the box of school memorabilia and old letters that was among the boxes in my parents' bedroom – there were letters from Willow, postcards from other sixth-form friends, but only one postcard from Oliver. I recalled a long-since-forgotten sensation of having been interrupted in a conversation with him. Now I realized that I had never heard from him again. I can't explain what instinct told me – us – that Oliver had something to conceal, but in that shying away from us he told us and we understood.

We flipped a coin. Best out of three: heads, you go, tails, I go. Corwin flicked it in the air a third time, caught it, and slapped it on the back of his left fist, pausing ostentatiously before lifting his right hand. 'Heads,' he said. 'You go!'

He looked disappointed. He was in need of confrontation. Sandra came into the kitchen to make herself some tea.

'What are you two up to now, then?'

'Assigning things to Fate,' said Corwin.

Sandra snorted. 'Don't you ever get tired?' she asked.

'Of what?'

'Of talking like that?' She was filling the kettle. 'Who wants tea?'

'I think you should go,' I said to Corwin. 'You're the one who really wants to.'

'No,' said Corwin. 'It's the right answer. He'll find it harder to lie to you.'

'I don't see why.'

Sandra was laughing. 'I don't even know who you're talking about, but I can see why!' She pulled three mugs from the cupboard. 'Tea all round, then?'

'What?' I said. 'Why?'

'There's something about you makes people want to smack you in the face with the truth,' she said simply. 'Who are you talking about, anyway? Not that it's any of my business,' she added, pre-empting me with a smirk.

'Oliver,' said Corwin. 'Do you remember him? Oliver Finch?'

'The Fairy?' She put a mug of tea in front of me. 'Don't you give me that look, Morwenna Venton. That's what we called him: the Fairy. You can't stop kids saying stuff like that.'

Before she went home that afternoon she came to find me. 'Say hello to Oliver for me,' she said. 'He was always nice to me.'

28.

I left at dawn the following day. Oliver had tucked himself between the moors. I drove along the edge of a river. There was light rain on flat water. Horses waded through the morning mists. I half expected him to have fled, but as I pulled into the courtyard of converted farm buildings I found that he was not hiding, after all, but alert to my arrival, coming to the door of his cottage and standing there while I switched off the engine.

His long hair was gone – now it was very short: salt and peppered, the hairline far back on his forehead. He wore small, thick gold hoops in both ears. As he came towards me the muscle shifted in his arms and under the fabric of his T-shirt and his jeans. He had exercised the girl out of his body, but when I got close enough to see his eyes they were still a little too full for his face, the lashes a little too long and curled, the expression a little too close to hurt.

'Hello, Morwenna,' he said. He kissed each of my cheeks. The cool gold touched my skin. 'No Crow?'

'Matthew's not well. Corwin's looking after him.'

'I'm sorry to hear that. I was just about to take the dog for a walk – do you mind? Come on in while I grab a jacket.'

Inside, I remembered his sobriety. The room was fastidiously clean. There was a range, a fridge, a large wooden table and chairs, a desk under the stairs, a laptop and mouse pad arranged geometrically upon it, and an empty floor space in front of a statue of Buddha and a candle. There was nothing soft to compromise his principles. The closest thing he had to a sofa was a large hairy blond dog.

'Do you live on your own?' I asked.

'No,' he said. 'I have a partner: Andrew.'

'How does that go down around here?'

Oliver laughed – he hadn't even smiled until then. 'Oh, they have some euphemisms for us. I've heard "nice boys" and "our gentlemen". I don't know what they call us behind our backs.'

We walked down to the river – it was still the flat water of early morning, moving in smooth dark planes. Oliver threw things up the path for the dog and the dog brought them back. Oliver said, 'You're looking very thin. And tired.'

'It has been a difficult couple of months,' I said.

'I'm sorry I ran away from you,' he said. 'That was childish. I don't know why I did it.'

'You must have some idea.'

'I don't know,' he said. 'It had been an overwhelming day. Every so often I try to make peace with my father. It's always upsetting when I can't. And I wasn't expecting to bump into you two.'

The river ran over furred stones. Trout shadows moved beneath the surface. The sun had appeared and was burning off the mist and the morning's rain. On the other bank was a tangle of red campion.

'How's Crow?' he asked.

'He's got compassion fatigue,' I said. 'It's turned him into a lunatic.'

'I'm sorry to hear that,' said Oliver, for the second time. 'What's he doing now?'

'Nursing a fixed idea,' I said.

It was akin to flirting, this verbal dancing. There was an electric tingle. I had no doubt that he felt it too.

'What are you doing, these days?'

'Working for the Wildlife Trust.'

'That sounds very worthy.'

'It's OK. A lot of it seems to involve sitting in an office at a computer.'

'I can't imagine you in an office,' I said. 'Somehow you and strip-lighting don't go together.'

'Most people don't get to love their jobs, Morwenna.'

I remembered the sensation of being permanently admonished by Oliver. He may have avoided us after school, but we had let it happen because it had been tiring always to be found wanting.

'No,' I said. 'I'm lucky, I suppose.'

'What do you do?'

'I'm still binding books. Living in London. Trying to avoid change – only Corwin won't let me.'

He was fussing over the dog, letting it lick his face. 'How do you like London? I don't think I could bear it.'

I'd had enough of this. I said, 'Do you know why I'm here, Oliver?'

Oliver's hands were still buried in the dog's deep fur. 'I have an idea.'

'Good. Well, let's stop pissing about. You see, Corwin thinks that Dad didn't die when he fell off the cliff. He thinks you know that.'

There was a pause in which a breeze hit the water and set off the first ripple of the day. The long grass swayed.

'Why does he think that?'

'Gut feeling,' I said. 'He's having a lot of those. I don't seem to get them myself. I just channel Corwin.'

'You always did!'

'Possibly.' I shrugged.

Oliver had been talking to the dog. Now he straightened up and said, to me, 'I really loved your father.'

'Yes. I remember you saying that before.'

'No!'

The dog jumped to its feet suddenly, guardedly, attuned to the pitch of misery in Oliver's single word. Oliver was undoing – dematerializing in the way that he had done as an adolescent. His eyes were awash. I felt the wonderful clarity of pitilessness. 'No?'

'I mean, I was in love with your father.'

His confession settled upon me gently, as if someone had dropped the lightest cashmere shawl on my shoulders.

'Curiouser and curiouser,' I said. 'And I always thought it was Corwin!'

'Well,' he looked straight into my eyes – a flash of defiance beneath the tears, 'Corwin too. We were all in love with Corwin. Even you!'

'Gosh, what a lot of tongues must have been wagging way back then!' I said. 'I'm amazed my ears aren't burned to cinders! But we seem to be straying from the point. Let's get back to my father.'

'You and Crow,' Oliver had re-formed, was solid again, 'you were so self-obsessed. You never *saw* anything. Crow was too busy looking off into the distance pursuing some grand idea of himself as a humanitarian – and you!' He paused, relaxed his shoulders, relenting, and said kindly, 'Well. You were just a bitch.'

I waited.

'You took your father completely for granted. He was a wonderful man. A wonderful, wonderful man. The soul just shone out of him.' Oliver was crying now, for his long-lost love. He wiped his eyes on the heels of his palms. 'I tried to kiss him once.'

My stomach moved in a lurch of pure revulsion. 'Did he kiss you back?'

'No. He rejected me very carefully and gently.'

'When was that?'

'Oh. A long time before that night. I used to help him in the garden, sometimes. I loved that garden. And he was sitting there, on the bench, and when I went over I realized he'd been crying. It was just after your grandfather had sold that land. And . . . Well. I tried to kiss him.'

'Jesus!' I said. 'You can't have been more than sixteen!'

'Yeah. I suppose,' he said, as though I had missed the point. 'He was amazing. He was so kind about it.'

Mainly, I felt rage. We stood in silence for a few minutes but there was a cacophony of rage in my ears. Rage that Oliver had dared to try to appropriate my father for himself and, worse, that he took it upon himself to make judgement upon the quality of our love. In the end I reached into my handbag and pulled out a tissue and handed it to him.

'Right,' I said. 'Let's move on. The night my father "died".' I waved my fingers in the air in the sarcastic gesture of quotation marks.

He wiped his eyes and blew his nose and looked at me. He hated me, pure and simple. I wondered if he always had.

'Well,' he said. 'I fell asleep and you and Crow went off to the cabin to do whatever it was that you and Crow always had to be so private about in that cabin of yours and eventually I woke up because I was freezing and it was about five thirty and I started to walk home.'

He stopped. I waited. I was all patience, all clarity.

'And when I got to the top of the cliff . . .' Oliver sighed – he wasn't looking at me: he was looking at the damp tissue in his hands '. . . I stopped. Because it was such a beautiful morning. I just stopped to look at the morning. The tide was right out and the sand was shining. And then I saw him – walking across the cove, across the sand. Just walking. And I didn't know then that he was supposed to be dead. I saw him walking straight ahead and I just thought he was out there, being part of the morning. And later, when I heard, I realized that I'd been watching him walk away.'

With this vision of my father – walking the length of the low tide, his feet shredded like Corwin's had been, perhaps, bleeding into the salt-glazed sand, walking right past us as we slept in the cabin – I felt my skin cool into an exquisite transparent fragility; a hoar frost encased me. I understood now why we had not been able to feel anything when we lost our father. The thief, Oliver, had stolen our grief. The thief, Oliver, had been crying our tears, and he was still crying them.

'What makes you so sure that it was him?' I asked – I knew that this was my last question for him. 'At that distance?'

'I'd have known him anywhere,' said Oliver. 'And, anyway, I remember thinking how strange it was that he was carrying his fiddle.'

'OK,' I said. 'I'm going now.'

'I couldn't tell anyone,' he protested. 'It would have been a betrayal.'

'It was a betrayal, Oliver. And I bet you have told someone. I bet you anything you've told your Andrew all about it – all about your strange and painful first love. I bet it lends you quite the air of romance.'

He started and opened his mouth as if to deny it, but he couldn't. As I walked away he called out to my back, 'I still look for him all the time.'

Without stopping or turning I called back: 'You don't get to keep my father, Oliver. He was never yours to claim – he was ours, mine and Corwin's.'

I drove for half an hour, my chest tight with rage, until I had to pull over to breathe. The river had widened its cut through the fields. I walked to the bank, stripped down to my underwear, climbed into the soothing water and put my head under. It was so, so cold. The water flowed over me and I let it wash away my vengefulness towards Oliver, and towards Andrew, whom I would never meet, but who had shared in the secret – they had nourished themselves on my father's deception. But I was calm. I had forgotten Oliver before. I knew I could forget him again.

29

The imaginary falling man now spread out his arms, as Corwin had done, and leaned towards the moon and stepped purposefully out. But I didn't know why.

Corwin wasn't surprised by Oliver's story. He said simply, 'That makes sense,' as though it did make sense, all of it. Except that it didn't – not to me.

'Why, though?'

'I don't know. I think we must have cornered him, somehow. He hated that job – he was never meant to sit at a desk. You should have asked Matthew while you still had the chance.'

'What about Mum – do you think she knows? Should we ask her?'

'What do you think? She's totally transparent. Just like somebody else I know. Leave her out of it!'

'How come she gets left out of it and Matthew doesn't?'

'You know the answer to that.'

So I whispered into Matthew's dreams of dying. 'Why did John jump off the cliff, Matthew?' I whispered into his ear, because I imagined the connections in his brain as a mass of soft filaments floating on the exhalations of my questions. I hoped for a gentle collision that might still produce a word. 'Where did he go?' I whispered. 'To take up with a lover? To unearth pirate treasure? To travel into Fairyland? Do you know where he is?'

But Matthew only breathed. What was left of him existed only to service his breathing and the plucking of his hands on the bedsheets. I had read about this in novels: the plucking of sheets by the dying. I had thought of it as something only the Victorians did, like fainting and sending children up chimneys. But then the nurses increased the morphine and the plucking stopped and we were left with the breath, percussive and persistent. And Corwin and I dozed in the room. Matthew rattled as if his organs had dried and crisped, like autumn leaves, and were being blown about inside him.

And then, one evening, it stopped. And Corwin and I both looked up at the interruption to the rhythm of this dream of ours, which had been Matthew's dying and in which there had been no time or substance and which had seemed like an always, as though we had stepped into a parallel life in which we existed as other versions of ourselves. We looked up, as if a blind had sprung open and let in the bright sunshine. It was late September; there was sun on the fields.

We straightened Matthew's sheets and arranged his hands and kissed his forehead, and I was about to call for a nurse when Corwin laid his hand on my arm and said, 'It can wait.'

I thought we would sit down again and simply stay and contemplate, but Corwin started rummaging about in the old cupboard in which Matthew stored his materials. I said, 'What are you doing? Leave his things alone!' But Corwin ignored me. He pulled out a bottle of white spirit and a box of cotton buds and went over to the map.

I said, 'Stop it. You can't do this now. Now's not the time. You're upsetting me.'

But he soaked the cotton in spirit, and picked up the magnifying-glass with his left hand and began to wipe over the canvas, over the sea below Brock Tor, saying, 'I've been patient. Now is the time.'

And Matthew lay dead with the sun from the west on his face and I held the magnifying-glass while Corwin desecrated the map with tiny, gentle strokes of soft cotton and the paint lifted, until there, at the base of the cliff, where it meets the sea, a creature appeared, looking out from a fissure in the rocks; a grinning creature, camouflaged in colour to blend in with the granite of the cliffs. It had horns and a forked tail and leered up at Brock Point – it was John Greenaway's Devil.

30

I asked myself, When did Matthew know?

And I remembered him, on the day of my father's death.

'Where did he fall?' asked Matthew. This was his first question.

'Just below Brock Tor,' said Corwin.

After the police had gone, Matthew left Valerie and Bob facing each other in the living room and went into his study and stood. There was only this standing and the absence of thought, and both the not moving and the not thinking drew all of his energy to a balancing point beneath the balls of his feet. Any loss of focus, and he would tip and injure himself. He had experienced something similar before, when his wife died, but this was different. When Anne died it was simple bereavement; his soul was stunned. But this . . .

An idea squirmed at the edge of his consciousness – a voracious maggot of an idea trying to bore its way into his brain, and he must keep it out or he must unbalance. And so he stood, still.

Fifteen minutes passed before he dared a movement. He took three steps, turned and allowed himself to re-form in order to sit down in his chair. Not a maggot, he thought. Maggots are for the surface, not the water. An eel. An eel with its blind vacuuming eel mouth twisting at the flesh to feed its black electric flicker. And in the time that it took to complete that thought the idea had perforated the membrane and was in.

At last he fell asleep, sitting in his chair, and slept for two hours the sleep of a man who was *too old for this*. After a while he completed the sentence: too old for this *counter-betrayal*. He should never have sold the land. John had begged him. Matthew had forced his silent son to speak: made him rehearse his plea. Working in the garden, out with Matthew on their evening walks, John had painstakingly fitted together the words. It had taken him ten days, and he had voiced them only the one time: 'Please, Father. Let me have that land. Please.'

Matthew had thought only of legacy and, for Matthew, legacy had always meant the house and the objects within the house and the stories that attached to the circle around the house and, within the circle, the triangle: house, church, cabin. The land, the soil of it and what the soil could achieve, was incidental. He had missed it. He could name every flower and tree, but still he had missed it. And John had punished him for it – *was* punishing him for it, perhaps. Or perhaps he was in the water, after all. How desolating, not to know, not to have proof.

Matthew waited for the house to fall silent. It was only one day off the full moon, but the rainclouds had come over; he couldn't see it. There were footsteps on the stairs. The plumbing shrieked, briefly. He couldn't imagine that anyone was sleeping, but no one, thankfully, could be heard to be weeping.

He pulled his stepladder over to the map and angled his light and his magnifying-glass towards the chine below Brock Tor. He picked up his palette and began to overpaint.

31

At Matthew's funeral I looked for my father. I thought, He must intuit it somehow. He'll come. But it doesn't work like that. Matthew had kept our grandmother's ashes and had requested for his own to be mixed with hers and dug into the soil around the climbing rose that they had planted on their wedding day: the rose that on his map wrapped itself around the house and which had grown year by year, a rose at a time, so that by now the house in the painting looked as if it were held together by the rose and would disintegrate without it.

I worried about what would happen when we sold the house. What if they dug up the rose?

Corwin said, 'We're not selling the house!'

And I said, 'We can't afford the inheritance tax.'

And Corwin said, 'Yes, we can. I've got it.'

'What do you mean, you've got it?'

'I've been saving,' he said.

For all those years he'd been saving. I'd had no idea. But, then, what should he have spent his money on?

'I'm not living here. You can't make me!'

Around me, the house, empty of its people, seemed to come out of hiding and reveal itself to me in its true state. Water seeped in; I watched it spread. The doors jarred on twisted frames. There were broken slates, gouges in the plaster. The weft appeared in the carpets.

Corwin said, 'I can't make any decisions until we've found Dad.' As though we needed to save the house for him. 'No,' said Corwin, 'that's not it. But don't you see? We are stuck now.'

*

I sulked, and as I sulked I thought about Ed. It was as if he were my connection to the outside world, so I phoned him.

'Morwenna,' he said. 'How are you?'

I said, 'Matthew's dead.'

'Are you OK?'

'Yes.'

We were silent for a while, and then he said, 'Why are you phoning?'

He made it sound as if there was a right answer to the question, but I didn't know what it was. I said, 'I don't know, really. I just thought that I owed you a call.'

'When will you be back in London?'

'Soon, I guess.'

'Well, why don't you call me when you're back?'

I wanted to explain to him that I had come into the world with my affections, my love, already parcelled out for me and that I was doing my best to reapportion them, it, my love, and that, with Matthew gone, surely there must now be some love released for me to bestow where I wished. But it wasn't the moment for that conversation. It must wait.

We carried on looking for our father. It was all we did, day in, day out, apart from when Mum insisted that we come over and eat sensibly; she assumed that we were taken up with sorting out the house. She was gentler than usual – had us bring our laundry, fabric-conditioned and ironed it. She made chocolate cake. We were grateful for it.

If Matthew had taken so much trouble to conceal, then there was something to find. We turned away from the map and the sketchbooks and started to go through the bank of wooden cabinets that contained his files. Matthew was an archivist – it was not in his nature to discard. Somewhere in his study, we were convinced, was a clue to our father's disappearance.

Matthew's sources hung in hundreds of drop-files, organized

geographically by parish and, within each parish, by subject, alphabetically. Thornton alone took up an entire filing cabinet. We started there and lost ourselves in Matthew's mind. We began to see the world as he had seen it – not in the two dimensions of canvas and paper but in multiple dimensions. In his view of the world there was no chronology: he experienced time through the finest historical layers, like so many sheets of the sheerest fabric, floating on the breeze, brushing against each other, lifting and curling at the corners to reveal other times altogether. In his world truth co-existed with invention, embellishment might be more truthful than fact, fact might be more magical than myth. Roses held up houses. Demons guarded names. Now when we walked down to the cabin in the evenings to bid the sea good-night on his behalf, the landscape shifted, broke up, rearranged itself. Matthew had lived within a kaleidoscope. Nothing had looked the same to him twice.

And then, suddenly, my four months were over. I wasn't ready. It was the end of October. At Thornton Mouth the sky was a violent orange, as if there had been a celestial tantrum. It was still warm in the evenings. We made a small fire on the beach and pulled in some mackerel for supper. We cast in silence, the fish so stupid that we caught them with the glint of metal. We gutted them quickly – they are bloody fish, mackerel; they quickly grow rank. We returned their heads and entrails to the sea.

Corwin said, 'I wonder what he calls himself now.'

I saw myself trapped in a tower with a chamber full of straw to be spun into gold. 'Rumpelstiltskin!' I said.

'Yes!' laughed Corwin. 'That works.'

I imagined the little wizened man, my father, dancing around the fire, singing out his secret name.

'I'll come back at the weekends,' I promised. 'We'll keep looking.'

Corwin drove me to the station. It was the season for dead

badgers on the road – the young, setting out on their own. I worried about leaving Corwin alone with his bitterness.

In London, a pile of mail lay on the table by the front door. I left it there and climbed the stairs, soothed by the familiarity of the sound and feel of each loose stair tread. I pushed open the door to my flat. Birgit was long gone. She had left a note and a couple of bottles of wine on the table. The flat smelt of neglect, of rain, of mice. Something clinked against my shoe. Ed had returned his keys. I opened the windows, poured a glass of wine and set mousetraps. In the early hours I heard a trap spring, unfeasibly loud; and then, half an hour later, another. I dreamed of mouse corpses, their stiff little tails, their flattened jaws.

Ana's black eyebrows lifted as I returned to work. She was pleased to see me back. 'I'm sorry about your grandfather,' she said, and asked, 'Everything else resolved?'

'Just about,' I said. She didn't want to know the answer: she was just reminding me that, even if nothing was resolved, I owed her the pretence that it was.

My hands were out of practice and ached at night. In the evenings I soaked them in warm water and massaged them with oil. If Corwin had been there, he would have done it for me – taken my hands one by one in both of his. Could it be enough – the life he wanted for us? I thought, If there were more words for love, if there was a word for Corwin and me, for our twin-ness and all that attached to it, could we make ourselves better understood? If Mum or Ed or Oliver or my father could have named it and said simply, It is *this* not *that*, would it all have been defined and obvious? Would they have been spared anxiety about it? Would my father have stayed? But there was no word for us.

I went through the pile of mail. Most of it was junk. There was a manuscript I had ordered for a book-design competition. It was *Aesop's Fables*, printed on beautiful thick ivory paper, into which the woodcut illustrations sank deep. I smiled. There would have to be a crow on the cover. I put it aside to think about later, and picked up a postcard – it was from Birgit. Her journeying had taken her to a bindery in Italy. She thanked me again for letting me stay and wrote that I was always welcome to stay with her in Zürich – the bindery there would be delighted to have me if I ever decided to do some journeying of my own.

I turned the card over and put it on top of the manuscript and went to the kitchen to make supper. I was cracking eggs into a bowl, the butter was foaming in the pan, when I stopped and wiped my hands and went back to the postcard. The image was from a Roman mural. At its centre a snake writhed within an eagle's beak. A sensation that was like heat, but which was fear and triumph and revelation combined, shot through me. I reached for my phone and dialled Thornton. The phone rang and rang. Eventually some-one picked up. It was a woman's voice. I said, 'Who the hell is that?'

'Hello, Morwenna,' said Sandra. 'It's Sandra.'

'Christ!' I said. 'Have you moved in or something? Where's Corwin?'

'Out.'

In the kitchen the butter was burning.

'When will he be back?'

'How would I know?'

'Well, when he gets back, tell him he needs to go back to the map. He needs to look for something small – like a mouse or a vole or something. Maybe even a snake. Something that a hawk might prey on.'

'OK,' she said slowly, appeasing.

'I mean,' I said, 'would you mind taking a message from me? Please. And thank you. And if you leave before he gets back, could you write it down? He'll know what I'm talking about.'

'Of course, Morwenna,' said Sandra. 'Whatever you say.'

Corwin didn't call back. And still he didn't. And he didn't answer the phone, and it was only Wednesday and I couldn't go back down until Friday night. I wondered if Sandra could have been spiteful enough not to leave the message, and then I realized she couldn't have been. She wasn't spiteful. I just wished her to be. I felt ashamed of myself.

I couldn't sleep. At last, at three in the morning, he called. 'I can't find anything.'

'Keep looking,' I said.

32

I went back down that weekend. Corwin met me at the front door. 'I've found something,' he said. I felt light-headed, almost nauseous. 'Not Dad,' he said quickly. 'And not on the map. I've found John Greenaway. He was in with the rector.'

It was obvious, really. Matthew had a whole drawer on John Greenaway's rector. He had lived a long life and had saved all his sermons and his correspondence, making copies of his own letters. There were some notes of Matthew's – he had toyed with the idea of writing a book about him.

'Where did Matthew get hold of all this stuff?' I asked.

Corwin shrugged his shoulders. 'Where did he get hold of *any* of this stuff?' He handed me a piece of paper. I tried to read it, but couldn't make out the handwriting. Corwin took it from me and read it out to me:

Dear Reverend Wingate,

You say you cannot hear my confession. That you don't hold with all that papist nonsense. Although some in the parish would say that your fancy collars might tell a different tale. Yet I know you to be my friend and will tell you, shriving or no. I came out of the sea named John Greenaway that day you pulled me off the beach. Now God and the Devil will sort out who will have me but I have fathered children in the village and left them without a father's name. I want them to know their father's true name and if they are not ashamed of it to use it for their own. Lastly I beg that I may be buried with my true name.

These are my last wishes.

Nathaniel Parvin
That was John Greenaway of Thornton

Corwin handed me something else. 'This was clipped to it,' he said. They were the pages pulled from the sketchbook. Across two pages was the Devil in various forms, grinning from the rock, as we had uncovered him, but also scowling, furious, being ridden through the water by a man.

I turned the pages over. On the reverse side of one was an illustration that took up the whole page. It was the cabin, but not as described by Ambrose Pearce. It was our cabin, our beach. The tide was out and there was a thick high-tide mark, which resolved itself into body parts. A man lifted an arm into a wheelbarrow, but it wasn't a portrait of John Greenaway. It was a portrait of Matthew. He had written two words at the centre of the bottom of the page: *The Sexton*.

My hands were shaking. 'We're getting closer,' I said.

'No,' said Corwin. 'This gets us no closer at all.'

The next morning I woke early and went to look in the grave-yard. I found him eventually, his headstone half buried in the ground, the words almost weathered away by the salt wind: *Nathaniel Parvin, died 1879*.

I went on down to the cabin to spend time with John Greena-way's ghost. I had the sense that I had seen the name Nathaniel Parvin very recently, but I couldn't think where. It was not until much later, when Corwin and I were sitting down to eat, that I remembered it. I jumped up from the table and ran upstairs to my parents' room and pulled out the box in which I had looked for letters from Oliver. I tipped it upside-down. There were all the things that Mum had kept from my primary-school days – pic-tures, my story-writing books and a folded piece of paper, which I took back to the kitchen.

I unfolded it on the kitchen table. 'Look,' I said to Corwin. 'It's the class family tree. The one we did with Miss Arden. She made a copy for everyone. You remember – when Sandra called me Morwenna the Witch.' There was the name, on the top row: Nathaniel Parvin. Not John Greenaway himself, but his grandson, probably. I followed the lines down, to our generation. He had several great-grandchilden. One of them was Sandra Stowe.

'That's how he knew the story!' I said. 'Matthew – that's how he knew the story. He got it from the Crab Man.'

But Corwin was right. None of this brought us any closer to knowing where our father might be. Corwin had now been home for eight months, living off his savings, and when he hadn't been caring for Matthew or obsessing about our father, he had spent his days walking and climbing and working in the kitchen garden with Sandra. Between them they had restored it to productivity, and had now turned to reviving the scrubby little orchard. They worked well together, trading light-hearted jocular insults. Corwin had filled out again. He was becoming strong and tanned from the work outside. Sometimes Sandra brought her children over. Corwin had given them their own corner of vegetable patch where they had planted pumpkins and sweetcorn. They had made a scarecrow – I recognized an old jacket and hat of Matthew's.

Now Corwin said, 'You see – we have a connection with Sandra.' I could tell that *he had been thinking*. A dread chill seized me. I steered him off the subject, whatever it was. He had been thinking far too much in general.

I bumped into Sandra in the boot room as she was getting changed out of her work clothes. She always wore jeans and DMs, but now I stumbled across her in red lacy underwear. She was all sinew except where her four kids had stretched her belly. There was a rose tattoo on her left hip. She had a smoker's face, rippled by the weather; brown eyes, bright with disdain. She belonged to the house now – whether I wanted her there or not.

'You and Corwin will be announcing your engagement next,' I said childishly.

'Crow!' She laughed. 'He's too pretty, and he's got all that going on in his head. I like my men simple: the sex, food and football kind. You know where you are with them. And,' she said, sitting to lace up her boots, 'they're easy to replace.' She pulled on her leather jacket. 'Don't worry, Morwenna. I'm not going to steal your precious brother.'

But Corwin cornered me. 'I've been thinking,' he said, 'about all this *space*. We don't need it all. It's too much for the two of us. We could split up the house – Sandra and her mum and kids could rent half of it from us for what they pay for their council house, and the place would be productive. It would be alive again.'

'Oh, yes,' I said. 'Alive with sex, food and football men and a giant Sky Sports screen.'

'You're such a snob, Morwenna!'

'Yes, I am. So what? That's my idea of Hell. It's not happening. And you need to think about what you're going to do next. When are you going back to work?'

'When we've found Dad!'

I said, 'I'm giving you until the end of the year. If we haven't found him by then, we stop this nonsense. I can't do this for much longer. I'm exhausted.'

'You think we can just do that? Just set a deadline? And then what? We stop wondering? We get on with our lives? Don't you see what he's done, Morwenna? He's put us in limbo. Disappearance is the worst bereavement. I've seen it so many times: there's no resolution – ever.'

And so we came to the crux of the matter: Corwin and his abstractions. I said, 'Don't come over all I've-been-to-Africa with me. Finding him doesn't help anyone – you don't get to do any saving by it.'

Corwin said, 'He did this to us deliberately.'

'No,' I shouted. '*You* did this to us deliberately. I was perfectly content when Dad was just dead! And what about Mum? She's remarried, for Christ's sake – you've turned her into a bigamist!'

'She won't ever need to know.'

'I didn't ever need to know, you selfish fuck! I've had enough of this. I'm going home.'

It was Sunday morning. I didn't say goodbye.

I was grateful for autumn, its shielding dark and thick knits. I didn't contact Corwin and he didn't contact me. I made dutiful calls to Mum, and we told each other nothing – she said, 'I've resigned myself, darling!' Although not, apparently, enough to resist exclaiming: 'God, Morwenna! Sometimes, surely, you must want something to *happen*.'

'No,' I said truthfully. 'I really don't.' Because I wanted my father to be dead. My father, with his slow grace, could never have done to me what Corwin said he had done.

I felt nauseous most of the time. I was losing weight. I worked on *Aesop's Fables*. The crows' skulls that Corwin had given me hung on the wall above my workbench. I took one and held it between the fingers of my left hand, away from me, at eye level: this tiny fragile miracle of nature's engineering. I let my right hand begin to make sketches. Dead, I thought. Dead.

I pared the black leather, shaped it, pressed it into the cover, gave the crow a small dark eyeball and attached ragged wings.

Vain, stupid Crow who couldn't keep his beak shut.

At the end of November there was the designer binding exhibition. The books were put out for display in glass cases in a wood-panelled guildhall. Ana came up to me and laughed. 'Morwenna, you have no pity! I've always felt rather sorry for the crow, myself!'

My book fetched eight hundred pounds. The buyer wasn't even in the room. Somewhere there was a library where my book would end up, to be looked at by . . . how many people? A handful of guests glancing over it after dinner? Its owner prising it gently from its slip case: 'Look at the workmanship. There aren't many people left who know how to do this.' Or maybe no one would look at it. It would sit on a shelf in a row of books that had cost more than my annual salary. The book was just paper and leather. It was all vanity. That was why Matthew had never bothered to make more than one painting.

An arm slipped around my shoulders. It was Corwin. He kissed my cheek. 'What are you doing here? And how did you know where I was?'

He didn't answer, but handed me a piece of paper. It was a photo, printed on copier paper, of a section of the map. An enlarged image, grainy, but clearly distinguishable: a pile of brown leaves, and protruding from them, the head of an adder, with its muted markings.

When you hear the word 'adder' you think: Poor shy endangered creature. It is almost your patriotic duty to love it. But then I said viper. You feel quite different about them. Vipers are viperous – they are untrustworthy, they betray. The V of brown scales was quite distinct on the creature's head, where it poked out from the twigs and dead leaves. Matthew had painted his son as a snake. He must have felt both things: poor shy vulnerable creature, who doesn't want to be found. But he would have thought traitor too.

Me – I felt, mainly, traitor. This man, our father, who had cheated us, who had tried to cheat nature, who had cost me my mother, my boyfriend, perhaps my most beloved brother, had cost me perhaps my self – perhaps there had been another, one who, at eighteen, had been about to launch herself into the world. I also felt – Leave him. He made his choice. Let him live with it. But, you see, he had stopped us. Corwin and I were stopped, stuck together. Simply put: It wasn't fair.

I said to Corwin, 'OK. I will do this. For you. For us.' I looked

228

again at the image – there he was, in Matthew's map; he had been unable to escape. I went cold at the thought, and said, 'But then we sell the house.'

'OK,' said Corwin. He was shining, gently vibrating with vindication. 'You have a deal.'

'So where is he?'

Corwin had blown up a section of the Ordnance Survey map. 'In this section, here. It's about ten miles inland.'

'So close,' I murmured. 'I almost feel sorry for him. I wonder how Matthew found him.'

'Maybe they were in touch.'

'No. Matthew would never have done that to us.'

'You're always defending Matthew,' said Corwin.

There was nothing on the map but a couple of lonely farms, patches of woodland, a warren of tiny roads, which would be lost between high, thick hedgerows.

'How do we even begin?'

'We'll just begin – grid it off like we did with the map. Walk it a bit at a time. Talk to people. We'll take our time.'

The following evening I went and knocked on Ed's door. When he opened up and saw me standing there, he winced at my poor taste in arriving unannounced. But he took command of himself and invited me in.

He said, 'I wasn't expecting to hear from you again.'

'I told you I would give you an explanation when I had the chance.'

He twitched with irritation. 'I feel that the moment for that has passed, don't you?'

I handed him the bag I was holding. 'This is for you,' I said. 'It's a present.'

'Oh,' he said, looking inside the bag. 'Thank you. What is it?'

'It's an aspidistra,' I said. 'They're ugly plants, but they're impossible to kill.'

He pulled it out and set it on the table and looked at its unpre-possessing dark, leathery leaves. 'Is this supposed to mean something to me?'

'Not really. It doesn't matter.'

Red Post-it notes were stuck all around the room. They had Chinese characters drawn on them in thick felt-tip pen.

'Is this for next year? Are you going to go?'

'Sort of. Yes,' he said. Then he said, 'Wen?'

'Yes?'

'I'm seeing someone else now.'

'Ah!' I said. 'Is she going too?'

'Yes. In fact, she's Chinese.'

'Well, that's good,' I said. 'It doesn't suit you to be single.'

'Don't patronize me!'

'Sorry,' I said. 'I didn't mean to.' I pointed to a Post-it note stuck to a chair. 'How do you say that?'

'Are you serious? Is that what you want to talk about?'

'Sorry,' I said.

'Would you like a drink?'

'No,' I said. 'You're right. The moment has passed. I'm just tidying a few things up.'

33

So we made a start. On Friday night I took the train down. I didn't tell Mum I was going. Corwin was in the kitchen, looking through old photos, trying to find one of our father. But we weren't a photo-taking family, and somehow he had contrived always to be behind the camera, or at the back of a group of people. Corwin had found one of him and Bob in their climbing gear from the 1970s. It was a good clear photo of him, but impossibly young. He could have been anyone.

Corwin had drawn a square mile around where the viper might be – Matthew's map had abandoned scale, and he had filled that empty landscape with outsize hedgerow plants, so we could begin only with a guess. We were to set off from the north-west corner of Corwin's square and work across.

We had an early breakfast and drove inland. The sky was closed. It seemed to be raining liquid slate, which settled and massed in darkness on the road, trapped by the hedgerows. We parked the car by a gate into a field, and began to walk. Corwin had scaled up the Ordnance Survey map and marked out our tangled route with a yellow highlighter. We were in a maze of narrow lanes. We waded through the gloom and found ourselves at road signs we had already passed. Every so often the wall of hedge opened into a gate and we had a view of winter fields, the cattle turned in against the rain, huddled together for warmth. We walked down driveways into empty farmyards, trespassed around the edges of fields. Corwin carried the photo of our father in his pocket, but there was no one to show it to.

After six hours of this, relieved only by a sandwich, we returned to our car and went home. My hands and feet were frozen.

Then we did exactly the same thing on Sunday.
And in the evening I went back to London.

During the week Corwin wrote to me. The email had been sent at three in the morning. I had not stopped to think of him alone at Thornton – whenever I saw him there he was in movement: waving his long arms, talking and doing. But now I pictured him sitting, still and silent, in that dark house, bereft of Matthew, quietly sinking into insanity:

> I imagine his conversations. He must say 'hello' and 'goodbye' and talk about the weather and I keep asking myself what he has gained by our eradication. Perhaps he has another family? Although somehow I doubt it. He was so overwhelmed by the one he had already. Until recently I felt as though we were chasing a ghost. But now I feel as though we are ghosts chasing him. We are silenced. We don't exist.

> I watched the sun come up over frost-trees this morning. I wish you could have seen it.

The frost gifted us a weekend of winter-blue skies, filigreed tree branches, ice-crusted puddles. We extended our search out-wards by half a mile. Neither of us was getting much sleep and our trudge through the lanes took on a hallucinatory quality, so that when, as it grew dark, we turned into a driveway and came upon a farmhouse flashing with coloured Christmas lights in the shape of a giant Santa sleigh, I truly believed, for a moment, that I had conjured it from my own mind.

What did we think we were looking for? There was nothing rational about our search, although we tried to give it logic with our grids and highlighters. On our third weekend of searching we walked around a tiny village with our father's photo and enquired at shops, and the people we approached were curious and asked friendly questions. Corwin answered with blithe lies. I hadn't foreseen this, and it made me feel furtive and sullied. It seemed as though we were cursed to do this for all time. I sat down on a bench in the village car park and refused to move and tried to make myself cry. Corwin stood over me. He was hollow-eyed and pitiless. He was never, ever going to give up.

But Corwin did relent, in as far as he decided that we should treat ourselves to a couple of nights at the only inn for miles around, the White Hart, which was one of those places that you normally drive past and wonder who stops there. The nearest building had a petrol pump outside it that looked as if it hadn't been in use since the 1960s. The pub was done up for Christmas with shiny fringed Merry Xmas banners over the bar and a flashing Christmas tree in the corner. There were dusty bowls of dried orange and cinnamon in the loos. A fire languished on a pile of ash.

We let them think we were a married couple. The room had a four-poster bed with lacy white polyester hangings and a deep window-seat overlooking the cobbled courtyard in front of the main entrance. We made tea from the plastic kettle with stale tea-bags and UHT milk. I sat in the window-seat and drank my tea and watched the slushy rain turn to water on the cobbles. At around six we went down for dinner. We were the only people in the bar. Corwin ordered vegetarian lasagne and chips. I wasn't hungry and nibbled stale bread from a basket delivered by an unhappy-looking fourteen-year-old.

'Don't despair,' said Corwin to me, as though the despair was all mine.

A few more people came in. They sat at the bar and chatted with the landlord and each other. They sat spaced widely apart and called to each other in loud voices. It was part of the ritual. 'We should make some friends,' said Corwin. 'They might know something.' He was cheering up with beer and festive kitsch.

'I can't just talk to people!' I said, horrified.

He laughed. 'Don't worry. Later. When everyone's a bit pissed. I'll make some friends.'

We drank slowly. The fire burned gently. The landlord came over and threw on a couple more logs. On the other side of the pub, someone started to tune a guitar. My whole being constricted briefly – a single pulse of instinct. Corwin and I looked at each other. He turned slowly to the landlord. 'You have music nights here?'

'Every Saturday.'

I was overcome with a desire to run away. I said, 'I need some air,' and left the bar. Outside in the courtyard the slush was turning to snow. A couple of smokers, shifting to keep warm, pulled on their cigarettes and chatted. I walked to the other end of the pub to peer in through the window at the musicians. I could make out the guitarist, and another man, holding a drum. They looked up to greet someone who had just come in – his body moved across my line of sight. I thought: I might not be able to recognize my father, even if I saw him. I can't remember him. How would I even know it's him?

As I stood there, a figure approached, a man, in his sixties, carrying a fiddle case. I thought, This could be him, and stared at him so hard that he looked up through the cold and asked, 'Are you all right, love?' And it wasn't my father.

I went back into the bar and sat down again. 'Feeling better?' asked Corwin.

'No,' I said.

The musicians began to play a simple slow reel. I said, 'What are we doing? This is pointless. Hopeless. We have nothing. We don't know he's ever been here. We don't even have a name for him.'

Corwin said nothing. He said nothing because I was right and there was nothing to add. I said, 'It's funny, you know. I really hate him now. I always thought of hatred as a hot emotion, but this is very cold . . . very heavy. I know now why people talk about hearts turning to stone.'

Corwin leaned forward and placed his hand flat over my heart. He said, 'It's not cold in me. Not at all.'

I said, 'You know that vow you wanted me to make? The one I said I couldn't . . . didn't?'

Corwin's hand was still on my heart.

I said, 'Well, I did make it, really.'

'I know you did.'

'But I was young. I didn't understand what it meant.'

'Neither did I.'

He sat back in his chair. I said, 'I think I want to go to bed.'

'One more round,' said Corwin.

'OK,' I said. And I was looking at him and thinking: I must sever myself from you – from your will – or I will be extinguished, when someone started singing. We immediately recognized the song, because it was one that Fuck Off Bob used to sing all the time.

Corwin and I were still looking at each other, but now we were waiting, because we knew that we were on the point of something. We didn't move, just listening to that voice, that stranger's voice, singing:

> 'A sailor's life is a merry life.
> They rob young girls of their hearts' delight,
> Leaving them behind to sigh and mourn,
> They never know when they will return.'

It's a good tune, and I had always liked it before I started to despise Bob. The singer sang the first verse unaccompanied, and still we were poised, and then a fiddle started and immediately we recognized the playing. Corwin's eyes blackened in triumph and purpose, and I understood that while I had been looking, not expecting or even wanting to find, Corwin had been hunting.

He scared me then. He whipped up straight and alert. He had our father's scent. I stood up very slowly and walked the long miles between our table and the bar, putting out my hands to the shiny mahogany for support and lifting onto my toes to look over the length of the bar into the room beyond, and there was my father, and of course I did recognize him. He was exactly as I had last seen him, sitting, playing, swaying. Only he was quite grey now and he was bald with a close-cut ring of hair and a well-trimmed beard and he wore glasses and looked more like Matthew, but it was him. And then I felt Corwin standing behind me, leaning into me, his hands either side of mine gripping the gleaming mahogany, his chin digging into my shoulder. And we watched, until the barman came over and asked us what he could get us, and Corwin asked, 'Do you know who that is, playing the fiddle?'

The barman looked over his shoulder and said, 'That's John Greenaway.'

34

We stayed at the bar, then, and stood and watched. The shock of his being there was less his being at all, but that it had been so simple, in the end. How easy it was for him to be dead and hide and be only ten miles away from all that had been his everything. That he had turned that everything to nothing, and how few steps he had had to take to do that, and then how few steps we had had to take to find him. All we had had to do was to look. It was an insult, almost. Or a test, maybe, I said to Corwin. In which case, we had failed – or, rather, fallen short.

Corwin said, 'Remember that birthday party? Ellen and Alice. Do you remember them? Remember how they always had to have their parties together, and the year that Alice hid under the table to see if anyone would notice that she was missing from her own party? And no one did notice.'

'I remember,' I said. 'She never really forgave us.'

'What if . . .' said Corwin, discussing this man, our father, some stranger, whom we had thought dead for the last seventeen years, and whom we were now watching, fiddling away contentedly. A sentimental tune – he had always been a touch sentimental, I had forgotten that about him; he felt too deeply, saw mermaids where there were none, communed with vegetables. Corwin and I felt very light in our conjoined soul, a dizzying release of tension – the end of doubt. We found that we were giggling. It was too absurd to take seriously, all our grieving and atrophying for this man who had been simulating all along, and who, despite his musicality, appeared quite, quite ordinary. We drank and watched (the music stopped and our father withdrew his fiddle from beneath his chin and cocked and straightened his head on his neck, a gesture that had always meant 'And now' – 'And now, children, to bed'). The bar had filled up, and the musicians' corner, framed as it was by the high Victorian bar, seemed illusory: a puppet theatre – you could see the mechanics, the figures didn't move by themselves, and still you believed in them. That was the magic. The music sank under the rising voices in the bar. To anchor myself back in the world, I looked around. We were among people, nothing more. Why would someone put himself through the inconvenience of being dead simply to end up among people – and, of all people, these people? They wore roomy zip-up fleeces and well-worn hiking boots. Perhaps they knew John Greenaway. Perhaps one or several of these women were or had been his lovers. That one, perhaps, who was in her early fifties, probably, and who had made the effort to dye her hair but hadn't got around to touching up the roots. Or that one, younger, my age – old men did that, didn't they, made themselves ridiculous over women as young as their own daughters? That one there with the tattoo on the inside of her wrist, some pagan symbol that signified something of great pagan significance.

'What if,' said Corwin, 'actually, he just didn't care whether we found him or not?'

We began to calibrate a scale for our father's betrayal, with wanting to be found and rescued at the top (best case). We argued a little – should not caring whether or not he was found go above or below him simply not wanting us to find him? Corwin felt it was worse: 'Indifference is always worse.'

'Not always,' I said. I often felt indifferent. There was nothing personal in it. You couldn't possibly go through life taking a view on everything; feeling, responding, to everything. It would be exhausting. No one could possibly live like that.

'You're wrong,' said Corwin. 'I live like that.' He glared in the direction of our father, the fiddle-playing puppet, who gave the illusion of being alive. 'Or at least,' he said, 'I used to.'

'There you go,' I said, 'that only proves my point. It wore you out.'

Corwin gloomed into his beer glass. I said, 'I suppose we ought to make some attempt not to get drunk and form a plan.' It was ten thirty. Soon it would be time. They still called last orders in the country.

'I think we should follow him,' said Corwin. 'See where he goes. Observe him.'

'We should wrap up warm,' I said wisely. I was finding myself most amusing. I felt slightly hysterical. 'I'll get the coats. You keep an eye on him.'

Back in the bedroom with the thick pink carpeted bouncy floor and the romantic bed, I realized I was going to vomit and brought up beer-bile into the toilet bowl. It had one of those plastic things in it, which release Mediterranean-blue chemicals when you flush. I had forgotten to eat. There were individually wrapped shortbread biscuits in a bowl on the tea tray. I stuffed them all into my coat pocket.

The bell rang: 'Time please, ladies and gentlemen!' Outside it was snowing with gentle conviction. We sat in our car and watched the pub doors. The man, our father, came out with two other musicians. One of them seemed to offer him a lift, which he declined, and he turned with a wave and began to walk away. Corwin and I got out of the car and began to follow. His shape moved against the snowflakes, which fluttered in the dim street lighting. Over his shoulder was the curve of his fiddle case. Even if he turned he would not be able to recognize us: two figures, like him, made shapeless by the layers of coats and scarves and hats.

While we were still on the main road we kept about twenty yards behind him, close enough to call out. But we didn't call out. We hadn't discussed what we intended to do, but we weren't ready for words. We were in a wonder of watching, not yet able to take in what we were seeing. When he turned off the main road into the sediment of dark between the hedgerows we held back a bit, sure that the narrow lane would compress our presence, make it felt to him, and when we too turned, he had disappeared and I felt a moment of furious despair that we had lost him, but we sank into the dark after him and as our eyes adjusted we could see in front of us a neat trail of footsteps laid out in the freshly settled snow and, of course, immediately I started to sing 'Good King Wenceslas' in my head, and so I followed my dead father's footsteps in the snow with the tune going round and round and round: La la la la la la *laa*, la la la la *laa laa*.

The footsteps turned abruptly at a stile. We climbed over, and could now make out his shape at the opposite corner of the field – a negative black space in the swirl of white – and still we followed. Over another stile, then another, then up a track overarched with trees, and down the other side, until after about a mile we came to a farmyard and the trail seemed to stop, but Corwin pointed and I could see the footsteps resume beyond a patch of cow-churned mud, and we skirted the farm buildings and I thought: This is it, this is where he has settled. But there was further to go, into the woods, and there were no more footsteps, because these were fir trees and the snow had not penetrated the canopy, but Corwin took my hand and we felt out the path with our feet and eventually we came down out of the wood and into a clearing by a stream where the snow fell, thickly now, onto a tiny stone hut. There was light in the window.

We watched the snow fall through the dark onto the roof of the hut, then Corwin took my hand, and very slowly we approached and sneaked up to the window to peep in. There were no curtains. There were only two rooms: a kitchen and a tiny bedroom. We watched our father move around his home. It was lit with candles. There was nothing decorative, no pictures on the walls. A table, a couple of cupboards, stacked boxes of fruit, potatoes and onions, shelves of preserves. We watched him peel and chop an onion, fry it in a small pan on his range, crack eggs into the onion, eat the onions and egg piled onto a slice of bread. I thought: He's pretending. That's what he's been doing for the last seventeen years, that's what he abandoned us to do – make believe.

After his meal he washed up in a stone sink and went to the door. We tiptoed around to the back of the house and crouched by the woodpile and heard his footsteps go off in the direction of an outhouse, and when he came back we followed him round and looked through his bedroom window. There was a bed and four walls of books – dog-eared paperbacks, mainly. We watched him undress. Naked he looked older, but wiry and muscular under his pale skin. I wondered when he had last allowed someone to touch him. He put on some thermal leggings and a sweatshirt and climbed into bed, turned, blew out the flame on his candle.

We turned and walked back to the pub. I would never have found my way back without Corwin. I had trusted him to do the navigating, had abdicated it to him. The hysteria had subsided. I felt so tired. I wanted to lie down there on the snow and go to sleep.

Back at the pub, we let ourselves in quietly, taking off our boots at the door and carrying them up the stairs. We lay on the bed on our backs fully clothed under the blankets, staring at the polyester lace and not speaking, until at last I whispered, 'I still don't understand *why*.' But by then Corwin was asleep.

I must have slept, too, because then it was light and the room was full of the silence of fresh snowfall. Corwin was awake with his head propped on his hand, watching me, and when I opened my eyes, he smiled and said, 'Come on, lazybones.'

I said, 'Look at you. All triumphant.' And it was true. He was iridescent.

'Not yet,' he said. 'It's not over yet.'

I still had an ice block where my heart should have been. I felt nothing, except a desire to know why, so strong that it was physical. Why? Why? Why?

'When do we talk to him?' I asked.

'I'm not ready to talk to him,' said Corwin. 'I think we should watch him for a bit first.' It was as though we were discussing how to discipline a child. As though 'watching him' was meting out a punishment that would cause our errant father to mend his ways.

We ate breakfast. I forced down porridge. My gorge rose with each mouthful. It was Christmas Eve and from the kitchen radio we could hear a relentless stream of Christmas hits. Corwin fortified himself with sausages and bacon. His lapses into meat-eating were becoming ever more frequent, as though his anger called on flesh for nourishment. Then we paid our bill.

In daylight, the walk did not seem nearly so far. Still, it was well off the beaten track. We would never have found him if he hadn't come to the pub. The cows were emerging from the milking shed when we got to the farm, milling around in the yard, steam rising from their flanks, white into the winter air. We walked around the farm and into the woods and found ourselves an observation post among the fir trees. Smoke rose from the chimney of the hut. A pile of logs was stacked behind the building, almost to the height of the roof. In front was a row of fruit trees, neatly pruned, the snow sliding from the branches in the morning sun. Some golden fruit still hung from a crab apple and drew a chatter of birds. A stream circled the hut and garden so that it looked as if it sat on a tiny island. There it was, our father's dream of a smallholding, all laid out in miniature in the sunshine, sparkling and clean and white, like a fairytale.

We walked around the clearing. There was a chicken run, a winter garden with fleece-covered brassicas. Tucked back in the trees well away from the stream was the outhouse. There was even a couple of beehives, but no sign of a goat. Then we returned to our look-out position. I sipped black coffee from a Thermos flask until I felt stretched to the point of snapping.

After a while our father came out to use his outhouse and feed the chickens and to split a few logs. As we watched, we began to remember things about him: his love of birds – the way he would pause mid-task and fix on a tiny bird in a tree, studying its markings, and would not return to his work until he could name it, pronouncing the name out loud, releasing himself. Through the binoculars we saw his lips move. The logs were slower to split now. We used to watch him, the swinging axe, *thud*, *thud*, *thud*, waiting to be old enough to wield the axe ourselves. We remembered his walk, the set of his shoulders, the way that one eyebrow was slightly higher than the other so that he seemed to be asking an eternal question. He fetched a bucket of water from the stream. He appeared to be quite alone. Treacherous, heartless Rumpelstiltskin, I thought, who parted children from their parents, in his clearing in the woods, alone and content. But we knew his name.

It was beautiful, though; truly a most beautiful morning. I whispered to Corwin, 'You know that poem "Stopping by Woods on a Snowy Evening"?'

Corwin shook his head. I murmured into his ear, as if it were a secret.

> *'Whose woods these are I think I know.*
> *His house is in the village, though;*
> *He will not see me stopping here*
> *To watch his woods fill up with snow.*
>
> *My little horse must think it queer*
> *To stop without a farmhouse near*
> *Between the woods and frozen lake*
> *The darkest evening of the year.*

He gives his harness bells a shake
To ask if there is some mistake.
The only other sound's the sweep
Of easy wind and downy flake.

The woods are lovely, dark and deep,
But I have promises to keep,
And miles to go before I sleep,
And miles to go before I sleep.'

I felt very sorry for myself then, because sleep seemed un-
attainable; I could not remember what it was to sleep, really
sleep, deeply. I craved oblivion. Corwin said, 'It's amazing that
you have all that in your head and you can't remember fighting
with Sandra over marbles.'

'It's a very clever rhyme scheme,' I said, ignoring the mention
of Sandra. 'Deceptively simple.'

We watched a bit more.

'I see what we're doing,' I said, at last.

'What are we doing?'

'We're watching him, and he doesn't know.'

Corwin smiled; my lovely malevolent brother. I said, 'It's a sort
of power over him, isn't it? We have knowledge. We decide when
to strike.'

Corwin smiled again. I loved him very much at that moment,
for being so clever after all.

'So,' I said. 'When do we strike?'

'Let's get Christmas over with.'

It was delicious, this waiting. 'Merry Christmas, Dad,' I whispered, as we turned to go back through the woods.

At Thornton the lichgate and gravestones were capped with
snow. The Atlantic was quiet and black. I could taste it on the
air. By the time I went to bed, the snow was melting. I slept

without dreaming and on Christmas morning the snow was all gone.

We were invited to Mum and Bob's for Christmas lunch. Mum said, 'Morwenna, darling! You look lovely! You've made an effort! Merry Christmas, darling!' I had made an effort. I had woken up feeling clear-headed and vengeful and incandescent with knowledge, and I wanted to look my best for this, my last day of orphanhood.

The oak banister was wrapped with evergreen branches and glass baubles. The table was laid with red and gold. There was goose and honeyed parsnips and spiced cabbage. I said, 'Thank you, Mum. That was absolutely wonderful.' And 'Great choice of wine, Bob.' And 'Oh, is that a new painting? When did you get it? It's lovely, isn't it?' And things like that. Mum brought in a flaming Christmas pudding, topped with a holly sprig. Her eyes flitted back and forth between me and Corwin, but she didn't say anything because it was Christmas Day.

After lunch, Corwin and Bob went for a walk and Mum and I sat on the sofa and watched *Great Expectations*. I said, 'I'm sorry about your wedding, Mum.'

She said, 'You've already apologized. One apology is enough.'

I said, 'But I was only half sorry then. I'm really sorry now.'

'OK, darling. There's no need to overdo it!'

'I would like to talk to you about Dad properly, though. One day. Soon. Before I go back up to London.'

'OK, darling. But not right now.'

Later, though, while Corwin and Bob were washing the dishes, Mum poured me a nightcap. She said, 'Perhaps we should get it over with. What do you want to know?'

'Was he unhappy?'

I expected her to make some flippant comment, but she thought about it. The red wine swirled in her glass. Eventually she said, 'I don't think your father aspired to happiness. He thought it was frivolous to pursue it. When Mark compared him to Sir Galahad at the funeral, I remember I felt an icy hand grip my insides! They were terrible those Arthurian Knights. Implacable! Your father was like that – austere and noble. Impossible in a husband. He was so single-minded. He thought that, because he loved me, I would transform into a farmer's wife. Me, of all people! So totally unsuited to nature. As you know, darling, I've never aspired to harmony with nature. I'm perfectly content to be a parasite upon it!'

She pulled back a little, as though reminding herself to take the question seriously. 'It's hard to live with someone who is always disappointed,' she said. 'He hated that job, and he blamed me – I think he felt that I'd trapped him in it. Perhaps I should have tried to get a job of my own, but, I don't know . . . I'm not sure it would have made any difference. And we should never have stayed in that lonely, spooky house, with Matthew always, always, always there. And the weather! Jesus! I just wanted to be safely back on the London borders where there is no weather.

'But,' she said earnestly, 'there was no affair. There was no thought of an affair. It wasn't a loveless marriage. It was just an unsuccessful one. Your father and I were simply a mismatch. It never occurred to me that it might be possible to do anything about it.'

We sat in silence for some time. Then I said, 'It was the view, probably. It fools everyone. You should have seen Ed when he came down. You'd have thought someone had slipped him a drug.'

Mum laughed. 'Yes,' she said. 'I think you're right. And then I always felt slightly cheated, as if I'd woken from an enchantment to find myself knee-deep in mud.'

35

It was time. I was ready.

I counted the church bells throughout the night until, at four, dazed by insomnia, I went downstairs and sat in the dark in the kitchen. Soon, Corwin followed. We found that we were talking in hushed voices, as though we didn't want to wake our sleeping rage.

It was still dark when we left Thornton, and dawn was breaking as we parked the car and set off down the lane. At the farmyard, the cows lumbered towards us and, suddenly, we walked right into him, driving them towards the milking sheds. He wished us good morning, surprised, perhaps, to see walkers out so early, but he didn't see us for who we were under our winter wrappings. He was treading slowly, like the cows, a familiar path that allowed no margin for the unexpected.

When we reached the woods we stopped. My heart was thudding. He had spoken to us. We had heard his voice. I looked at Corwin. He was shaken and turned to lean against a tree, pressing his forehead into the bark.

At our father's hut I sat on the doorstep, listening to the stream, the waking birds, the chickens gently clucking. Corwin was pacing, bracing himself. All at once he stopped. 'I can't do it!' he said. 'You have to do it on your own.'

'No way,' I said. 'Calm down. We agreed.'

'No,' he said. 'I can't do it.' He began again to stride up and down. 'I feel . . .' He looked at me imploringly. 'I feel . . . Shit! I think I might harm him. I just want to kill him. I just want to fucking kill him. And I think I might. I think I might.'

'Coward!' I said. 'Fuck off back to the car, then. I'll meet you there.'

I watched him disappear into the woods and sat back down. I was surprised to find that, as my anger with Corwin subsided, I began to feel very peaceful, very patient. I was apprehensive, obviously, but suffused with a sense of expectancy that gave the morning a pleasant glow. I must have sat for a couple of hours, because a weak light was coming through the top branches of the fruit trees by the time I saw him come out of the woods. He saw me sitting there, and walked towards me with his questioning eyebrows, and still I sat and looked at him. And then I saw, in his eyes, the quizzical look of half-recognition, then the full glimmer of understanding, but I didn't say anything. And he walked right past me, where I sat, and went into his house and shut the door.

So I waited.

After about ten minutes, the door opened again. My father said, 'I'm sorry. Please come in.'

I followed him into the house. He said, 'Please. Take a seat.'

I sat down. He sat opposite me and laid his hands on the table. He still takes care of his hands, I thought. And remembered him carefully washing and creaming them after manual work, 'So that I can play,' he once explained.

Still I waited, while he looked at me. He is *searching my face*, I thought. But I won't let him find anything.

He took a deep breath, and said, 'You will have to excuse me. I have lost the habit of speech.'

I waited. I thought: Let him speak. I, too, can be implacable. I am magnificent in my hatred of him. I am Boudicca in her chariot. There are knives on my wheels.

Outside, the winter solstice had passed and there was the kernel of the idea of spring. From where I sat I looked out onto a plum tree, perfectly centred in the window. This is what he does, I thought. He sits here and can sense the bud forming in the bark. He watches this tree all year. And then the next year. It is sufficient for him.

'How did you find me?' he said at last.

'The map.'

He nodded – of course, the map.

'Matthew painted you as a viper,' I said.

He nodded again. Then asked, heavily, carefully, 'How is Matthew?'

'Dead,' I said. I admit to enjoying that, inflicting pain. I enjoyed my father's flinch.

'How did he know?' I asked.

The question took some time to penetrate his grief. He was crying, silently, for the death of his father. He drew back on his pain, forced a voice: 'I sent him a grid reference.'

'When?'

'Not long after . . .'

He was looking for a word, a name for the point between Before and After, but there was only one point – *the* point: there was no need to name it.

'Why?' I asked. 'Why did you want him to know?'

'For the map,' he said. 'I thought that he would know and that he would need it for the map.'

'That's not good enough,' I said pleasantly.

He tried again. 'I thought,' he said slowly, 'that he would know, and that he would think it was his fault. We had been a little . . . estranged for a couple of years, and I thought he would understand that I had settled. That it was all right.'

'That it was all right?' I repeated. 'Interesting choice of words! Did he ever seek you out?'

'No. I just sent him the grid reference. No words. Nothing else.' An appeal formed on his face. He was about to express it. I held up my hand to stop him.

'Once or twice,' he said, 'I thought, perhaps, that there was someone watching me. I thought, perhaps, that Matthew was there. But it was just a feeling. Nothing more.'

The tears dripped off the end of his nose – for his father. Not for me. I had never seen him cry – almost, that time, when

Matthew sold the land. But he had stopped himself then. Now, apparently, he allowed himself everything. He wiped his face and said, 'Where's Corwin? Was that him and you I passed at the farm?'

I said, 'What should I call you? I can't call you "Dad".'

'John,' he said. 'My name is still John.'

'Of course,' I said. 'Well, I shall call you John. Well, John, I think I would like a cup of tea.'

He looked at me then, as though remembering something he disliked about me – my tendency to flippancy, perhaps. But I wanted a cup of tea, and I wanted to watch him, see what he was made of, what held him up.

'Of course,' he said, and stood up and went to the large jug in which he stored water. I thought: Every morning he draws water and he says to himself, *I am drawing water from my stream*. In the haze of his memory is the action of turning on a tap with its effluence of chemically altered water and this act of taking water from the stream is akin to a morning prayer of thanks. He poured into his kettle the amount of water required for a cup of tea and a top-up each. This, I thought, is the same about him, the way he measures water into the kettle. He placed the kettle on the range and we waited for it to boil.

'I'm surprised,' I said, 'that you permit yourself tea.'

'Some things,' he said, 'I can't produce myself. I have to work. I help out with the cows. It's impossible to do completely without money. There are rates. I can't risk the attention of not paying them. I buy oil, flour, tea. I found that I was unable do without tea.'

I left that sentence to float about the room with all the things – the people – that he had found himself able to do without.

He took the pot to the kettle and warmed it and counted out three teaspoons of the precious tea for which he had milked however many cows at dawn. Pedant! I thought. Fuck you! That is your legacy to us? Your pedantry? The parsing of tea leaves?

It was pleasant, though, this slow life – I was prepared to grant him that. I drank his tea without asking if he allowed himself sugar. I assumed that he didn't.

'So this was it,' I said. 'Your dream? You just stepped off the world?'

He said, 'Will you tell me about Corwin? About your mother?'

'No,' I said. 'You're dead. The dead don't ask questions. What happens is that the living send out soundings, and echoes come back from the Other Side.'

'I had forgotten,' he said, 'your cynicism. Your inability to value anything that can't be expressed in a pithy sentence.'

'And now,' I said, 'you remember! Do ghosts remember? Or are they simply trapped memories? Am I this way because you remember me like this, over and over again? No, *John*! Don't answer. I'm not looking for your opinions. I have a set of questions. I will ask them. You will answer. And then I will go.'

And this, I thought, is different about him: he has forgotten how to smile – it is too arduous, this being dead, even if he believes that he has corrected himself. And despite his care of them, his hands are coarser, the knuckles beginning to swell. And he has the skin of a peasant, which perhaps is his secret vanity.

'Very well,' he said. 'Ask.'

'I'll tell you this,' I said. 'But only because I want you to know it: these are our questions, mine and Corwin's.'

He nodded.

'The first question is: how?'

He looked surprised that this was my first question – the technicalities rather than the emotions. He had to think. Then he said, 'I had often thought about it. Since childhood. Whether or not it could be done. I was pretty sure that it could.'

He stopped. It was a lot of speech. He wasn't sure that he had the stamina to continue. 'May I ask you one question?' he said.

'You may,' I said. 'But I may not answer it.'

'How did you know to look for me?'

'That,' I said, 'is a long story. And we don't have time for it. But,' I relented, 'in a nutshell: John Greenaway.'

He looked relieved then. He said, 'So you know.'

'No,' I said. 'I don't. You have to tell me.'

He closed his eyes – his stern grey eyes that admitted of no colour other than grey, so that life was always in earnest. It was a relief to see him blind and not to have to return his gaze. He said: 'I hadn't planned it. I had always wondered about that jump, whether it could be done, or whether John Greenaway was simply a great romancer. And then there I was, standing on the edge of the overhang, looking down. It was such a calm tide. I had never seen a tide like it, a mirror tide. It seemed like an invitation. I had fifty pounds in my pocket – I can't remember why. I remember thinking: That will do.'

He opened his eyes. 'I did think about my children,' he said, as though I wasn't one of them. 'Yes, I did. I thought about how they had outgrown me and that that was only natural. And I thought about my wife. I thought: I can free her. She might stop being so sad. It was such a waste, her sadness. She wasn't built for it. I thought about Matthew, of course. I worried about him.'

I said, 'Gosh! You've been rehearsing that, haven't you?'

He looked grey, spent. I allowed him some recovery time.

'You didn't go very far,' I said. 'It's almost insulting – just popping around the corner to buy a hut!'

'When my mother knew that she was dying, she gave me some money. Just for me. It was our secret. By then it was obvious that your mother and I were . . . incompatible – that I would never persuade her to share in my dreams. And I put the money away, in an account. No one knew about it. Not even Matthew. I thought, When I have my land I'll use it as seed money.

'And then, when Matthew sold the land, I took out the money and closed the account and bought this. For me. My sanctuary. I bought it in cash, from an old farmer, without a lawyer. My old name is on the deeds. Then the old farmer died, no one knew me here, no one knew I had the land. I just started calling myself John Greenaway.'

'So you did plan it?'

'No. I don't think so. I just wanted somewhere for me. Somewhere safe. And I used to come here regularly to renovate the hut, clear the garden. I planted the fruit trees.'

'So you've been here all the time?'

He nodded.

'And you've never bumped into anyone who knew you?'

'No,' he said. 'I limit my movements. And people are like rats. They move along runs. None of the people I knew come out here. Their runs don't extend out into these lanes.'

I laughed. 'So you never even left Matthew's circle. You went to all that trouble simply to come here! Why?'

'He sold the land!'

It was the closest I had ever heard him come to shouting. He composed himself. 'I begged him not to. After that, there was nothing left for me. I wasn't interested in the house – all that stuff. Things and more things. I don't know how it happened, but Valerie and I were in different camps: my wife and her radio and her television, the constant stream of banalities. And it has only got worse. I see how it has become. People walking along, talking into the air, like morons. Everyone has quite forgotten how to look about. No one sees anything. I was absolutely right to take refuge.'

'But you can't do completely without people. We saw you playing in the White Hart.'

'I can't do completely without music.'

'So,' I said, after a while. 'You despised your wife. You thought your children were in an incestuous relationship. Your father wouldn't give you your perfect fifteen acres, so you jumped off a cliff. You didn't think, for example, that divorce might be a less drastic option?'

'Stop! Please. Stop.'

I stopped.

'What did you think,' I asked finally, 'you were doing?'

'I didn't plan it,' he said pleadingly. 'I just jumped, and then I thought, I could have some peace. I just wanted some peace. I thought we could all have some peace. Divorce – it's so messy. People are so messy.'

'What? You think you didn't leave a mess?' I was incredulous now. It mitigated my rage, my disgust.

He rallied, straightened up, said, 'I thought – I still think – that grief is better than slow, torturous alienation between people who have loved each other.'

I was stunned by the neatness of his self-exoneration. Corwin was right – he hadn't faked his own death, he had faked ours. I wanted, for a heartbeat, to scream this into his face, but I stopped myself. He should have nothing from us – not our thoughts, not even our anger.

I said, 'You haven't used my name since I arrived. Say it. You gave it to me.'

'No, I didn't,' he said. 'That was your mother's idea. She was over-compensating for not being local. She wanted you to have West Country names. Matthew explained to her that it would be false to give you Cornish names. You can imagine. That absolutely set her mind in opposition. I wanted to call you Anne, after my mother, and Corwin, James, after my grandfather. Those are real names.'

I was glad of this note of bitterness. It allowed me to leave.

'You never got a goat,' I said, standing. 'You always wanted a goat.'

'I had one for a while,' he said, taking my question seriously. 'But they are unruly animals. It kept chewing everything.'

He had no sense of humour, I realized. I wondered if he had ever had one. 'One last question,' I said. He looked up at me and nodded. 'Did you see the Devil in the water?'

He had to think about this. Then he said, 'I didn't *see* him, but I met him there.'

'I'm going now,' I said. 'You won't see me again.'

'Yes,' he said. 'Goodbye.'

He didn't stand to see me out.

I had been there a long time for so few words. The sun had moved above the hut. I left the man who once, seventeen years before, had been my father, but who had not been since then. I felt nothing for the person sitting in the hut.

Corwin was waiting in the car. I got in. 'You drive,' I said. 'And I'll tell you on the way home.'

36.

The imaginary falling man picked up his fiddle and stretched out his arms. He laughed and tipped himself forward into the air. He hadn't planned to jump. Simply, he found himself standing there on the edge of the overhang, looking down onto the bowl of water and the sea was calling to him. Bob was sinking to a sitting position, about to pass out. John had seen him do that many times before. Once out, he would be out for a while.

John Greenaway had survived it – if he was to be believed. And he had not known, as John Venton did, that this was a tube, a hollow – there were no rocks directly beneath – and that on a spring tide, such as this one, the water was deep and descended to sand. John knew this because he knew every last fold in the rock on that stretch of coastline.

He might still die, of course. But anyone might die. It would not be such a bad thing. And he might live, and that would be most interesting. Then he could decide. He could continue to be John Venton, or he might be a ghost, move invisibly through the world. Nothing would attach to him. He would be free to look, to think, and not to speak. What a boon that would be – to shed the weight of language.

Bob was lying on his back, laughing at the moon. It was important to lean forward, as the fall would rotate him backwards. John Venton pushed off the edge.

He felt nothing as he fell, and thought that this might already be death. They say that a person is killed by the fall itself. Perhaps he and his body had already parted, which would be a surprise, because he did not believe in a life separate from the body. The fiddle fell from his hand. Some instinct told him to straighten out, and he sent that message to his body, which, indeed, responded and he fixed his arms to his sides and pushed out his legs and entered the water feet first. For a moment he was suspended, he was under and in and of the sea. He put his head back and looked at the moon through the water, broken into a million silver fragments by his impact on the surface. And then his body began to rise and as he reached the air a pain in his ribs told him that he still inhabited his body. He swam back towards the cliff face, where he would be obscured by the overhang. This was instinctive, he did not think about it in those terms at the time. There he felt about for a hold – despite the calm of the tide, the sea was buffeting him against the shards of rock, and for the first time he felt panic. It was not so easy to die, after all. Not a slow death by abrasion. But the panic came to his aid. He found a foothold under the water, and a sort of seat where he might perch and wrap his arm around a rock and wait for the tide to go out. He clung there, and experienced something like sleep. In his dream he was found and returned home, and self-pity welled up from his navel like bile and burned his throat. Then he started awake.

The receding tide was showing a patch of sand below where he sat, a good twenty feet above the base of the cliff. He climbed carefully down the cliff face. The sun was coming up. When he came to rest on the soft sand the knees of his jeans were shredded and his fingertips were bleeding. He sat for a few minutes before pushing himself awkwardly onto his hands and knees, and from there to a standing position. And then he saw, as though the sea had affirmed his act, that twenty yards away on the seaweed tideline lay his fiddle case. The instrument would be ruined, but, out of habit, he picked it up.

Already the freak stillness of that night had passed and there were waves on the outgoing water. The spring tide had peeled so far back that all he had to do was walk along the shining dark sand and make his way carefully over the rocks. Then he walked across Thornton Mouth, leaving a trail of footprints on the rippled surface of the sand, as though he were the only inhabitant of this shore. He walked on, past the cabin where Corwin and I slept, and on and up onto the coast path. He kept on walking in his wet clothes but he removed his shoes and walked barefoot, turning inland, past the cows moving towards the milking sheds, past the tourists sleeping in their caravans, invisible at last.

37

Corwin was silent as he drove. I talked and he listened. When we got back to Thornton he went down to the cabin for a few hours.

When he came back he said, 'It's not enough. How could you sit there and not speak? He should *know*! He should know what he's done. What it's cost us.'

'There was nothing to say,' I said. 'If there was something you wanted to say, you should have stayed.'

'You can't just disconnect!' he shouted. 'You can't just stop and turn in on yourself! We're all connected. We are all responsible for each other or we are nothing.'

'You should have stayed,' I said. 'Then you would realize. He is nothing. He has nothing to do with us.'

'I want him to pay, somehow. He stole seventeen years from us.'

'It's not like you to be so vengeful,' I said.

'I went away and stayed away,' he said, 'because that was the last thing my father asked of me before he died. To go away until my relationship with my sister "corrected itself".'

'You didn't tell me that bit.'

'Well, I'm telling you now. It was my father's dying wish – only he didn't fucking die. I want him to suffer.'

'He is suffering,' I said. 'We've punctured his dream. He can't dream it any more.'

When I got up the next day, Corwin was gone with the car. I went down to the church to sit there quietly and read the memorial tablets: the novels they contained, the potted tragedies. I thought about my father reading them, and Matthew: the one with its litany of dead sons ending with the extinction of a 'most antient and respectable family'; the couple who had married there but 'died in South Africa where they lie in widely separated graves'; the soldier 'who received a wound at Waterloo'; and the one that warns:

> *See. See. Spectators, and behold*
> *Whether you're young or whether old*
> *What you in time must be*
> *For Strength nor Beauty cannot save*
> *Nor wealth protect you from the grave*
> *You shall be dust like me.*

I did that because I knew that I was done with Thornton, now. I would be leaving the circle. I went down to the cabin to say goodbye to the sea, stopped at the war memorial on the way back and recited the names out loud. Corwin showed no sign of coming back, so I ordered a taxi to take me to the station. Two evenings later he phoned. He said, 'It's all right. I've thought it through. I have clarity again.'

I didn't ask him where he had been.

We sold the house, but without the cabin. We gave the cabin to Sandra so that she could do it up and rent it out to holidaymakers – it seemed apt that she should have it. We donated the contents of Matthew's study to The Sands Museum and auctioned off everything else, apart from the map, of course, and the curse spirit – we thought we might need his protection. And we bought a nice little terraced house in central London not too far from the bindery, so that Corwin can have somewhere in England to come back to. And I have drawn a circle around myself, but not too tightly. I will permit myself to leave it now and again. I think I might go to Zürich. Perhaps I will visit Corwin in Africa. Perhaps I will even go on my own to Chile. I like the sound of Chile – it is hard to be too far from the sea there. I am reading Neruda, just in case.

But I kept thinking about what Corwin said: that our father should know the cost. I thought, perhaps, he was right. We had let him off too lightly. So I wrote it down. For John Greenaway. So that he might *know*.

I won't bind it. I will print it out on unbleached eco-friendly copier paper and tie it up with jute string, and perhaps – but only perhaps – I will go at night and leave it on his doorstep, and then, when he is done with it, or if he does not care to read it, or if, for any reason, he has disappeared from there, it will compost nicely.

Acknowledgements

I owe thanks to readers of early stages of this book for their insight and encouragement: Katie Burns, Leo Klein, Ralph Rochester, Sophie Rochester, Sibylle Sänger, Lydia Slater and, especially, Martin Toseland, who can always be relied upon to re-orient me when my writing goes astray. I am indebted to Kate Rochester, for bringing her book-binding expertise to the manuscript, and to Peter Moffat for drawing my attention to Robert Frost's poem 'Neither Out Far Nor In Deep'.

Thanks also to my agent, the unstoppable Karolina Sutton, and to Norah Perkins at Curtis Brown; to my deft and tactful editor, Mary Mount; and to Hazel Orme for her incisive copyedit.

For everything else that matters, I thank Scott and Inês.

He just wanted a decent book to read ...

Not too much to ask, is it? It was in 1935 when Allen Lane, Managing Director of Bodley Head Publishers, stood on a platform at Exeter railway station looking for something good to read on his journey back to London. His choice was limited to popular magazines and poor-quality paperbacks – the same choice faced every day by the vast majority of readers, few of whom could afford hardbacks. Lane's disappointment and subsequent anger at the range of books generally available led him to found a company – and change the world.

'We believed in the existence in this country of a vast reading public for intelligent books at a low price, and staked everything on it'
Sir Allen Lane, 1902–1970, founder of Penguin Books

The quality paperback had arrived – and not just in bookshops. Lane was adamant that his Penguins should appear in chain stores and tobacconists, and should cost no more than a packet of cigarettes.

Reading habits (and cigarette prices) have changed since 1935, but Penguin still believes in publishing the best books for everybody to enjoy. We still believe that good design costs no more than bad design, and we still believe that quality books published passionately and responsibly make the world a better place.

So wherever you see the little bird – whether it's on a piece of prize-winning literary fiction or a celebrity autobiography, political tour de force or historical masterpiece, a serial-killer thriller, reference book, world classic or a piece of pure escapism – you can bet that it represents the very best that the genre has to offer.

Whatever you like to read – trust Penguin.